The Killing Face

Book 2 of The Killing Arc

Kenneth B. Humphrey

ISBN 978-0-9963659-3-2 (Print version), 978-0-9963659-4-9 (Digital version)
Cover design © 2015: Kenneth B. Humphrey

www.kenhumphrey.com
Twitter: @kbhumphrey

DEDICATION

When I speak to people about writing, one of the first questions I get is along the lines of: "What kind of stuff do you write?"

To me, that's a singular answer.

I write fast-paced books designed to keep the reader turning pages. Whether it's my youth series *The Hunts of Raimy Rylan*, or my adult thriller collection *The Killing Arc*, the stories are written in a very sparse manner. That is by intent.

You could say it's laziness on my part to avoid typing more, or that in today's attention-deficit world I need to cut to the chase. Both are to some degree correct. Mostly, it's because those are the types of books I like to read. So if you're looking for long descriptions of flowery fields, or in-depth technical explanations of forensic procedures, wrong bus stop.

Maybe someday I'll try a literary tome packed with prose and feelings. Or not.

Every book is a collection of input, ideas and edits. The author gives birth to the original concept (usually), and throws it out there to his network of friends, confidants and experts. Everyone serves a purpose: The wife who has a good eye for missing or transposed words; the buddy who isn't afraid to tell you when an idea is really REALLY bad; the industry specialists who provide grounding and advice for realistic details.

This book, more than my others, required significant assistance from my publishing network. I can admit I struggled in a number of areas, from the story scope all the way to tracking the timeline of characters. Right to the end I waffled on certain items. Without all those folks I doubt whether this book would have seen the light of day.

There are too many to name here, but if I've spoken to you over the last year about this story, then you have contributed in some way.

For that I cannot thank you enough. Enjoy the read.

~KH

MORE BY THE AUTHOR

Young reader series
The Hunts of Raimy Rylan
    Book 1: The World Serpent
    Book 2: Chase of the Samurai
    Book 3: Origins (2016)

Adult novels
The Killing Arc
    Killing the Man - 2014
    The Killing Face - 2015

PART 1

CHAPTER ONE

Monday, July 12, 1999
11:51pm

The cop's belly stretches his uniform tight. A white t-shirt peeks through the gaps between buttons. He's large and round. He uses that mass and the weight of a badge clipped over his heart to stand his ground. His nameplate, pinned to the other side of his chest, states *R. Alberts*.

It's not my first time at a crime scene. I've been at many during my time as a beat cop. But it is the first one with my shiny new detective's tin clipped to my belt. I sign my name into the logbook and square myself to him. He doesn't give any indication of moving aside. It's a symbolic gesture. I could simply

1

walk around him, but that would be giving ground, showing weakness. He's blocking my direct route, thereby making a statement.

"You mind?" I say, not so much as a question. This is *my* scene.

Hostility colors his eyes. The emotion is visible even in the dark. "Or what? You going to lawyer up and cry if I don't?"

There's no witty or sarcastic reply at the ready on my tongue. Comebacks are not my strong suit and that pisses me off even more. How long before these people get over it?

"Hey. Alberts. Stop busting on him, yeah?" My partner, Griffin Toms, appears behind the hostile cop. "You can't be a dick every day, can you? Oh wait, yes you can. It's your name."

For good measure, he reaches up and flicks Officer Richard Alberts' hat off. It lands in the dust with a puff.

"Dick," is all he says and chuckles as he waves for me to follow him.

I keep silent and do as he indicates. He glances over his shoulder as we walk. "You going to let the old salts keep walking over you like that, Detective Aramis Archibald White?"

"I've told you a dozen times, call me Arch." My legs are longer than his and I pass with ease.

"I know, but come on. Young, proud, black detective, named White. You're just white. Tell me that's not funny." Griffin laughs, a high-pitched giggle that sounds odd coming from a mouth just months away from retirement. No one will admit to it, but I'm sure his impending departure is why he got me as a partner. He's close enough to the end of the tunnel that he doesn't give a rip any more. As evidenced by Officer Dick Alberts, there are still plenty who do.

"Yeah, well..." I reply. "You're old." It sounds lame even to me. Damn.

Ahead an orange cone emerges from the darkness. It's one of those traffic cones used in road construction all over the country. Yellow scene tape is knotted to the top, stretching forward to the next one. Beyond that sits a third cone. This is our path in and out of the crime scene. Someone is holding tight to the book on this and I wonder why.

Griffin pauses next to me. He doesn't say anything at first, then: "Tell me what you know and what you do."

I take my time, remembering other tips he's given me since I walked through the station doors last month. We're at the outer edge of the parking lot for an abandoned factory of some type. Even though it's almost midnight, the sound of constant highway traffic drifts over us, coming along with the cars on the Stevenson Expressway rolling out of Chicago. The city of Cicero is rarely quiet, whether from traffic, planes on entry to Midway Airport, or the shouts of violence, despair and hopelessness. I've never quite seen a place like Cicero, but then again, my life existed mostly in the small towns of South Carolina. That was before all this.

Ahead of us two identical buildings are nestled close together, creating an enclosed courtyard between them. A dry fountain - covered in graffiti - stands between the parking lot and courtyard, a forgotten sentry.

Halogen lights have been set up in the courtyard, just on the other side of the fountain. In the glare of those lights I can see a single forensic tech moving with care, snapping pictures and making notes.

"Single homicide, male, early 50s." This I got from dispatch on the way out. I snap a glance at my watch. "Scene entry at 11:51. First responder Officer Alberts stationed at front, logbook present, six sign-ins, plus mine." Other cops and our sergeant have already been here. I wonder why none are still around.

Griff stays silent, letting me process in my own way. He's giving me a lot of rope, either because he believes I need it or want it. Or he simply doesn't care anymore.

"Marked entry, leading in. Location is between two buildings, site of..." I stop. "What did this place used to be?"

"I think Middle Plains Plastics, or something like that. It's been closed near two decades now."

I nod and something triggers in my brain. "Why is there only one tech? Where's the rest of his crew?" The fact that they are already here means Griff arrived a while ago and called them in. Dispatch didn't notify me right away. Did he have them hold off? Or is there some other reason?

"You'll find out in a bit. Keep on here. Pay attention to the things that look out of place."

Moving toward the fountain with even steps, I continue. "Technician Johnny Nayaki from Evidence Services present. He's capturing the scene from all compass points. Did he do the separator shot yet?"

Griff barks a short laugh. "Dare you to ask him."

By now we're within earshot of Nayaki. His black hair is streaked with shots of gray, pulled back into a ponytail. Round, silver-framed reading glasses are perched on top of his head. He spares us a quick glance, then digs into his belt pack and removes a single sheet of paper. With efficient movement, he crumples it up and throws it at me. "Your sheet, detective."

I unroll the paper and glance at it. Neat lettering provides dry details about the scene from a forensic standpoint: Time, date, temperature, address and such. This is the first picture in the series, to mark the beginning. I suspect Johnny just uses a new card for each scene. He seems particular that way.

"That's still called a fanny pack, you know," Griff says, taunting him.

Johnny switches out lenses on his camera, flipping us the bird in the process. He doesn't say anything.

A car sits a dozen yards off to our right, a late model Mercedes. The door is hanging open, dome light still glowing. "Vehicle present, VIN and tags will be traced for ownership. I'm thinking the victim's. He parked here and..."

"Don't speculate," Griff says, cutting me off. "Observe the scene and note only the facts. Form a theory based on what exists, don't make what exists fit into a theory you've created."

"Gotcha." I turn my attention to the body. "Victim is African-American, dark suit, lying prone on his right side, facing away from us. No visible murder weapon from this angle. Signs of struggle in the dirt. Identity unknown at this time."

I step around, taking care to stay wide of Johnny as he snaps his mid-range shots. My eyes track along the ground surrounding the body, looking for anything that seems out of place. I've only held my detective's shield - my tin - for a month so I'm not really sure what 'out of place' would even look like, but I try anyway. My heart is beating so loud I swear the other two guys can hear it and my throat is dry.

Stay calm, Arch. Don't let it show.

"Coroner will set time of death," Johnny notes. "But from early indications, the victim has been dead just a couple of hours. There's some rigor set into the eyelids and neck, the lips, but the rest of his body is still flaccid."

He points to the ground around the body. "You'll note the numerous footprints. There was a struggle. Due to this, it will be difficult for good impressions to be made. The dirt is too thin and there are very few imprints whole enough to cast."

It looks to me like any other concrete base that's been left untended for years. Dust and dirt coat everything, weeds poke through the cracks, some grown several feet high; more than a few of the slab sections have heaved, small-scale tectonic plates of concrete lifting above their brethren.

I nod in response as Johnny continues speaking and I continue my controlled idle around the near-perimeter. The stark glare of halogens create knifed shadows, turn the scattered drops of blood black on the ground, etching each forgotten rock on the ground in silhouette.

When I get to the front side of the body, my eyes move to his face. It's cast in false shadow and I move my legs to let more light shine on him, to reveal his features.

My feet stop with a jerk.

His eyes are wide open, staring at me in accusation. The tie is cinched tight to his throat. An empty wallet lies near his stomach. His face is twisted in agony. Blood tracks from cracked lips, a busted nose, swollen cheeks. This man has been beaten, and beaten hard, before being strangled with his own tie. Screw Griff's advice about theory and evidence. I know a robbery when I see it. I also know something else.

"That's Noah Bell." I blink, slow and steady. *Keep calm, Arch.*

This makes Johnny stop. He lowers the camera and stares at me over the tops of his silver frames. "Sorry, Detective White." He steps back a respectable distance and starts to fiddle with his camera controls, but I can tell he's just buying me time.

Noah Bell, the crown prince of Chicago. His presence was a beacon in the night for the utopia of racial harmony. He joined causes for the singular purpose of erasing the divide between white and black, or any color for that matter. He served as a champion for the underdog, the disenfranchised segment of society that just needed a break to go their way, no matter how small or large. Judges befriended him, councilmen consulted him, mayors hosted him.

My father used to talk about seeing Martin Luther King when he was younger. He spoke of him in tones that revealed just how much he respected someone with that depth of fortitude, someone who put everything on the line. I thought I'd be saying the same thing about Bell to my kids someday.

"You okay?" Griffin asks. "Need a second?"

For the first time I notice a cup of coffee in his hand. Some detective I am. Steam floats off the top. If he's been here long enough to call in Nayaki, that means he's on his second cup. Griff never gets his own, he always ropes a young beat cop to do it, but there are none here. Something doesn't sit square with this.

I nod. "Yeah, I'll be fine."

"If you want to pull back, I can take this one."

"I said I'll be fine. Let's just get to work here."

He doesn't say anything at first, watching me watching the victim. He sips from his coffee and makes a little hissing sound. "Tell you what. Johnny's got a lot of stuff left to do. Let's leave him to it and come back a little later. There's something else you need to see."

Without another word, Griff spins and starts walking, heading for the back of the courtyard. He passes out of the circle of halogen and disappears into the dark like he was never there.

I don't follow right away.

It took me almost a year to get onto the Chicago Police Department, a year of stress, bad press and far too many legal briefs. It also required a champion to take up my cause because he believed in my right and saw my desire. I'm young for the job, damn near the youngest ever for this city. There were many others with better credentials applying for the vacant position, many who deserved to win. That doesn't intimidate me, it makes me more determined. This corner of the city, Cicero and the surrounding areas, are my new beat, my new chance. I'm going to prove to everyone that regardless of the lawsuit I filed to get this tin shield, it's not a badge wasted; that it was never about the racial claims I made, only about getting me into a place I needed to be. I owe it to everyone who stood behind me and those who stood before me as well.

I follow in Griff's wake, giving a backwards glance at the victim, at Noah Bell, the man who won me my tin.

TWO

I catch up to Griffin near the back of the courtyard. Trash is strewn across the space: old newspapers, cans, broken glass. Windows adorn the face of both structures, matching pane for pane like a mirror image, but most are broken and black now. Glass crunches under our feet, a combination of bottle and window. The sound is quickly swallowed by the night.

Even at this hour it's hot. We got heat back in my home territory of South Carolina, but it was often leavened with breezes washing towards the Atlantic. This stuff is stifling, like the air drips with liquid and every move I make springs new sweat to my brow.

We emerge from the courtyard at the back of the factory grounds. The paved brick gives way to grass and weeds. Someone must still do the occasional mowing job, the growth is only knee high. Ahead a chain link fence marks the outer edge of the property, though it's missing most of the links now. Trees loom over the fence posts, Mother Nature staking a claim to land that once was all hers.

"Where the hell are we going?" I ask Griff, casting a look over my shoulder. The glow from Johnny's light is still visible, but he and Noah Bell's corpse are now blocked by a building corner.

"You'll see."

He leads me into the woods, following a path that looks to be a forgotten walking trail. The asphalt is old and cracked and neglected. I don't know what's on the other side of the woods, but I can see light filtering through the tree trunks, hear the noise of activity, of voices. The color is wrong for streetlights, it's something else.

"Is that a park?" I squint my eyes but the night conspires against me to keep our destination a guess.

Griff doesn't answer. He blows over the rim of his cup. It sounds like he's trying to make a tune.

We exit the woods into the glare of more halogens. I get a sinking feeling. "Is this what I think it is?"

"Likely worse."

A basketball court holds center stage in the small park. One lonely hoop with no net is all that remains to indicate what it once was. To the other side of the court sits rusted playground equipment: a carousel listing to one side, two of those rocking horses on springs; a swing set with no swings, just chains hanging empty.

The middle of the court is littered with bodies. I count six as we approach. Now I know where the remainder of Johnny's team is. They circle and stalk the scene, multiple cameras in play, duplicating the patterns of their boss back with Noah Bell.

Griffin stops at the edge of the blacktop. Scene tape has already been strung around the perimeter and the buttons of his sport jacket brush up against the plastic.

"What the hell happened here?" It slips out before I can pull it back.

"That, my friend Aramis, is what we find out. Did you miss the opening lecture of Detective 101?"

I ignore the sarcasm - his default tone - and start walking around the perimeter. The victims are all young black men, late teens, early twenties, dressed in shorts, t-shirts, sneakers; a sweatshirt with the slogan 'Just Do

It'. A basketball rests up against the hoop post, setting the stage. Blood pools around the bodies, some more than others. My mind leaps to gunshot wounds, despite the need to resist assumptions.

There's a seventh body, apart from the main group. He's at the far edge of the asphalt, black like these kids, but older and beefier. Jeans, a collared dress shirt with two neatly placed bullet holes over the heart; dark wingtip loafers. One of these bodies is not like the others.

Let the facts drive, Arch.

I come to the opening in the tape. A young black cop is manning the logbook but he doesn't give me the same attitude as Alberts. Maybe he thinks our shared skin color means a shared brotherhood. I tin him, pulling back my jacket to expose the detective's badge clipped to my belt, and sign into the scene. He just returns a slight nod. Griff scribbles his name beneath mine and follows me in.

"We don't have this one too, do we?" I ask, feeling naive about the process.

Griff nods to the far side of the court where two detectives stand with several beat cops. I can imagine the conversation, I've been on the other end many times. They're laying out how they'll canvas the area for witnesses.

"Stewart and Towney have lead. All of us will support. Why? Do you want to take this one instead?"

"No, just wondering why we're here if someone else is handling."

Griff jerks his head. "Follow me is why." He walks towards the older victim and stops in the space between him and the other bodies.

I look down. A small yellow flag rests on the pavement, indicating a piece of evidence. It marks a credit card lying on the ground. I kneel down and study it closer. The halogens provide enough light to illuminate the embossed letters on the face of the card.

Noah J Bell.

"Hard to resist the theory that just jumped into your mind, isn't it?"

I stand back up and nod. "How can you not?"

"Then let's hear it."

"You said not to speculate."

"I also once said I was wrong. That was a mistake. Tell me a story, Arch."

I gather my thoughts. "For whatever reason, Bell shows up at the Middle Plains factory. Someone of his stature never travels alone or unprotected. He's always accompanied by a personal security detail." I point to the older victim. "That's that guy. Bell is doing whatever he's doing at Middle Plains. At some point, these kids jump him. Maybe they see a Mercedes and an easy mark. Maybe they're just street thugs looking to jump anyone. Somehow they subdue and kill him. The bodyguard gives chase and catches up to them here. Shots are exchanged. Before he gets tagged, he manages to bring them all down."

"Case closed, right?" Griff has a strange look in his eyes, visible even in the shadows cast by the evidence lights.

"I don't know."

"Good, hang onto that skepticism. We'll need it later." He wanders off towards Johnny's team. They are done with the long range pictures and are now setting up the grid. They want to create a model that duplicates distance and relationship for all the elements of a scene like this. Griffin starts talking to one of the techs as she stands up a tripod.

I spin in a slow circle, trying to absorb my own details, capture the little impressions that don't translate to digital snapshots for my own photo book.

We're six months away from a new century, a new millennium, and there's so much unknown looming in the near distance. It's created this sense of shared apprehension that covers us all in suspended anxiety, because no one knows what it all means. We could wake up January 1 and life will be exactly the same. Or, if you listen to enough news, nothing will be the same. I hear reports of computers that may not be able to perform the simplest calculations because they won't know if it's 1900 or 2000. This one issue will cause worldwide chaos because at the heart of nearly everything we do today, there is a computer controlling a part of the process. Some people are saying we'll be thrown back to the Stone Age, a world where technology no longer works.

I don't pretend to understand but that doesn't sound logical. In fact, it sounds ridiculous.

In any case, I don't spend much time worrying about that. Who knows what January will bring but I suspect some things will never change. People will be people. They'll commit crimes against each other and I will be one of the good guys trying to figure it all out. At least I hope that makes me a good guy, but compromises are everywhere. Sometimes we have to do not-so-good things to make bad things better.

A great man once told me that the world would be a better place if people did two simple things: *Stand up for yourself, stand up for others.*

It was a profound statement at the time, but look where it got us. He's lying dead in the dirt, strangled by his own necktie, and I'm staring at two crime scenes that appear related but don't make sense when you try to tie them together.

Just beyond the crime scene boundary, locals have gathered, attracted by the whirling lights and the sound of more squads arriving every second. At the entrance to the park two cars block the drive, accompanied by a cluster of street uniforms holding back the news vans from getting too close. I can see reporters jostling for position so their cameramen can catch the basketball court in the background of the video.

Nearer to us, I spot a group of Chicago brass. I'm guessing the magnitude of this scene has brought out everyone up my chain of command. If nothing else, they need to maintain the appearance of control. It looks like every detective from my district is here, hovering close to the outer edges, watching inside, watching the crowd.

I can sense the restlessness of the bystanders. It's in their body language, in the snatches of conversation that float my way. They see the young boys, the blood, and they form their own conclusions. Based on my short time here, I know those conclusions are not complimentary towards the police.

This area of Chicago is depressed in every way: economically, socially, racially. In my short time here I've already encountered it in the words of people I've interviewed, in the way others act on the streets. The racial bias is perhaps the most damaging. Because I'm black, maybe some of them think I share their view of racial oppression or whatever term is popular now.

They couldn't be more wrong.

My own troubles are far afield from worrying whether someone like Dick Alberts' approves of my appearance in his life.

Most of the bystanders are black, with an equal Hispanic presence as well. That seems to be the nature of our world at the cusp of the new millennium. Whether we like it or not, there are other races and cultures that share our oxygen. We either have to encompass them or withdraw. So that makes it tough for those who cannot adapt. Sure, they can form little hate groups and scream about conservative values or the erosion of American culture, but what do they really expect to happen? Do a bunch of guys stomping around with Nazi tattoos and face paint truly think they are going to change the tide of racial immersion? It's already here and covering all of us.

Noah Bell understood that from a rational man's point of view. He wasn't just some victim crying racial foul. He didn't take the path of some of his peers, using another wrong to prove their right. His life was dedicated to finding that middle ground where everyone could stand as equals. It earned him a nickname of the Crown Prince. He was Chicago's new royalty. If it comes out that he fell victim to the very segment of society for which he fought, that will undercut a life's work. It will betray the values he espoused and prove to an outside world looking for justification that blacks truly are their own worst enemy.

That thought bothers me.

Off to one side a white man is quietly watching the events. He's small and hunched, timid looking, and it worries me. He's a perfect target if the crowd gets charged up. He's cut off from his own herd and when packs of animals form, they seek out the weak.

That's all we need to cap this night, riot squads clamping down on restless citizens tired of seeing death. We have enough on our hands inside the tape.

"Not a bad crowd for opening night," Griff says as he pulls up alongside me. The coffee cup is now empty. "But this is just the warm up act. The house band. All the top shields are here, to draw media attention. This keeps the other scene off the radar for a while, but that won't last forever. Wait until they hear about the headliner."

"Noah Bell," I say.

"Noah fucking Bell," he repeats, then turns to look me in the eye. "This one is going to carry a lot of heat, Arch, just because of who it is. Bell was an icon around here, the flame tip of hope in city hall and down on the streets. When we release his name, the real flames will erupt. You will get burned. How much and where is up to you, though. I'll try to help, but I'm an old white guy with no hair and a pension calling my name. No one listens to me, and you're still carrying baggage from your arrival. There's only so much I can help with."

I nod, looking over his head at the busy techs. "Thanks, I'll be fine."

He stares at me a second longer, like he's measuring something, then clicks his tongue. It's one of his quirks I've come to learn. "This party is going to run all night, partner. I need more coffee and a pisser. You do too. Well, at least the coffee part. I'm assuming you can piss on your own."

We sign out of the scene and head back through the woods away from the most significant murder Chicago has seen in decades. He's right, this is going to get messy. Despite my words to him, I'm not sure how to stay clean through the end.

THREE

Tuesday, July 13, 1999
7:26AM

I fiddle with the stack of papers in front of me for the hundredth time when Griff walks into the briefing room. Aside from a short break to run home and shower, we've been together all night working the scene. No greetings are necessary.

He pokes at the tray of donuts on a side table. "You know," he says. "If we had more high-profile cases, I would just wait until I got here to eat breakfast. We only get fed when the bosses show up. Oh, hey. A cherry turnover."

I level a hard stare at him.

"What?" He replies.

Nerves rattle inside of me, scattering my focus. Noah Bell served as the battering ram to get me in the doors of the Chicago detective's unit. Now he's dead and I've landed it as my first case in the lead investigator role.

This cannot be a coincidence.

On the massive whiteboard behind me are arranged pictures shot by Johnny and his crew. The right half of the board is dominated by a large press shot of Bell, the way I remember him. A strong champion for the people. Juxtaposed against that image is a photo of his final position. It doesn't show his face clearly, but it does display the desolate location, the unnatural angle of his limp limbs, the vacated car in the background. I hung them that way on purpose, to contrast the man in two phases and drive home the injustice of murder. At least that was my intent. Smaller scene shots revolve around the two large ones like a constellation.

The other half of the board belongs to Detectives Stewart and Towney, lead investigators for the park massacre. They hung several mug shots front and center. Turns out three of the dead kids had priors. In addition to those, there are a number of photos showing the basketball court from different angles.

Neither detective had said a word to me when we were setting up. I haven't seen them since.

Common sense says that both scenes are

related, that cause and effect are in play. The math - as we know it right now - plays out and supports the theory. Ballistics, DNA and trace evidence may come back and prove otherwise, but that's still a couple of weeks away. The labs take time to process all this stuff, leaving us to old fashioned grunt work and guesses.

There's a part of me that doesn't want this to be so easily tied up. For one, it would reduce the myth of Noah Bell to a footnote. It would take all that he had accomplished as a voice of racial harmony and turn it into a twisted, sad joke.

"Oh, he fought to elevate the plight of minorities? He tried to bring equivalency by showing how we're all not so different after all? Yeah, too bad his own kind didn't hear the message. They beat him down for a couple credit cards and $28. Now who's the victim?"

Another part of me wants this to be harder. To require effort and deduction and savvy. I want to earn the resolution to Bell's murder and prove that his efforts to get me on the force weren't just racially motivated, but that he believed I had what it takes to be an agent for good.

If Stewart and Towney clap the case closed by saying *'Yep, black kids killed their savior. Next.'*, then I'll be cheated of the chance to redeem Bell and prove myself. I'll be a secretary in this case, relegated to copying down notes and appending them to my case file. That will cement the thought that I only got this job because I'm black and don't have the chops to do it. That if a more seasoned officer had been awarded it, he would have made more of a difference.

I cannot stand thinking about that angle.

Griffin sidles over to me. He's already deep into his second turnover. No wonder the guy's stomach overlaps his belt by a large margin. I think I can hear his arteries straining.

"Penny for your thoughts?"

I take a sip of coffee, but it doesn't wet my dry throat. "You're going to need a lot more than that."

He raps a knuckle against a binder lying on the table before me. It's the case file I assembled last night, containing everything we know so far. He calls it a murder book. "Your stuff in order? They'll tear it apart if it isn't."

"I didn't change anything from what we put together." Now my nerves are the keening pitch of a violin bow drawn slow across the strings.

My partner shoves the rest of the pastry into his mouth and smiles through it. Red turnover filling stains his teeth. "Am I making you more nervous?"

"Yes, now shut up."

He leans in close, bringing with him the scent of cherries. "Look, better to show it in front of me than anyone else. People don't like the way you earned your tin, by having Noah Bell hand it to you in a courtroom, but this is your best chance to show them it wasn't a mistake. Forget the lawsuit, forget the news. Focus on the crime. Everyone coming into this room wants the same thing you do: To resolve the case."

"Just that some want it for different reasons than others. This is a political hot potato."

"Unfortunately, yeah. But true. This case will ripple across the city, hell the nation. The guy was the next Martin Luther King. If it comes out that he fell victim to the types of kids he tried to champion, well...you can bet the brass doesn't want to be the one to deliver that news. When they do, their information needs to be airtight. That's what you need to focus on, Arch. The truth will come out if you collect all the facts."

The door to the briefing room opens.

Here we go.

Captain Michael Donald is first. He's commander of the district and remained neutral in my lawsuit. My hiring didn't affect him directly.

Four other detectives follow him, including Stewart and Towney. They're laughing at something but when our eyes meet, both shut it down. Behind the two detectives follow a half dozen unis. I recognize the young black cop from the park scene but am surprised to see my friend Dick Alberts is not among the group. The young guy gives me a nod and I return it.

Black power, people.

Chief David Hecker slides into the room as the door closes, like he couldn't be bothered to push it open wider. He's pale, with reddish blond hair and a face that looks like he suffers from high blood pressure. It's perpetually red and strained, stranger to a smile. He leads the Bureau of Patrol and someone on his squad didn't make their tin because of me. It's no secret that he resents my presence in this station house. While he doesn't have direct command over me, his badge still carries weight and influence.

One second after the door shushes closed, it opens back up for Hector Gonzales, Deputy Super for the Bureau of Investigative Services. This guy is the top dog in my chain of command. He pulls the door handle with smooth control and steps into the room, stopping to survey everyone present. The man carries a reputation as someone deliberate in reaction, who needs to take things into consideration, before coming to a decision. I've heard other cops bitch that it takes him too long to decide anything. Those things are true, but I've also come to realize the guy is rarely wrong.

He's been fair to me since my arrival, we'll see if this morning alters that.

Hecker moves straight for the pastry table and looks over the offerings. "I told them to bring turnovers, dammit." He grabs a donut instead and slams down his notebook as he takes a seat. His freckled face carries a sour expression.

Griff belches and wipes his mouth.

I wait until everyone is settled at the rows of tables, coffee steaming in front of many, before I begin.

"Good morning everyone." I kept my words deliberate and even, to help control my nerves. "As you are all aware, last night Noah Bell was identified as a homicide victim in the 11th District. The location was the site of the old Middle Plains plastics factory near Lauren and 26th street."

I point to the portrait on the board behind me. "Mr. Bell's presence and work in Chicago has been well-documented. It will be certain to bring scrutiny once his identity is released. Evidence Services, under Jonathan Nayaki, presented and processed. The preliminary report was received around 4am and forwarded to everyone here. Hopefully you had a chance to review it."

None of the expressions change. I'm not telling them anything new.

Hecker taps his pen against the table, a staccato rhythm, and is the first to say what everyone else is likely thinking. "We need to talk about the investigation lead. Is White the correct officer? All eyes will be on us, do we really want to hand it over to a rook?" He casts his eyes around the room, seeking support. I could be invisible for all the attention he paid me.

Gonzales responds. "It was his slot in the rotation, his case. If we break protocol in order to assign it to someone more senior, we open ourselves to scrutiny."

"Yes, but..."

"Let's just get through this, David. You will have a chance to speak your mind after."

Even though Hecker holds a lower rank than Gonzales, he's been acting in the vacancy of Deputy Super for Patrol and conducts himself as if they are equal. It's a testament to Gonzales' self-control that he hasn't verbally slapped Hecker down more often. It's no secret the two men dislike each other.

I wait a moment to ensure no other comment is brewing. There isn't. Gonzales may have a rep, but he's well liked and more importantly, well respected. If he suggests a room remain quiet, it remains quiet.

"If you did not review the packet, here's a quick recap." I walk them through the evidence collected thus far, trying to avoid painting a picture not yet supported by facts. Griff's face hovers at the edge of my periphery, watching. I'm conscious of his expressions, expecting him to shake his head or frown at something I say. He doesn't. He does pick at his nose, however.

It only takes me ten minutes to rewind through Johnny's evidence report. From a facts standpoint, it's straightforward. If you set aside the public name, it boiled down to: A black man was found beaten and murdered in a shady part of Cicero, wallet emptied, car abandoned. This description could fit every third homicide case that rolled through the city.

"At this point," I summarize. "We have no witnesses identified. As such, we have not developed a suspect list, or even persons of interest."

The room remains silent, expectant with replies that are still forming.

Stewart gets up from his chair and walks to the other side of the board. He points to the mugshots of the kids. "Gang thugs. Weapons. Bell's credit card. Opportunity and motive. Here's your suspects. Bang, case closed." He claps his hands like he's closing a book.

Towney and several beat cops laugh. Even Hecker smiles.

I take a deep breath. Time to test the confidence of my supporters. "Sounds great on the surface, but I don't think the two events are related to each other."

FOUR

Stewart's smile disappears. He's a middle-aged guy with a blond buzz cut and stocky limbs. We've only interacted once, mostly introductions and a five-minute conversation. Griff says he's a good guy and well meaning. Still, I'm casting doubt on his case, which means I'm casting doubt on him and his deductions.

I ignore his stare but before I can speak, he takes a step forward. He's got a formal look on now. "Prior to the Bell report, we received an anonymous tip of shots fired in Paluski Park, on the back side of Middle Plains property. Officer Lands handled first response, officer Rollins was also in the area."

At that, Griff snickers behind me, but I don't know what he's laughing at.

"Officer Lands discovered six youths, aged 16 through 21, all GSW victims, all deceased. The seventh victim was a 32 year old male, also a gunshot wound victim, identified as Guy Johnstone." He gives another wave to the board behind him. "Three of the kids had prior arrests, two for assault, one for illegal firearm possession. Tattoos paint them as members of the Two Two Boyz."

Captain Donald glances over at one of his patrol officers, then back to Stewart. "Two Twos? Isn't that park on Latin Kings turf? Those guys have been going at it for years. How do we know this wasn't a gang gunning?"

"It's a possibility, but we've all seen plenty of those scenes. This doesn't fit the profile. Too many dead, all from one gang, precise shots. We'll need evidence to chase that angle. As White noted, ballistics and other processing will take a few weeks, though we've pushed priority on this. Thanks for the assist, supe." He nods at Gonzales. The inference is clear: Our top dog put in a call on their behalf to expedite a return. "But visible evidence at the scene included shell casings, weapons, and a credit card in the name of Noah Bell. As well, Johnstone has been confirmed as an employee of Travian Security Associates, assigned to Bell as personal protection."

This grabs Donald's attention. "Travian? As in William Travian?"

Stewart nods. "Yes, sir. One and the same."

He shakes his head. "Great, now that guy?"

I don't know who William Travian is, or why he will be a problem.

Heckler places both palms down on the table. I notice his donut is not eaten. "It seems to me the case is closing itself. These kids attack Bell in an isolated location, beat him to death for his money; your typical crime of opportunity. The bodyguard chases them through the woods and catches up to them at the park where they shoot it out and knock off each other. Black-on-black violence, happens all the time. I think we can wrap this up quickly."

He gets up to leave, as if everything is settled. I open my mouth to protest and am cut off again, this time by Gonzales.

"David, sit. Nothing is that easy, you know better than to speculate theory before evidence. We cannot leap to case conclusion. It will taint officer review."

"Screw that, Hector. A shit storm is brewing on this thing. Bell was Chicago's favorite son. Once we release his name, the liberals will go ape shit. They'll probably start picketing City Hall and blame us in some way. We need to nail this shut ASAP. The gang attack is logical. Why make our lives any harder?"

Gonzales stands up. "I said: Sit. We do things right, at the expense of fast if need be. Precisely because this is Noah Bell will we do this right. All eyes are on us."

"And you want to give it to White? It's only been a couple of months since his suit settled out. People still remember, he doesn't have a fan club watching his back. You want to court disaster when he screws up? It will be a PR nightmare."

I notice he says 'when', not 'if'.

"What I want," Gonzales says as he sits back down and sips from a cup almost empty. "Is to hear what one of my detectives has to say about the case. I will worry about my team. You worry about innocent bystanders getting run over by your patrol officers."

That shuts up Hecker. He shakes his head, but he's shrewd and ambitious. He knows he can't afford to make an enemy of someone who outranks him and who will have say in his application for the vacant spot of Deputy Superintendent. At this point the two men are disagreeing on a professional point, but if he continues to push it, things could escalate too far. He sits down and pushes away his donut.

"You going to eat that?" Griff asks, but gets no response.

"Now, Detective White, care to share your thoughts? Repeat what you told me earlier." Gonzales turns and addresses the rest of the room. "As a blanket disclaimer, none of what is to follow leaves this room. It's all speculation and part of our internal process. It doesn't need to scroll across the news."

The faces in the room are once again on me. Off to one side, Stewart crosses his arms and remains standing, staring at me.

"Let's start chronologically," I say, and flip open my murder book. "Page 5 of your brief. The first call came in at 9:02 PM. Report of several gunshots in the vicinity of the park. A few minutes after that, another call, this one anonymous, no mention of shots, but specific about location inside the park. Twenty minutes after that, another anonymous call about the factory. This one was much more vague."

Captain Donald and Hecker exchange glances. "Inconsistent 911 calls are common, White," Donald says. "In fact, it's rare that callers are accurate about what they're reporting. You should know this from your time on patrol."

I nod. "I do. I'm not questioning that. However, how many gunshot wounds?" I look over to Stewart.

He doesn't pause. "Eleven. Several victims had two."

"That many shots attract attention, even here, right?" For this I look back to Griff, seeking to bring him into the conversation.

My partner gives a confident nod. "It does seem strange that more calls didn't come in."

No one says anything to counter his statement so I continue. "There was no weapon around the bodyguard. Where did it go? Those two shots were on point and probably killed him instantly. If he took out six kids and died in the process, you'd think his gun would be close by."

"You're assuming there were only six kids total on that court," Stewart says, voice flat. "Could have been more. The ones that lived took him out, took his gun, and high-tailed it out of there. We'll never hear from them again, until that weapon shows up at a different crime scene. When we get ballistics back, then we'll know which guns killed who. I've got teams heading back out there this morning to scour the woods. If the bodyguard's gun is anywhere around there, we'll find it."

"In the meantime, we have other questions." I'm not backing down from my thoughts. Gonzales frowns at me over the top of his reading glasses, but I can't tell if it's from doubt, concern, or something else.

"Let's play Connect Four. If those kids did rob and beat Bell, how did that happen? Where was the bodyguard the whole time? The car was less than thirty yards from where Bell's body was found, so in that space we have to assume Johnstone was close by. If he was a professional, then he knew Close Protection Tactics dictate a tight perimeter set by protective details, no more than ten yards to a stationary target. At that distance, help is seconds away. How could those kids have jumped Bell with Johnstone hovering nearby?"

Before anyone can respond I plunge further. This is where I test my Deputy Super's allegiance. "Further, it appears Bell was beaten after being strangled."

Hecker's eyes widen and several of the other detectives lean forward.

Gonzales holds up a hand to forestall any conversation. "What makes you say that, Detective White? Lab results aren't back. Be careful making leaps in logic with that fact level."

"I spoke with Johnny Nayaki and he is of the same opinion, from his preliminary review. Ligature marks on the neck are consistent with strangulation by some type of garrote, like his tie, but that is not an instant act. Unconsciousness can happen in sixty seconds, but brain function doesn't fully cease until four minutes. So what was going on while that's happening? And once he is dead, why beat up the body?"

"Speculation," Donald says. "It's something to consider, but not much to work with."

"Also," I add. "The blood spatter and quantity is inconsistent with expected results."

"I saw the blood under his head," Stewart says.

"Yes, but not much anywhere else. They shattered his jaw, guys. He lost teeth. An orbital fracture ruptured the skin of his cheek. Bell was pounded to a pulp. His blood should have been everywhere, but it wasn't, because his heart was no longer pumping."

"The autopsy is scheduled for this afternoon," Griff interjects. "That may give us some answers around the order of things. Based on what we know so far, I expect ballistics to give us some *very* interesting information."

"Like what?" Hecker demands.

Griff simply looks over to Stewart. "You want to talk? Or me? I can do it with an accent."

Stewart shakes his head, visibly irritated. "Stop sneaking around my scene." To the rest of the room he says: "Two of the kids were shot in the back, in a direction that suggests they were fleeing back towards the factory. One was shot in the forehead from what looks like close range. The basic layout doesn't add up."

"Well, you know how these punks are," Hecker says. "Shoot while running away, scatter bullets like they're throwing parade candy. Shit, for all we know those two were shot by their own friends."

A plausible, if dismissive, answer.

I know what he's talking about. Kids get their hands on a gun and think it makes them tough. They watch movies and think that teaches them what to do. But once real bullets fly, survival instinct kicks in and the response is to flee from imminent danger while firing back at it. There's no discipline, no training on proper grip or weapons practice. That's how innocent bystanders become a statistic.

A phone buzzes somewhere in the room. Gonzales stares at the board, deep in thought, then jumps slightly when he realizes it's him. He pulls out his Blackberry and studies it through his glasses. He turns to Hecker. "Come on, David. Jacobs is ten minutes out. He wants us to take a look at his press conference brief before he goes live."

Jacobs is Superintendent Randall Jacobs, the top dog over us all. Gonzales and Hecker answer to him. I've never met the guy, he rarely shows up in this district according to what I've been told. He prefers to stay downtown where the power centers are. If he's coming out this way to deliver a presser, that tells you how high profile these cases are.

Gonzales pauses at the open door to the briefing room, turning back to us before he exits. "Good job, White and Stewart. I don't have to remind everyone of what we're handling here. News crews are already stacked five deep out front. Give them nothing. Nothing. Not until we finish the press conference. We're going to keep Bell from them this morning, see how long we can hold out. Once his name is released, all hell will break loose so let's postpone that inevitability as long as we can. Let the process be our guide. Work out of this station for the time being. There's desk space for two teams, Stewart and Towney, Toms and White. The detective force the Chicago PD will be at your disposal, so use them as you need. There's no room in this case for cowboys so rely on each other."

He gives me a long look. There's some kind of message there, but I don't know what it is.

As the room empties, I remain standing in my spot, thinking a thousand different thoughts. Today is looking like it's going to be a mess and the timing couldn't be worse.

Griff walks over and claps me on the shoulder as the door swings shut, leaving us alone. "Good job, Arch. You presented well and held your own when Hecker came at you. Be proud of that, he's made more than one guy come undone with that style of his."

I shrug. "I'm not sure I pushed my case hard enough. Stewart and Towney are going to try and tie these two together, aren't they? Seal it up nice and tight before we get a chance to dig in deeper."

"Probably. We just have to keep producing pieces of the puzzle to prevent that bow from being tied on top." He pauses. "You know what you want to do next?"

I nod. "I'm calling William Travian, whoever he is."

FIVE

I hang up the phone twenty minutes later. Griff is still in the briefing room, no doubt snacking on the leftover pastries. As soon as I exited, other cops who were not present at the briefing drifted in like scavengers. Griff stayed back to protect his precious glazed favorites. I catch his eye through the glass plate wall and nod him over. He grabs one last donut and exits the room.

"You get in touch with Travian?" He asks, sucking sugar off one finger.

"No, but I got his schedule for the day from one of his flunkies. We can pay a visit. Have you ever dealt with him before?"

Griff shakes his head. "He lives above my pay grade. If Bell was the crown prince, Travian is the court counsel. He's connected with everything that goes on in Chicago, but you don't usually see his name in lights. He lets all his business partners take credit."

"Yeah? Well, it turns out he was also partners with Bell in several business ventures."

"Doesn't surprise me. Guy knows everyone. But I bet he's got great snacks at his place."

We exit the detective's room. The Ogden avenue station is from the 70s and some of the design reflects that. In some areas you can tell work has been done to upgrade cosmetics. Glass partitions section the space up across the lobby, often making it hard to judge depth and distance. The detectives are kept towards the back of the station.

Through all this plate glass, I can see out the front of the building. Gonzales wasn't kidding about press scrutiny. The entrance is packed with people, nearly all of them wielding the armament of the fourth estate. I see cameras, microphones, sound mikes and other equipment I can't name. Several beat unis have been assigned to create a cordon in front of the building, keeping everyone back from the podium that's been set up just outside the doors. This is where Gonzales - maybe even Jacobs - will set forth the facts of the case as we know them, or as we want them to be known.

Beyond the crowd of people, I can see news vans with satellite dishes mounted high. There's no sense of organization or order; they are parked every which way. The press conference is thirty minutes out yet. I wonder what Hecker, Gonzales and Jacobs have been discussing. There's no sight of any of them.

"Let's duck out the side," Griff says, sizing up the crowd.

"You read my mind."

The station has multiple entrances, most closed to the public. I make sure to avoid eye contact with anyone out front as we cut through the lobby and walk down a side hallway. Griff is first out into the harsh morning sun, swearing under his breath when we get blasted with humidity. This stuff rivals some of the hottest days back home. I never realized Chicago got this warm.

The side of the station holds a parking lot reserved for official vehicles. This is where police squads and other employees park. It has a barrier arm preventing entry into the lot without a badge swipe, but there's no other barrier or fence around the space, so someone could just walk around the gate assembly.

That's how she sneaks up on me.

"Detective White." It's a statement, not a question, terse and professional.

Griffin swears again, louder this time, and picks up his pace.

Sheila Walters emerges from the shadow of the building, direct in her line of approach, aimed at me. Her polo shirt sports the logo of FOX 32 Chicago, the local affiliate for FOX News. A voice recorder is clenched in her hand like a weapon. She must have seen me trying to escape out the side and ran around to cut me off.

I slow. "Ms. Walters." My tone is non-committal.

She spits aside all preamble. "Okay, spill. What's going on? Who is it?"

I debate playing dumb, but nix the idea. She's sharp and will know I'm playing her. I don't need that extra hassle.

"You can find out with the rest in a few minutes. If you stand by the Ficus tree, it gives a great side angle to the podium. Good luck."

She moves in front of me, blocking my progress. I could easily push her aside. She's petite, dark-haired, near my age and quite a head turner. Her looks are beauty pageant quality, with hints of Hispanic origin and a fire to match. But that's not the reason she gets camera time as a field reporter. To assign her success to mere physical looks undercuts her intelligence. I've seen her in action before and she's got some chops. Griff tells me she blew into Chicago a few weeks before I did and has been making her mark. This is not our first time speaking in a professional capacity.

But I resist the urge to blow past her. This day and age, everything is under scrutiny. Just my luck there would be a camera pulling B-roll and I'd get caught in the background. That wouldn't go over well. So I take a respectable step back and meet her eyes.

"Knock it off, detective. I know this is your case."

"How would you know?"

"It doesn't matter. Someone else is handling the kids at the park, so you were next on the docket. What happened at Middle Plains? Is that what brought Jacobs here?"

"The murder of seven people in a forgotten park isn't enough to bring the Superintendent down?" I counter. "It's the worst homicide scene since Al Capone and the St. Valentine's Day massacre. I'd say that warrants a presser from Jacobs."

"You're covering. Something happened at Middle Plains, something you guys want to keep under wraps. What is it?"

By now Griff is halfway to our cruiser, walking with his shoulders hunched like he's expecting to get shot on retreat. I bet if Sheila barked his name he'd jump out of his slacks. For a seasoned officer, he sure does shy away from contact.

I start to formulate a response, minding Gonzales' parting words, but before the first words emerge she's already fired off ten other questions. None of them I can answer, so I stop her with an upraised hand. Surprisingly she stops talking.

"There's nothing I can give you right now. You'll have to wait on the press conference with the rest."

"But you can later, right? Once the conference is over, you'll be able to talk on those points?"

"Possibly."

"No, not possibly. Certainly. Call me first."

"Look, I'm in the middle of a case. I've got more important things to do than give interviews."

Fire ignites in her hazel eyes. Against the tan complexion and blue-black hair, they look like molten gold. It's hard to ignore her. She truly has a face for TV. "There's a reason you have this one. A reason beyond it being your turn at the plate. That's where the real story is. Promise you will call me first, White. Promise."

From beside the protection of our car, Griff hollers out: "Just give in Arch. You know you want to."

"Fine," I reply, to get her out of my way. "Whatever. We'll talk later on."

Sheila Walters, field reporter for FOX 32, holds my gaze for a long second and there are many thoughts churning behind those eyes. I try to stare back but end up breaking first. Dammit.

She steps aside. "Do not leave me hanging."

Without another word, I stride towards the slickback cruiser assigned to us. Griff watches Sheila make her way back around to the front of the station. She bends over to dip under the drop arm barrier and he lets out a whistle.

"Grade A beef right there, son. If I was twenty-five years younger I'd..."

"...still trip over your tongue like a nervous schoolboy." I interject. "She'd chew you up and spit out Dunkin Donuts bits."

He sniffs at my comment. "I never liked pushy broads anyway."

"Broads?" I echo as I slide into the passenger seat. "Christ, Griff. This is 1999. No one uses that term anymore."

He doesn't respond and I don't follow it up. No sense prolonging this kind of conversation. I have my own thoughts on Ms. Walters and no inclination to share them.

Griff pauses at the lot exit and waits for the arm to lift. The road is clogged with vans and cars, worse than it looked from inside the station. Remote shots are being filmed from every conceivable angle. They all know something momentous happened last night and everyone wants to break the story first. Most probably think the basketball court massacre is the lead topic, but those like Walters with good instincts are sniffing another trail.

Many of the other reporters don't know me. They may know of my story, might remember the talking points of my lawsuit or Bell's intervention, but for most I'm a footnote lost in the chase for the next big thing.

That's fine with me. Preferable, actually. I need to focus on pulling together the doubts I cast on Stewart's case while resolving my own. Ideally, both happen together.

Griff spins the cruiser out into traffic. A male reporter stands near a CBS van, adjusting his ear piece. I watch as the cameraman counts down with his fingers.

3...2...1...

Just as he hits zero, Griff lays on the car horn. The reporter jumps, startled by the sudden sound, right as the camera goes live. He frantically tries to regain his composure and stutters into the mic.

My partner laughs. "Oh, man, that worked perfect. What a schlub. Stupid newsies."

I smile out the window. The guy may be pushing retirement, but he acts like a frat boy at times.

"You still want to swing back to the factory?" He asks me.

"Yeah, let's walk it in daylight, see if there's anything we missed."

"You know, if Nayaki thinks you're casting doubt on his work, he will track you to your home. You know those old Pink Panther movies? Where Clouseau comes home and has to hunt through the place for his Asian butler before the guy attacks him? Yeah, that'll be you and Johnny. He's small but scrappy."

I smile again, letting my eyes wander across the crowd gathered in front of the station. I see Walters walking across the lawn towards the FOX van. She points to me in a gesture that I don't really understand the meaning of. "I'll take my chances."

We wheel through the western suburbs of Chicago, my home for the moment and hopefully much longer. It's not that I have new love for this city. In honesty, it's not my kind of place. Too large, too crowded, too fast and I haven't even been through a winter yet. I'm a southern guy, used to things a little slower, people a little simpler. My life to date existed in a smaller world, where everyone somehow knew someone who knew someone that you knew. Conversation revolved around the things we saw or heard, cemented to people, not ideas.

But, as with many twists that turn our lives in strange directions, fate conspired to bring me north. Before coming, I knew very little of Chicago, and even less about Cicero. Sure, I'd heard about Al Capone and the infamous St. Valentine's Day massacre. Over a half dozen mob members were gunned down in a garage during the time of Prohibition. Two of them took shotgun blasts to the face after they had fallen, obliterating their features. That's sending a message.

Until yesterday, it was the single bloodiest event in Cicero's history. It encapsulated the troubled history of this near-city suburb. Griff told me a saying on my first day: "If you smell gunpowder, you're in Cicero."

I laughed when he said it, but I'm not laughing now. No one is.

In any event, circumstances brought me here. I may not have arrived under the best of conditions, but deep inside I know I made the right decision. No one will ever know the reasons unless I decide to share. I'm not inclined to do that, to reveal the reasons I raised a lawsuit against the entire city, claiming discrimination in the hiring process.

They had dismissed my application based on lack of experience, and rightfully so. I'm a young guy with only a few years under my belt, and there were more qualified guys in line ahead of me. But none of that mattered. I had to get up here, for reasons personal and intense.

Speaking of which...I look at the dashboard clock, calculating.

"We need to finish up at Middle Plains by 11:30. I got a quick something at noon. You can just drop me back at my car."

Griff gives me a wide-eyed stare. "You are not serious. Arch! You've just had a career-changing case dropped in your lap. Whatever else you got going on needs to come in second for now."

I shake my head. "It won't take long. Maybe an hour, then we'll get back after it."

His eyes narrow. He's not watching the road and we drift over the center line. A car honks coming in the other direction. I tug the wheel, pulling us back into our lane. He doesn't take the hint, or take his eyes off me. "You keep doing this, disappearing at weird times, no reason given. What's up? What's so urgent that it can't wait? You got someone on the side? A married lady, maybe? Handsome buck like you probably can pick the litter."

"No, nothing like that. No married lady."

"A married man?" His voice quivers.

I wave off that question too. "Christ, no. Look, it's really no one's business, not even yours. I have something already planned and missing it isn't an option."

My partner moves his eyes back to the road, but it's a slow movement, indicating he isn't sold on my answers. "You sure don't inspire much trust," is his only comment.

I know.

SIX

We pull through the open gates of Middle Plains Plastics. In daylight, I can see many of the details that were not visible last night. The driveway is bordered by trees standing tall. At one time this would have been a nice entrance. The trees give an impression of soldiers at attention, tracing your path in silent judgment and watchful care, making you feel small for daring to intrude.

Now, weeds choke out the trunks. The leaves are thick and unruly, growing with anarchistic intention in every direction. The asphalt driveway is faded gray, with thin-stemmed vegetation pushing up through the cracks, the concrete curbs chipped from years of neglect.

As the tree-lined drive opens to the parking lot, I see Bell's car still in the same position. The door remains flung wide open, exposing the fine German leather to harsh sun and swirling dust eddies.

A dozen feet away from the Mercedes a police cruiser with full light rack blocks any further entry into the parking lot. Griff haggled with Hecker long past midnight to get a street uni stationed there. It's not normal procedure, but due to the victim's identity and amount of care we needed to show for this case, Hecker relented. Unhappy, but relented nonetheless.

"Where's the watch detail?" I ask, looking around. There's no sign of the cop who should be standing guard. The cruiser itself doesn't prevent someone from simply walking around both cars and entering the scene. That's what the uniformed officer is for. If someone just dumped a police car here for show, who knows what could have happened.

"How would I know?" Griff grunts. "Probably out back taking a piss."

I get out of the cruiser and take a moment to scan the area. The sound of traffic is muffled, like it belongs to a higher altitude and we're only privy to the bass notes this far down. There's a stillness in the air, the buzz of nature, heat waves rippling off the old asphalt.

Something doesn't seem right.

Griff points to the passenger front fender of the squad car. It's crumpled and dented. "Rollins is on watch. No wonder he wasn't at roll this morning. The dumbass hit some pedestrian last night. Sitting his ass out here in the heat must be his punishment. Ha. What a dipshit."

To the immediate south is a train yard, visible across the open expanse of property. Dozens of tracks mark the boundary between the factory grounds and the outer edge of the yard. Rail cars occupy every inch of track, most sitting silent and empty. I hear the occasional voice of a yard worker hollering to someone else but like the ever-present traffic sounds, it belongs to a different segment of the world.

Opposite of the yard, to the north, is the tree line that hides Paluski Park from view. Maybe Rollins walked over there to check things out. That would be breach of duty.

I place my hand on my holster and start forward. Griff notices and shakes his head. "Really? This ain't some stupid thriller novel, Arch. Nothing's going down. Rollins!" He hollers. "Get out here!"

Ignoring him, I circle the cruiser. Nothing seems out of place with it, other than the damaged front fender and the smashed headlight. Rollins is going to take heat for a long time over hitting someone. Cops can be the biggest assholes sometimes, and over the dumbest shit.

The orange cones marking the line of entry are still in place. In fact, aside from Bell's body, which was removed last night, nothing has changed. I trace the cones and walk into the scene. Griff follows in my wake, humming a tune under his breath. I don't recognize it.

"I'm telling you," I say, low. "Something is not right."

"Yeah," he sniffs. "It smells here, like I stepped into a community latrine for homeless people. That is what's not right."

A sound lifts out of the building to my left, soft but unmistakably human. It's a shout of pain, quickly muffled like someone clamped a hand over the mouth of the person yelling. I yank my weapon out, thumb on the safety. Griff does likewise.

Oh, now he takes it serious.

I raise my voice enough to project across the courtyard, but short of yelling. I like to think of it as my authority tone. "This is Detective White with the Chicago Police Department. Whoever is inside, make yourself known."

"Whomever," Griff whispers behind me.

My ears fill with the sound of my accelerating heartbeat.

There's no response. I glance back at Griff as I approach a single service door set in the middle of the building. "Stand down, anyone inside. Make yourself known. We are entering the building."

The service door is already cracked open; I push it wider with the muzzle of my weapon and lean back. Inside is dark, despite the morning sun. Rays of light punch holes through the interior, entering through windows and holes in the roof, but can't do much to illuminate the sheer volume of space. I step through the doorway and off to one side in a single move. Griff follows suit, setting up on the other side of the door.

We pause a few seconds, letting our eyes adjust, trying to get a sense of the layout. A ceiling hangs over us, the second floor, which I guess are the offices and break room. Past it I can see the open factory area. Stairs off to my right lead up to that second floor.

Another sound leaks towards us, coming from a point by the stairs. It's a grunt, the scuff of footsteps. I slide over and crane my head around the railing, leading with the sights of my gun. The sound of someone landing on the floor and running away echoes back to me.

On the landing halfway up the stairs is a body, wearing officer black, crumpled in a heap. The feet twitch. I vault up in two steps. "Officer down!" It's Rollins. Even in the dark I can see his shock of red hair and freckled face. His eyes are closed but one hand scrabbles for grip on the metal grate landing. It's a reflexive movement only, but signals that he's alive at least.

Griff rushes up to help, but I wave him off and point to the far end of the building. "Someone's running that way. Go!"

He shoves me aside. "Yeah, send the old fat guy on a foot race instead of the young stud. Terrible plan. You go."

I leap over the railing and drop to the floor, tucking into a shoulder roll. I come up in a sprint and wind my way through the space, leaping over tipped barrels, darting around discarded piles of machine parts. My eyes strain to pick up any sign of movement, detect anything that indicates where the suspect is.

Because that's what he is to me: a suspect.

Anyone running from the site of a fallen cop automatically tags himself as worthy of cuffs, even if only to get the true story. Maybe it's a homeless person who panicked and knocked down Rollins. Griff has said this place is very popular for them because it's large and dry for the most part. I can understand someone with a couple of warrants outstanding trying to escape arrest. There have been plenty of times in my career when desperation made someone do something they normally wouldn't.

Maybe it's another kid from the gang last night, coming back for something, and he intentionally assaulted Rollins. If that's the case, I need the kid. More than anything, I need that kid.

A door opens farther ahead, letting in a spark of light that crests over some kind of huge generator. I alter my course, picking up speed. If the suspect gets outside, my chances dwindle. He can easily disappear into the woods that surround this place. I can't afford to let him get away. Desperation fuels my legs, pitching aside caution for speed.

Which is why I don't see the metal pipe swing out from behind the generator. It catches me flush across the forehead and the impact fills my skull.

The world tumbles to black.

***

I feel myself being pulled to a sitting position. Voices come from a distant place, light pierces my vision and I squint back against the pain.

Everything resolves down to a flashlight wielded by a paramedic. He's repeating my name, waving the light back and forth. I grunt and push it aside. "Get that thing out of my face." I get off the stretcher and stand silent for a moment while everything shudders and shakes. The dizziness passes and I feel somewhat normal, except for the sensation of being two degrees removed from my own brain. It's like watching myself from a tiny corner in my skull.

I'm in the shadow of the building, next to the service door. They must have wheeled me this far and stopped when the light got better. Police cars litter the entrance to the factory, lights whirling in silence, unis moving in and out of the scene. Two ambulances idle next to Rollins' car. Griff must have called it in as a 10-52, officer needs ambulance. Great. Now I'll get thrown into the hazing bucket with Rollins.

Griff emerges from the building. "There's my Sleeping Beauty."

I rub my eyes. "Did he get away?" I already know the answer but have to ask anyway.

"Oh yeah, long gone. The way you knocked the weapon out of his hand with your forehead scared the shit out of him." He thumbs off to the side where an officer walks with a length of pipe in a plastic evidence bag. I see one of Johnny's team members writing in a notebook. There must have been a couple of them over at the basketball court to get here so quick. Or I've been out that long.

"You talk to Rollins? What happened?"

Griff motions with his head to the row of windows above us. Most of them no longer have glass. "He heard a noise and saw a face in the window, peeking out. When he came in to investigate, he got jumped. Guy used some kind of strap to choke him out."

"He's okay though?"

"Yeah." Griff points to one of the ambulances as it starts up and wheels down the drive. "They're taking him back for medical, just to make sure he checks out. Looks like the guy didn't want to kill him, just put him to sleep."

"You think it was a homeless guy? That's pretty aggressive."

"Only if they got something to hide."

"Or, if they know what happened here last night. Like maybe, their friends are lying all over the basketball court, bleeding out."

He nods. "I thought of that. Strange as it sounds, that may be a good scenario for us. Maybe we get evidence that points us in a direction. Johnny's inside now. They will sweep the place after they've finished cleanup at the basketball court, but it's a lot of ground to cover so we may not find anything. Even if we do, don't expect much today. Those guys are maxed out and there's no help coming soon."

I give a disgusted sound. Can't believe I got jumped by some punk. "And I'm assuming Rollins didn't see much."

"Nope. He saw a flash of face, went into the dark and next thing he knows, he's waking up from the dark. Hey, that sounds like a Friday night for me."

My forehead throbs. I touch it and bite back a wince. There's a large knot on the right side. Tomorrow is going to bring a whopper of a headache. I glance at my watch. It's nearing eleven. I lost an hour to slumber land. My cell phone shows several missed calls. I angle the screen away from Griff so he can't see the names or numbers. "Can you drop me back at my car?"

"You should take the next ride in the bus to where Rollins is going, Arch. That was quite a blow."

"I'm fine. Let's go."

He stares at me and I can hear the wedge driving deeper, widening the rift between us.

But I'm not ready to share.

"Okay, whatever." He says at last. "Take care of your shit and get your head in the game. I don't have time to babysit."

I stumble twice walking to our cruiser but he says nothing.

SEVEN

The roads of western Chicago are subdued at 11:30 on a Tuesday morning. I pilot my old Plymouth with a heavy foot through the side streets towards the Palmer Square area, several miles north of Cicero. The car struggles to blow cold air against the July day, so I settle for open windows. Sweat trickles down my temple.

My mind bounces through a hundred different thoughts, fragmented and unpredictable in their patterns. I don't know if it's because of the blow to my head or the implications inherent in that blow. If there's a witness out there, some gang kid too scared or unwilling to come forward, I need to find him. If this kid knows that he was implicit in the murder of Chicago's favored son, that might be enough to drive him underground, to send him to the places that my rookie experience can't bring me, losing this case in the process.

If that happens, I'll have to rely on Griff more than I want to. The guy means well and knows these streets like the back of his hand, but I can't simply ride his coattails to resolution. I have to show everyone that I have the chops to solve it on my own. There is no other option.

I pull over to the curb on Humboldt boulevard, easing my car into an open spot. Just ahead a church points to the heavens with a brick steeple that soars above the roofs of the surrounding houses. It is telling us all to look up, to see a brighter day ahead when the calendar turns to a new millennium, but like many, I can't afford to send my eyes that high. There are too many things right in front of me that demand my attention and if I don't watch out, they will trip me up.

Across the boulevard is a long stretch of green, an open expanse of nature several blocks long, but barren of anything except unkempt grass and weeds. Maybe someday the city will dress this spot up, install playground equipment for local kids, make it a place where those who can, can come outside and soak in the sun.

I turn back to the row of houses lining the sidewalk. From the outside they resemble any other block of two story brick structures, with deep porches and garages stacked along an alley out back. The last six houses leading to the church don't bear any outward difference, but the insides carry a new purpose. Instead of families inhabiting those spaces, a special kind of promise lives behind the oak doors. An outreach program for disabled people had purchased these houses and renovated them to be function-specific.

Now those unable to care for themselves had a unique place where those who cared, could.

I take the front steps two at a time and cross the porch, conflicting emotions of joy and sadness stirring my gut. My forehead throbs, but that's nothing compared to the burden others carry and I don't allow myself to acknowledge the pain.

The front door is unlocked, as it always is during the day, and I enter. The house is quiet. From upstairs I hear the movement of people slow-walking along the hall. Low murmurs of encouragement accompany the heavy steps. Someone is doing therapy.

I head down the first floor hallway towards the back of the house. The layout has not been significantly changed from what it originally was, as far as I can tell. Kitchen, living room, bathrooms are all in the expected location. The house is large, six bedrooms in all, and I suspect it was designed to have upper and lower apartments when built. Those rooms have now been substantially modified in purpose to suit the mission of this special place.

At the end of hall, three bedrooms await behind the doors. I enter the one on the right.

A young girl is lying on a Stryker medical bed, one that cost thousands of dollars and is purpose-built. Tubes run under the rails, providing life and sustenance. The steady beep of a heart monitor fills the room, marking her existence like a clock hidden somewhere beyond the horizon.

Her name is Anna. Today she turns six.

I kneel down next to the bed. "Hi, baby. It's daddy. Happy birthday." I rest my hand on her forehead.

At my voice she twists, eyes unfocused, arms and legs and voice unable to convey the message of her damaged mind. Faint sounds dribble from her mouth, a way of speaking back.

Anna is afflicted with *Athetoid Cerebral Palsy*. It's a severe case, marked by slow, writhing movements that are involuntary and uncontrollable. As if that wasn't enough, she's also hypotonic, indicated by decreased muscle tone. Even if she could coordinate her unwieldy limbs enough to stand, she doesn't possess enough strength to stay upright. Doctors trace it back to hypoxia in the womb, of such sufficient degree that there is no recovery. They speak only of prolonging her days, using statements like 'quality of life' and other vague terms that can never fully express the horror of being trapped within your own mind and body.

Doctors have also told me time and again that she cannot comprehend or process external stimuli, that any response is a general reaction with no inherent meaning. They say that deep in the silence of her skull I don't exist.

They're wrong. I do. And she knows I'm here. She knows I will always be here.

I stare at her as I caress her head, her forearm. She looks so tiny in the bed, shrunken body kept alive by the nutrients fed through tubes. Her body has not grown and developed, as if in solidarity with her mind. She may never get much bigger. Her wrist, the diameter of my thumb, twists. I place my finger in her hand and feel weak pressure as she closes her fist around it. It could be pure reflex. Or it could be my daughter grasping onto the anchor of her life, desperate to connect to another human. I feel the burn in my eyes and my peripheral vision goes fuzzy with tears.

Where society at large wrings its hands over the unknown state of our world in six months, everything I am and everything I need is right here. There may yet be years ahead for Anna and I want to spend every one of them holding hands.

Hold on tight, baby. Hold on to daddy. I'll never let you go.

A slight noise from the corner of the room interrupts my solace and I turn my head, wiping at my eyes. "When did you get here?"

Sheila Walters gets up from the armchair, the only other piece of furniture in the room, and moves to the bedside across from me. "Just a few minutes before you."

Her eyes, smoky and intense when she's chasing a story, are red and swollen. Six years now, carrying the guilt of our daughter's condition like a sword of Damocles. The doctors have said many times there was nothing she could have done, that it was an unpredictable incident, but those words have never penetrated Sheila's armor. Six years and she still thinks it's all her fault.

"I told Michelle to bring the cake when you got here. I hope that's fine."

"That works," I respond, eyes still fixed on Anna. She squirms her head a fraction towards me. Small mewling sounds leak from her lips even as her eyes trace a blank stare to the ceiling. Her expression is slack, an effect of the hypotonic_muscle condition. She will never smile, or frown, or laugh. The muscles necessary to do so won't respond.

Michelle, Anna's caregiver, ducks into the room with an ice cream cake and a subdued greeting for me. I don't know how she can do it, day after day, confronted with the helplessness of others in the house. There are six residents in total, all similar to Anna, but with varying degrees of affliction. It takes a special heart to be that giving and I know I could never do it. I can barely look at my daughter without cracking. I'm not that strong.

It's chocolate ice cream cake. The room is silent as Sheila cuts it into pieces and places them on paper plates. She even cuts one for Anna, who can never eat it.

We exist in silence. No birthday music, no laughter, no shrieks of other children at play outside. That kind of celebration is beyond my daughter. The scene is so depressing that I don't even want to contemplate the next decade or two.

How can we go on like this?

When I'm with Anna, time is suspended, life is suspended. There is only the moment that exists between a father and daughter as they hold hands. In that moment are the school dances, the bedtime reading, the struggles with homework and boys and hard teachers; the driving lessons and goodbyes at the entrance to the dormitory. In the contact of skin on skin exist glimpses of a fullness she will never attain, snatches of experience unneeded for her daily survival.

"Arch," Sheila says after a while, breaking the atmosphere. She cannot stand silence.

"The next words better not be about Middle Plains."

She gives a faint smile. "You know I would never do that. What happened to your head? You have a pretty good bump."

"That's not what you really want to ask, is it?"

A moment of held breath from her. Then: "No. I want to talk about us."

"How many times can we hash this out, Sheila? There is no us."

"But there could be. There should be. I followed you all the way up here because I believe that. This," she motions around the small room. "This is our 'us', this is our family. We can make a life with what we've been given. Not all fairy tales end the same."

From the front of the house comes the sound of the door opening and closing. Subdued conversation follows, too faint for me to understand the words, but I hear Michelle's voice. Maybe another set of parents is visiting their child right now, opening up the same kind of wounds that never heal. I've never met any of the others - we've only been here a month - but I feel a sense of remote kinship. We are all tethered to the same orbit.

Sheila makes it seem easy and simple in the way she answers her own questions, she always has, but there are no answers in me that sound the same. Maybe it's her ability to cut through the chaff and see the core story. I don't know. Together we created a life. Through some fickle and cruel twist of fate we unwittingly consigned it to eternal imprisonment, thereby imprisoning ourselves with a different set of shackles.

I get up and toss my plate into the trash. There's very little cake eaten. I follow it with Anna's plate, which has no cake eaten. "I'm sorry. I can't talk about this right now."

"Then when, Arch? When will you stop carrying your cross and look up at what's in front of you? Ten years now; ten years since you kissed me under the tree on the Fourth of July. You were my first, you are my only. There was an 'us' before Anna, what happened to them? How can they have disappeared so completely?" There's no acrimony or accusation in Sheila's tone, she's not that way. It's how she excels at her job. The woman can compartmentalize emotion from the circumstance and assess the situation from the best perspective. I've never met someone with her amount of clarity and focus.

But I do detect a hint of fear in her voice.

"I don't know. I just don't." Leaning over, I give Anna a kiss on the forehead. She releases a raspy groan. In that I hear a message meant only for me. "Happy birthday again, little girl. Daddy loves you very much."

Sheila's eyes are glistening when I stand back up. I open my mouth, knowing that whatever emerges will be insufficient for her needs. It's a futile gesture. She waves me off and turns away to stare out the window. I wait a heartbeat, then spin to leave.

Time to get my game face back on. These moments with Anna are few and far between, but they drive me. If I want to stay in this area for her, I need to find the reason why Noah Bell was murdered last night. If I don't, I have a feeling that Anna and I will be looking for yet another facility that can meet her needs.

Michelle re-enters the house as I approach the front door. She gives a shy smile and ducks past as I push open the door and step out onto the porch.

Griff leans against the railing, waiting for me.

EIGHT

My partner and I stare at each other, deciding how to proceed through this lie. I've kept Anna a secret from everyone I've met, including him. In law enforcement, you trust your partner with everything, because you are trusting him with your life at some point. Hiding Anna this way can be taken as an act of small betrayal.

"Why didn't you say anything?" He finally asks.

"For what purpose?" I hear the defensiveness in my tone but can't help it. I am defensive. He's just seen my greatest vulnerability. "Sympathy? Excuses? Frankly, it's no one's business but my own."

"Arch, you sued the city of Chicago to make your shield. You played a race card which I haven't seen again since we've been teamed up, which tells me you don't really believe you were discriminated against because of your color. You enlisted Noah freaking Bell to create a public relations campaign, all based on the racial discrimination that I don't think you think really existed."

He scrubs his hand through the layer of thin white hair atop his head. "That set a lot of people against you, man. A lot. No one likes to be told they've done something wrong and they really don't like it when it's been told in public. Hecker is a perfect example. The guy is a Grade A prick, but he's also fair to most everyone. You come along, swing your lawsuit hammer and suddenly one of his guys is bumped to the back of the line for a promotion. Now he's got you in his sights. Don't you think if others knew about your situation they'd adjust their attitudes?"

"Listen, Griff. I needed to get my daughter here. This program is one of just a few in the country with an opening. Making grade and moving here helped get her placed. That is the only reason I filed a suit. I had to be near her. Nothing else matters, including what Hecker thinks or knows."

He shakes his head. "I get it and don't

blame you. Can't imagine what you've been through. I just think it would make your life easier if others knew your motives. You've got a force of Dick Alberts waiting for you to screw up so they can knock you down. Why live life so hard?"

I step closer to him, using every inch of my six-three to look down at him. "Do not tell anyone. It's my story, my right to reveal if and when I want. I don't need a bunch of pity-slaps from old timers who can't see beyond their noses. Nor do I need a partner following me around because I don't tell him every little detail of my life."

Griff backs up, hands raised. "Okay, okay. Ease up, cowboy. I got your back. I'm just saying...Any more secrets you want to clear out before we get our asses back in gear?"

"No, let's get goin..."

At that moment Sheila emerges from the house, dabbing at her eyes with a tissue. She looks back to Michelle and says goodbye before turning to me. She freezes when she registers Griff's presence.

He looks at her. At me. The pieces click in place and his eyes widen in shock.

Sheila says nothing. She hurries off the porch and gets in her car. The sound of exhaust is still hanging in the air before he says anything. "Holy shit, Arch. Is that your...?"

There's no escape for me. Time to own up. I can sense my control slipping away. "She's the mother."

"Oh, good lord. Now it all makes sense. She showed up a few weeks before you did, landing that spot with FOX. You'd already won your case and the appeal was pending, but everyone knew the city was planning to drop it. Once you had a start date, she was clear to move up here."

I nod, short and abrupt. "There was a lot of logistics to moving my daughter cross-country. I handled that while Sheila got herself settled."

He shakes his head and ambles off the porch. "You are a master of secrets. Should have been a priest. Now come on. We got a meet with Travian ahead of us."

***

I blink against the bright sun as Griff wheels the cruiser towards Chicago proper. The harsh light is causing sparks of pain to flare in the back of my head, but I push the sensation away. There's no time to attend a concussion.

We cut east on Cermak before heading north on State. "He's got an office at Monroe and Wabash. That's right downtown," Griff says, playing tour guide. Maybe he thinks I don't know my way around Chicago yet.

He'd be right, but I'll never tell him that.

We pull over to the sidewalk and he stops in a No Parking zone. The plates on our cruiser identify it as an official vehicle so there's little chance of us getting towed. Elevated train tracks stand over us, a massive glass and steel tower stands over them. I still haven't gotten used to the vertical nature of this city. I came from a place where ten stories made up the tallest building. Here, I think ten stories is the low-rent district.

There's noise everywhere. The train racketing above us on the tracks, cars honking, somewhere I can hear the repeated beep of a large truck backing up. The sidewalks are crowded with the lunch crowd making their way back to work. A short heavy guy chattering into a cell phone bumps into me and gives a dirty look before proceeding onward. Asshole.

The sounds are cut off abruptly as we enter the lobby and cross the tiled space. There are people milling around, a central receptionist and the buzz of conversation hanging in the air. No one pays attention to us as we stand before elevator banks, waiting.

"Travian has a rep as a bulldog," Griff says as we board. "I met him once a few years ago at some police function. He's a friend of Jacobs, Gonzales, Hecker, the mayor, and anyone else who signs your paycheck. He seemed okay, so maybe his rep is overblown. Or maybe he turns it on and off when needed. But I've heard stories of him plowing through people who stand in his way like they weren't even there."

"What's his business? Besides the security company?" I ask, looking out the glass walls of the elevator. We clear the first few floors and I turn away from the view. I'm not fond of heights.

"More like: What isn't? He does a lot of commercial development, he's on the board of several companies, he's got a stake in the *Tribune* and WGN news. Hell, I even saw him on an episode of *Oprah*, cooking with her. Cooking!" Griff chuckles, as if the thought of a powerful businessman cooking on TV is some kind of hidden secret.

"Anyway," he continues after a bit. "Travian calls the shots and most likely will be a handful. If you want me to take the lead, just say the word. I've dealt with these types before."

"No, I want to handle it."

"Have it your way, champ."

A chime sounds as we near the top floor. The doors swish open to a vast lobby space, all chrome and glass. Two couches sit off on one side, at angles facing the flat screen TV hanging on the wall. I've only seen those things in stores, they're out of my income range. It does look pretty cool though.

Across from the elevator a receptionist sits behind a desk. She looks up, a generic blond young beauty. Her eyes are red-rimmed from crying. It doesn't diminish her attractiveness.

"Detectives White and Toms to see Mr. Travian," I announce in my official business voice, and hold out my shield for her to examine.

She doesn't even glance at it. "Are you here about Mr. Bell?"

"We are, yes." We haven't announced in the press, Gonzales wants us to hold his identity tight as long as possible, yet this girl already knows. Someone in my own department has obviously made a call to Travian.

I skip over further commentary. There's no benefit in going down that road. "Is Mr. Travian in?"

She nods and wipes at her eyes, waving to the dark double doors behind her. "I heard a gang of black kids killed him for his money. Is that true?"

I glance over to Griff and his expression darkens.

"Did you hear that on the news?" I ask, trying to keep my tone neutral.

"No, some people here were talking about it. If that's true, I hope you make them fry." She reaches under her desk and I hear the click of an electronic lock being released in the double doors.

"Someone has a big mouth," Griff whispers as I put my hand on the doorknob. "Probably Hecker, feeding this office some insider news to make good with the power players so he can get promoted. What a dick."

"If that girl knows, it's more than leaked info from Hecker. It's filtering down to the lower levels."

"Still, he's a dick."

We enter the office. Four men turn to us. Three of them are sitting off to the side where several flat couches form a square. The space is done up in black tones, offset with gleaming chrome accents. Shelves line one wall, but instead of books, pictures are displayed. I recognize more than one celebrity, politician or prominent figure. The guy likes his photos and autographs.

The fourth office occupant stays against

the back wall, watching us with hawk eyes.

One man gets up from the couch and approaches us, hand outstretched. He's medium height, white-haired, close cut white beard and salt peter mustache. His suit jacket is draped loosely across his square shoulders but it's an expensive cut. I place him in his mid-50s. He's made of hard edges and lean times, a guy comfortable in his own skin because he's survived the trials of a harsh life to stand atop the mountain.

"Officers, I'm William Travian."

Griff shakes his hand first and takes the cue. "Detectives White and Toms." He stresses our title and I wonder if Travian is pulling a little power play by calling us officers. He may simply not understand the difference. I notice his eyes are also red, like his pretty receptionist. People here are taking Bell's death hard. That's something to note.

"Please," he waves to the couches, including the men occupying them. "Have a seat. These are my business partners, Steven Rothchild and Wayne Radd." Both men nod but don't say anything. Business cards for all three men are set on the coffee table in front of the open seats, indicating where we should sit. I remove my own card and slide it to the middle of the table.

Griff points to the man against the back wall. "And who else do we have today?" His tone is aggressive. Maybe he took the officer comment hard. Or maybe we're doing the good cop-bad cop routine.

"That is my head of security, Turk. We can speak freely in front of him."

"Turk? Is that a first name, last name, or legal description?"

Turk is short and squat, powerfully built. He looks like he could bench a truck. His spiked hair is white at the tips in contrast to the lighter brown that seems his natural color. He appears a little old for that kind of cut; I'm placing him in his 30s. The goatee is thick, almost black. He pins me with eyes the color of sand then moves them to my partner. They track slowly, like mechanical objects.

"It's a warning." His tone is flat, grating.

"Oh goody. Someone brought a clown to the show."

Travian interrupts. "Turk is by my side at all times, especially given recent events. Now, let us know how we can help you."

NINE

I pull out a little notebook and take my time finding a blank page. This gives enough mental space to adjust and plan my thoughts. Travian's eyes watch me, patient but with hints of wariness.

I keep my tone professional and restrained. "You've been apprised of recent events by our district, I presume, so we can confirm that last night, Noah Bell's body was found at the site of the former Middle Plains plastics factory. This information has not been given to the press yet. I understand you two were close?"

"We were."

"We all were," Rothchild interjected. His hair is black, slicked back with gel, revealing a strong Widow's peak. If he had a long dark beard, he'd look like one of those old time magicians. "Noah had a vision that was hard to ignore. His passion was contagious. How could anyone not want the same future he fought to create?"

"And what future was that?"

"One where equality is not a campaign slogan but instead an achievable goal. One where we stop talking about race because it no longer matters. Noah wanted to bridge this cultural gap that separates us from each other."

It sounds good, but it also sounds like a rehearsed campaign statement.

Wayne Radd clears his throat. "Look, this is rather awkward. Detective White, we're all close to Noah. Or were. We know of his role in your lawsuit against the city to claim that detective's badge you now wear. Stephen, William and I supported Noah's efforts as he fought for you. He called every single bureau chief, commander, and deputy super to plead your case. We lent our voices to his. You were a young officer from a small town trying to get into a position that your resume didn't warrant. Noah believed in you, so by extension did we. Please dispense with the normal interview tactics and just ask us what you need to know. We all want the killer found."

Radd's voice is gentle and smooth. Unlike

his two partners, he has no hair, just a gleaming pate. There's a softness about his features, rounded cheeks and fleshy lips that give him the appearance of a man used to easy pleasures, not one who clawed and scratched his way up. He and Travian are opposites in their aura. Radd's pants are pulled high to cover an expanding waist line and his belt is cinched one or two notches too tight, like he refuses to believe his belly has grown.

The other two nod. "Yes, we want to help," Travian murmurs.

I take a moment to look each man in the eyes. "Okay then. Thank you. Both for your attention before and now. Tell me what Bell was doing at the factory."

Rothchild meets my stare. "I sent him there."

"Why?"

"He wanted to set up a community youth center, a safe haven for at-risk kids. That area is rife with examples of kids falling to the wayside, especially from the black community, so he wanted to establish a place for them to go. I tried to talk him out of it, to start with someplace less risky. He'd never led this kind of project before so I wanted him to keep it manageable, but you have to understand Noah. Once he sets his mind to something, no one dissuades him."

I find it interesting that we're discussing the disadvantages of minority youth, yet I'm the only black man in the room.

"So he was there to meet someone and take a look around?"

At this Travian nods. "Yes. I referred him to an agency that I use for low volume engagements. They have experienced agents in all the market segments."

"And who was that agent?"

"Jerold Rosenfel...Rosenthal...something like that. I've never met the man personally but he came highly recommended." Travian nods over his shoulder to Turk, who disappears through a side door at the back of the office. Griff watches him with an intent expression.

"Has anyone spoken with this agent today?"

"We have not," Travian replies. "There is an investigation process you must follow; we wanted to respect that and keep the lines of communication clear. You can be the first to contact their office." Travian pauses, as if something has just occurred to him. "Do you think the agent might also have been attacked by those kids?"

Turk returns and holds out a business card. Griff reaches for it but he ignores the gesture and hands it to me. It's the card of one Jerold Rosenfel, featuring a head shot photo of a middle-aged pale man, with thin sandy hair and ruddy cheeks. The street address and contact numbers are all local.

"How do you know about the kids?" Griff asks, challenge in his tone. "Nothing has been reported to connect the two scenes."

All three men glance at each other. When Radd turns back to us, he has a sheepish smile, as if apologetic for what he's about to say. "Our information doesn't wait on new cycles, I'm afraid. We walk in different circles and our paths afford us access to higher privileges."

"So Hecker leaked it to you."

The smile drops. "I'd rather not share the conversation."

"That means there should not be another question on this topic," Turk spouts as he resumes his position along the back wall.

I switch gears to more conventional interview tactics, borrowing some tips from the Reid technique. I direct my questions to Travian, but make frequent eye contact with Radd and Rothchild.

"Noah used your security agency? A man named Guy Johnstone?"

"Johnstone and several others. Three-sixty coverage is what we provide. I've had assignments on him for years."

"When did you last speak to Mr. Bell? How often did you two speak on average?"

Travian looks up to the ceiling, thinking. "It would have been last week, Wednesday night. We traded voice mails. He called to thank me for the referral and to let me know he had an appointment arranged. I returned his call to say only 'good luck'. We normally touched base once a week."

"When was the last time he spoke about anyone who might have posed a threat?"

"Oh, never." Travian's eyes widen. "He made plenty of enemies with his unwavering focus, but the worst of them still respected Noah. They were only enemies because he presented a challenge to the known way of things."

"Is there anything unusual, a recent event or interaction, that you can recall?"

This causes Travian to go still. He looks over to Radd. "What about that Covenant case up in North Haven. Do you remember him speaking about that?"

Radd stares back and I can see the gears churning. "Vaguely. I think he knew one of the victims."

"What's North Haven?" I write the name down in my notebook and double underline it.

"It's a town up near the northern border near Wisconsin. A couple of months ago they had some murders, racially motivated crimes. Several men with ties to white supremacist groups were killed in hideous ways. Following those, several minority victims were found, setting the stage for racial tensions the likes of which we haven't seen since the 60s. Riots, police patrols, National Guard on standby...it was apparently very unstable up there for a month or so. From what I know, a white separatist group named the Covenant Church of the New Millennium was behind it all, instigating some scheme to pit whites and blacks against each other." Travian gives a shrug to indicate he knows nothing more. He makes eye contact with me. "No offense."

I have no idea what he thinks may have offended me, other than speaking about race relations in front of a black man. This world is really becoming a weird place.

"So you think this Covenant group may have had something to do with Bell?"

"No, no, no." Travian waves his hands. "I didn't say that at all. You asked a question and I answered it to the best of my ability. Please do not infer any direct links from that to Noah."

I look over to Griff, who's stayed quiet for

the most part, letting me run things. "You know about it?"

"A little. I got an old buddy up there we can call if we need more info."

Before anyone else can speak, Turk pushes off the wall again and interrupts us. "That's it for now, detectives. Mr. Travian has a meeting in five minutes, so I'm going to ask you to leave."

I pick up all the business cards from the table, making a show of inspecting them. All three men have written their cell phone numbers somewhere on the card. That's an unusual vote of assistance. Men in power rarely give out personal contact information, relying on layers of administration to hide them.

"And what about you, chubby?" Griff says to Turk. "You got a card? Or do you just scratch out an 'X' for your name?"

The bodyguard says nothing in reply and simply moves to the office door. He holds it open for us in a clear message.

At the door, I turn back to the three men, kings of the city, traders in wealth and privilege. "I appreciate your time. Please expect that there may be follow up questions so I will advise making yourselves available as the need arises."

They stare at me. Maybe they aren't used to being spoken to that way. Maybe they don't know what to say back. But as one they nod, allowing me a brief glimpse into the power of an alpha male.

"What was that?" Griff says as we pass by the receptionist. I note that there is no one waiting in the lobby for a meeting that begins in five minutes.

"You first. What the hell were you doing with Turk?"

"He reminds me of my daughter's ex-husband."

I give him a hard stare. "I can't tell if you're serious or not."

"Serious as a heart attack, Arch. Guys like him annoy me."

The ride down the elevator is silent, both of us wrapped up in thought. At least I am. Griff whistles and draws a smiley face on the wooden rail with his pen.

Afternoon light draws down to gray as we descend into the steel canyons of shadow. I try not to let the metaphor stick in my mind. We get into the cruiser just as a call goes out for a response unit up in Wicker Park. Victim was a bartender found stabbed in the back of his business. "Man," I remark. "Shitty week. Too much death. Who's taking that call? Not us, right?"

"No, Leeds and Schmidt are up, I think."

I grunt. "So what did you think of Travian and crew? Anything we need to key on beside Rosenfel?"

"I think they're a bunch of rich snobs with little understanding of life below the 20th floor, but they didn't trip any triggers for me."

"Yeah, me either. Travian especially seemed eager to help."

"Try the numbers for Rosenfel. Let's see if we can grab him on the way back."

I pull out my cell and punch in the number for his office. It's one of those systems that allows you to dial directly to his extension. It rings a dozen times and never goes to voice mail.

The next call is to his cell. This one goes to voice mail. His greeting is standard business, thanking me for calling and promising to return my call at his next convenience. I leave my name and number, but no details as to the reason for the call.

"Try the office again but punch out to zero. That should get you to a secretary or something," Griff suggests.

I follow his directions and press zero instead of his extension. The phone is picked up on the second ring.

"Weber and Hall Realty, this is Amanda. How may I direct your call?"

"Jerold Rosenfel, please. This is Detective White with the Chicago PD."

A long pause followed by a confused tone. "I...I can't, sir."

My internal alarms trigger. There's something in her voice. "Why not? Has he come into work this morning?"

"Um, no. He hasn't come into work for weeks. No one's heard from him. We all thought he just quit without notice. Did something happen? Do you know anything?"

I snap my phone shut and look over to my partner. "Head back to the station. We got a problem."

TEN

Griff drops the paper down on my desk. It's a sheet of thin fax paper, trying to curl up at the corners. I note the heading is another precinct in the Tennessee area. There's a picture in the upper corner, blotted from the fax transmission, but I can see enough of it to recognize Rosenfel's features. I raise my eyes to Griff and wait.

"So the guy heads out on vacation with his family at the end of May. Wife, two teenage boys, going to someplace like the Outer Banks, Hatteras...I think off the South Carolina coast."

"You know, I am somewhat familiar with the geography down there."

"Oh, right. Your old stomping grounds. Anyway, they stay a couple of days in Tennessee, Gatlinburg and Pigeon Forge area, before heading over the Smoky Mountains towards the coast. That's what they told the owners of the house they rented anyway."

"I'm assuming they never made it."

"The wife and kids were found dead in the car, high up in the national park, shot point blank through the skulls. Jerold was found scattered across the next few miles, like someone had chopped him up and threw pieces out the window as he drove. A lot of parts were never recovered, probably taken by wild animals. Luckily a hand was found mostly intact. He had prints on file from a juvenile arrest several decades ago, so they were able to ID the hand."

"No suspects?"

Griff shakes his head. "Or witnesses. It's a thin jacket. Several tourists reported seeing the family posing for pictures on one of the overlooks, just a family like any other. Then they drove off into something that got them killed."

I don't know what this all means. Coincidences hover in the air, bats on a wing just beyond my sight. I lean back, mulling over nascent thoughts.

The station has a hum to it, electric and invisible. Even in Cicero the events of the last two days are extreme. Griff was right about

Leeds and Schmidt. They took the case of the dead bartender up in Wicker Park. Even now I can see their heads through the window of a conference room, talking back and forth much as Griff and I did. So much of our work seems to be spouting theories and saying things out loud to see how logical they sound.

Stewart and Towney are nowhere to be seen. In fact the station is empty of all detectives other than us and I wonder what leads they're chasing with the kids at the park. The two cases are intertwined. I feel pressure to nail down my budding theories before they do theirs, as if first one into Gonzales' office wins.

I look over to my partner. He's chewing on his index fingernail. "How long do you sniff at something before saying it stinks?"

"Truth or dare? Go."

"Truth: Travian recommended the agency that provided Rosenfel's name."

Griff records a hash mark on the fax paper. "Point. Dare: Travian didn't know anything about Rosenfel's fate."

"No point. Wouldn't the agency have told him?"

"Truth: Things work much slower at the top floor. These deals take months and years to put together." Griff shrugs, like he's apologizing for the pace of big business.

"So, dare: He could have done introductions and references prior to Rosenfel's murder. He did say he'd never met the man personally."

I sit back, staring out the glass walls of our detective room. Across the lobby a number of unis are talking. Judging by the animated looks on their faces, someone is telling a funny story. I look back to Griff.

"Truth: Bell went there to meet someone. So who was it?"

"Rosenfel is dead and someone took his place; that throws the idea of a random crime out the window. Now we're talking assassination. But why go through the trouble of setting up a meeting, using men like Rothchild to proxy, when a well-placed sniper shot does the same thing? What's to gain from that?" He shrugs.

"Dare, double-dare: We press Travian, see what he gives up from the realty angle. Bring him in for questioning to add pressure."

At that my partner's face goes a little sour. "We're going to need solid evidence indicating he had motive. You don't just house call guys like Travian and Rothchild on a whim, pecking away at their stories. They can drop a dime to Jacobs and suddenly we'll find ourselves working peripheral leads. If we go back to those guys, we'll need a stack of questions that we're fairly certain we have already answered."

"We need to build our case and use them to confirm, rather than building our case off their information. That's backwards." I feel a sense of frustration.

"It's also reality when you draw down on names like theirs. These guys aren't Joe Schmoe working retail at the Hyper-Mart. They control things." He shrugs again, apologizing for a broken system in which we are relegated to pawn status.

Johnny Nayaki emerges from a door behind the detective room, one that leads to the basement where his team has their equipment. I sense something in his posture and straighten up in my chair.

Griff follows my gaze and cranes a look over his shoulder. "Give us a poem, Nayaki. One that helps out."

"Yeah, try this: Once upon a time a lazy detective looking at retirement got a case that would make his career, but he ignored the science and blew it. He disappeared into anonymity afterwards, forever forgotten."

"That's terrible. It doesn't even rhyme."

Johnny drops a folder on my desk. "Appreciate at this time how very special you are, Detective White. Somehow your case cleared to the front of the line for processing. Meanwhile, other evidence items I sent to the lab a week ago are still idling."

I reach for the folder, but he slaps a hand down on top of it. "One question, Aramis: Will you follow the science, unlike your slovenly partner?"

"Call me Arch, and yes. I will."

"Good, because there's another story buried somewhere in here. As we suspected, Bell did not die from his beating. Ligature marks indicate strangling, which we saw at the scene, but the beating took place after death."

Griff leans in. "Someone strangled then beat him?"

"According to my version of this fairy tale, yes."

I sift through the photos and skim the write-up. "Did the kids' hands at the park show any signs?"

Johnny's eyes crinkle at the corners as he lets a smile drift onto his face. It's not a normal look for him, in the short time I've known the guy, he hasn't smiled once. "Now you're following the trail. No, none of them bore marks. Based on the level of damage to Bell's face, at least one of those boys would have severely swollen knuckles, if not broken."

Griff and I cross stares. "There's someone else." I say.

This prompts Johnny to drop his smile. "You think there were more suspects present."

"I'm beginning to talk myself into it. At least one, if not more. And I think he was back at the factory scene this morning."

"Because," Griff picks up my line of thought. "He's afraid there's something that identifies him. This kid, he doesn't want to go down as a killer of Noah Bell. No matter how 'street' he is, he knows he'd be crucified."

Johnny nods and turns away. "Well, this is where you earn your paycheck, gents. I just bring you reports." He starts to walk away.

"Hey," I call out. "How long for ballistics? I'm interested in the rifling matches and firing angles. We've got missing guns, ammunition counts that don't add up and weird drop patterns."

"Maybe later this week for both. The lab committed to Friday on ballistics, again a rush order, and my team is reconstructing the scene. But we're tapped tight and it may take longer, especially if people keep turning up dead." Johnny waves in the general direction of Leeds and Schmidt.

He passes Stewart and Towney as they enter the station through the same side exit we used to escape this morning. From the look in their eyes, they also have something for me. Their body language is direct and they cut straight across the room to my desk. Must be my lucky day.

Towney drops a piece of paper on my desk. "This should interest you, rook."

I ignore the jab and read it. "GXE548. Geoffrey Moller, North Haven." The location doesn't escape me, but I raise one eyebrow. "And?"

"It's the plate tag from a black Tahoe seen entering and leaving the Middle Plains factory last night."

Both Griff and I shoot to a standing position. "How did you get this?" We say in unison. Griff mumbles 'jinx' under his breath.

"Working our scene. There's a gas station down the block so we pulled the security tapes. One of them has a good angle to the factory entrance. This Tahoe was recorded in and out, at the right time frame for you. I tracked the registration to Moller. You're welcome."

With that he spins and walks away. Stewart follows without a word, but he does give me stink-eye. Maybe he's still pissed from this morning's briefing.

Griff stares at the paper. "You know this isn't coincidence, right?"

"So, what's the protocol? Do we have someone from up there pull in Moller for us?"

"No way, Arch. Not with this case. If one thing slips, we're in the noose. We handle it. I know a guy up there, George Warren. He used to work south side down here but got burnt, so he took his shield north. I'll have dispatch call ahead and track him down. I'm driving."

***

We hit North Haven not long after the dinner hour. I crumple up the burger wrapper and toss it into the back seat. My attention turns outward.

Suburbia incarnate surrounds us as we roll down a road named Jordan Way. All the trappings of a new world are present: Target, Home Depot, Starbucks, and a host of other chain restaurants. Main street America disappeared long ago, along with many of the mom and pop stores. Now we're a civilization of franchises, with detailed market plans that define the size, type, and location of the next expansion opportunity. As a result, I often see the same stores nestled in close proximity to each other, regardless of the city.

Griff provides me a breakdown of the area. North Haven serves as the hub to dozens of small towns. They cluster loosely around the perimeter, as if wary of predators lurking in the undeveloped fields and lakes. There's no actual city center to North Haven, no gathering of local shops to which longtime residents brought their business and spent hours chatting up the owner on a quiet Saturday morning.

If you want to get anywhere around here, you need a car. I see a few bus stops as we drive, but they are lightly attended. There's no graffiti on any of them, so either there's a good civic response to clean up, or there's enough respect that no one bothers defacing them in the first place.

With the pending millennium around the corner, North Haven seems like a place equipped to handle it. The gleaming signs lining Jordan Way hint at things that say: 'We're new and flexible. We can adapt to anything and will be here tomorrow for you.' It seems odd to me that this place, full of it's shininess and upscale modeling, would suffer from the kind of racial unrest that recently happened. To me, riots over skin color are a legacy of the distant past, when opportunities for my people were much less.

Now, we're limited only by our own ambition. That's my belief anyway.

"Lots of money up here," I remark as yet another fancy car rolls past us. I've seen a heavy presence of German luxury automobiles, along with numerous higher end sports cars. The houses we've passed also stink of money.

"Got that right, brother. It's all the technology people, I guess. Like Internet web sites and stuff. They pulled their wallets out of the near North suburbs and brought everything up here. You can buy twice the house, twice the land, yet you're only ninety minutes from downtown by rail."

"Sounds like they also brought some of the same problems with them, though."

"Yeah, you can't ever get away from that. The stuff they had earlier this year was shit that not even Cicero deals with. The Klan, black lynching, a riot that tore up one of the smaller towns. Some guy was hung from a tree in shackles, some other guy got burned in white robes. I'm telling you, it was tense up here from what I heard. The Feds were one call away from pulling together a task force."

He leans forward and looks out the windshield at a passing road sign. "Yep, here it is," he says out loud. "North Haven police station."

I follow his look. My eyes widen. "Holy cow, Griff."

ELEVEN

The station down in Cicero is pretty nice, far more so than what I left behind back home. It was renovated a few years ago, according to Griff, to bring in more light. Windows were enlarged, ceilings raised to give the impression of more space. All in all, the precinct should be proud of the place they call home.

North Haven makes Cicero look like a dump.

The building shines white in the early evening sun, brilliant marble curved for the facade, tall windows stretching up two stories. We idle up the main drive. Manicured hedges line either side, making me feel like I'm entering a country club. Patrol cars can be seen at parade rest alongside the building and each one gleams with a fresh wax. I peer up at the roof. Along the front of the building, statues line the peak, replicas of Greek and Roman gods. I think. I have no idea what any of them are.

"The money that stood this place up..." I mutter.

"Whole different world, partner," Griff adds.

The lobby is vast, two stories high, with fabric draped from the ceiling. It's more like a museum entrance than a place of law and order. We check in at the front desk and pass through a metal detector. Our weapons are handed back to us on the other side. A beat cop named Borden points us down a long hallway to Warren's office.

The detective is in, sitting behind his desk, typing slowly into a computer. He glances up at our entrance and recognition colors his face. "Griffin Toms! Dispatch said you were on the way up. What brings you out of the swamp?" They shake hands and my partner introduces me. We all sit around the desk.

George Warren looks like the short detective from the cop show *NYPD Blue*, I kid you not. Same build, more hair, no mustache, but they could be brothers. I can't shake the image from my head as they indulge in small talk for a few minutes.

Griff steers the discussion back on topic. "We got some footage off a case we're working. Plate traces back up here so we need your help."

"You drove all the way up just for that? Why not call?"

I interject, establishing myself in the conversation. "There's some sensitivity to this. We needed to handle it in person."

He looks at me and the dots connect. "Shit. It's true. Rumors have been circulating all morning that Noah Bell was killed."

I glance over to Griff then back. "It appears there are some big mouths in the 11th District. We haven't released anything yet on his identity. I feel like I'm chasing a gossip trail."

"Hey, it's a small world when you break it down. Noah Bell is a name. Someone like him drops, there are going to be cops calling other cops going, 'Did you hear?' Pull on your big boy pants and deal with the fact people love juice."

Warren doesn't mince words, I'll give him that.

Before I can respond, he plunges ahead. "I hear that a gang of black kids took him out. Mugged their social savior for a few bucks, and that his bodyguard took them all out. I got that right?"

"There was a nearby homicide involving a person enlisted from a local security service, yes. At this point, we don't have enough information to confirm any connection..."

"Cut the shit, kid. I ain't the press. You don't have to watch your tongue around me, we're all wearing tin." His tone is sharp, a teacher rebuking a student about some lame excuse given for not completing his homework.

I look over to Griff, to see if he's going to intervene, but he doesn't give any indication of speaking. He's picking at something in one of his fingernails.

"Honestly, we don't know. I'm not sold on it being a direct connection. Everything is set up to appear that way, but there are some inconsistencies."

"Like what?"

"Scene evidence, manner of death, ammunition counts versus shots fired. Those types of things."

Warren leans back and gives a dismissive wave. "I hate shit like that. Do yourself a favor, don't get too wrapped up in it. Take the surface story and write your report around that. Trust me, your life will be much easier. Those evidence techs think they all can solve everything from the lab."

Suddenly I get a glimpse of the inner man. He doesn't want sticky, avoids hassle. When cases get complicated, he's not the type to stay in there and untangle the knots. He'll just toss the whole ball of string onto someone else's lap and wish them well. That's not my way and never has been. I feel a drop in respect for Griff's longtime pal.

My voice turns formal, a way of letting him know I'm not taking his poor advice. "We pulled plate numbers from a truck near the scene at the right time window. The owner lives up here. This is just a courtesy stop to let you know we're in the area."

Warren grunts. He likely doesn't care whether some young buck is going to listen to his advice, as long it keeps him above the fray. "What's the name?"

I glance down at my notebook. "Geoffrey Moller, has a place in the village of Marewood."

His eyes go flat and piercing, as if he's just heard his own name called at a funeral. "Tell me you are joking."

"He don't joke," Griff says. "I've tried, but he refuses to lighten up."

The jovial tone from my partner fails to alter Warren's expression. He shakes his head and looks off into the distance. His fingers rattle a pen against the desk. I said something to upset him. What?

"Moller ain't your guy," he finally says, turning to address us both. "Go back and work the gang angle. Pray for that to be your case resolution."

"You sound awfully certain. Why is that?"

"Because Geoffrey Moller has been breathing through a tube for the last month or so."

I take a moment to process this. "Well, the video was clear so I don't think we have a crossed plate number."

"It would be better for you if you did. Otherwise, it means there's a whole new complexion to your case. And you especially," he fixes his gaze on me and points. "You really don't want to be at the center of it. Trust me."

That's twice now he's asked me to trust him. This guy is cryptic and there's something he doesn't want to talk about, something he's reluctant to say. "It sounds like you have a story to share."

Warren gives a bitter bark. "It's not my story. I'm just the shit head who got stuck cleaning up the mess." He writes down an address and slides the paper across the desk to me. "I'll let the man in the middle tell it. He was ground zero and knows more than anyone else what really happened."

The North Haven detective who failed to stick with the mess of south side Chicago leans back in his chair, hands behind his head. The tangled ball lands in my lap. "You want to talk to a guy named Rick Killing. Go have a chat."

He laughs. "And good fucking luck with him."

***

We navigate our way through winding roads bordered by yards taken from landscape catalogs. I see many crews mowing, trimming, laying block for a patio or running some kind of landscaping machine. It doesn't escape me that most of the faces are Hispanic, enforcing the stereotype. I've never been a big racial proponent, never felt like I've been victimized for my skin color. I realize that my very public suit against the Chicago PD paints me as one of those types who cry foul and hide behind race, making me a hypocrite. But as I delve deeper into this case, the reality of discrimination keeps poking at me. Is this truly becoming an issue between white and black? All the disconnected data points are confusing. Thinking about it from the standpoint of a racial matter changes my mindset completely and I'll be the first admit I'm not well-equipped to address all the issues that led to Bell's death.

But I'd never say that aloud.

The entire drive Griff babbles about this guy we're going to see. "It has to be him, right? I mean, how many Rick Killings can there be in the world? Has to be him. Has to."

I get enough after the first ten minutes. "What are you talking about?"

"Killing. Rick Killing the player. I watched him at Illinois a few years back. Guy was incredible, probably the best I've ever seen. Thought he was a lock for the NFL but after he banged up his knee, he disappeared. I heard he was picked up by the Minnesota Vikings this spring in the draft."

"We're heading to a talk to a football player? A professional athlete?"

"Has to be him."

I look over at my partner. His eyes are gleaming with excitement. "Well, make sure you don't drool on him."

Griff turns us into a subdivision called Windemere Fields. The name is spelled out in a wrought iron arc between two massive pillars that flank the entrance. "What the hell is a 'windemere'?" I ask, but he doesn't respond. He's scanning the house numbers as we roll down a road called Hunter's Run. Killing and Moller lived on the same street, and judging by the house numbers, not all that far apart. Coincidence?

The cruiser slows in front of a huge Spanish-style house, with white stucco walls and red tile roof. I'm not sure I've ever seen an uglier place. "This looks like the kind of house a pro athlete would own." It's not a compliment.

"Just be cool, Arch. Be cool." By the tone of his voice, I'm wondering if Griff is talking to me or himself. He throws the car into park, turns it off and lets out a long exhale.

As we exit the car and start up the long brick driveway, the front door slams open and out comes the most beautiful woman I've seen in a long time. She's Asian, with long black hair that glints in the sunlight, lean legs in shorts and a full tank top. I open my mouth to speak, reaching for my badge in the same motion.

"Fuck all your kind!" She states and storms past us without another glance. She hops into a Jeep parked in the garage and tears away to the deep sound of all-terrain tires scrubbing on asphalt.

What the hell was that?

Griff stands there, staring in the direction of the departing vehicle. A low whistle slides out of his pursed lips. "Good Lord in heaven, Arch. The angels have been released."

A deep voice comes from behind us. "Wrong direction, pal. You need to look down, not up."

I turn. Standing on the front patio is one very large man. I'm tall and used to looking down on a lot of people. He's another inch or two taller, but that doesn't convey his sheer size. There's at least a thirty pound difference in our builds. He's wide at the shoulders, thick in his chest. The loose t-shirt can't hide his muscle. Blond hair is cut short to near military length.

I glance back at Griff. "I'm going to guess this is your guy."

Griff eyes are fixed on him. "Should I ask for an autograph?"

Shaking my head, I approach the patio. "Rick Killing, I assume?"

"Never assume. It makes an ass out of you and me," he replies. I've heard that phrase a hundred times in my life. It wasn't funny the first time and still isn't.

His eyes are blue, but so light they look almost clear. It gives him a glacial aspect, like he can look right through you. It's unnerving.

"But to answer the question you actually asked, yes, I'm Rick. Warren tells me you want a story."

TWELVE

Rick Killing throws himself down on a living room couch and motions to the leather chairs opposite him. "Cop a squat, fellas."

There are boxes stacked throughout the kitchen and entry. I spot an open door at the end of the hallway on our right, leading to a bedroom. More boxes litter that space. Despite his wise words to the contrary, I make another assumption.

"It looks like someone's moving out. You or the angry Jeep lady?"

He scrubs his stubbly jaw and looks at me through those colorless eyes. "Both. Need a place?"

I look around at the shiny tile floor, granite counters and stainless steel appliances in the kitchen. "I doubt I could afford the water bill."

Griff clears his throat. "Mr. Killing, we need to ask you some questions. Do you mind?" I don't think I've ever heard him speak so formally, not even to our brass. How nervous is he?

"Call me Rick, and no. But I don't know what else to tell you that hasn't already been told to Warren, the FBI and whatever other agency that's knocked on my door."

"Actually, I was going to ask for your autograph."

Killing stares, a direct look that women probably loved and men hated. Then he laughs. "Wow, something I can answer. Will wonders never cease." He gets up and walks over to the den across from the kitchen.

"I watched a ton of your games at Illinois. Easily my favorite player," Griff calls after him. "That last one, when you were on track to break the single game receiving record, when your knee..."

Killing returns and interrupts him. "Here." He sets down a small replica football on the end table next to Griff. Across the face, just under the laces, is a signature scrawled in permanent marker. I can't read it.

I butt in, before Griff can slobber over this

guy any more. "We'd like to talk about the interaction you had with a Geoffrey Moller."

"An 'interaction'? Is that what it's being called now?" He gives a short laugh, devoid of humor. "Interaction is something that happens at a store when you run into a friend or someone you haven't seen in years. Interaction is conducting a purchase of goods. This guy tried to kill my best friend, my girl and me. I can do without those kind of interactions."

Griff looks up from studying the football. "He tried to kill her?" His head jerks in the general direction of the long-gone angry woman, like he couldn't believe anyone would want to harm someone so beautiful.

"No, that was my wife you saw. This was someone else." For the first time his frosty stare cracks. "Crap. That came out completely wrong. It's...well, let's just say it is rather complicated."

"He tried to kill you?" I repeat. "How did that come about?"

"I drank too much of his good liquor."

When I don't respond, he continues. "Moller moved into a house farther down the block early in the year. He came off as a king of trade. If you needed an actor to play the president or some kind of high-powered executive, Moller is who you'd look for. He had the look, a certain way about him. Very dignified and intelligent. It took a few months for us to meet but I came to learn that that was by design. There was absolutely nothing random or by chance with that guy."

"So how did you meet?"

"I'd like to say it was because he looked at me and thought: 'Hey, that Killing guy sure looks swell. I should go introduce myself.' But it was part of his plan. He walked up the block one day and stuck out his hand. That's when everything kicked into gear."

"What's 'everything'?"

"Come here, let me show you."

Killing gets up from the couch with a move sudden and startling, like he was shot out of a gun. We follow his lead as he takes us downstairs to a finished basement. A large workout area dominates the floor space at the bottom of the stairs. There's a theater room beyond that, with several rows of interconnected chairs that look like they were taken straight from a movie house. Except they are padded leather and several are still in the recline position. I didn't even know you could buy something like that. The space is vast. The entire first floor of Anna's group home isn't this large.

A Smith machine dominates the center of the workout area. Weight plates hang off the side. Along one wall are arranged a treadmill, elliptical and recumbent bike. Opposite of them is a rack with rows of dumbbells, from twenty pounds all the way up to one hundred. I'm no stranger to working out or gyms, but my experience is mostly working my way through the various machines. This place reeks of purpose-built lifting for power and speed.

He points to the floor near the Smith bench. It's covered by thick mats like you'd see in commercial gyms. Dark stains mar the surface. "Some kids came here in the middle of the night, sent by Moller. They came to kill me, to stage some kind of scene that played into his grand vision."

"That seems to have failed," I note dryly. Killing comes off as a guy with a smart sense of humor. Maybe I can use that to bridge some rapport.

"No, it worked. The resale on this place is dead now." He picks up a forty-five pound plate from the floor and hangs it on the weight rack. I notice he only needs one hand.

"See, Moller was a smart guy, probably one of the smartest people I've ever crossed. He had a way of talking that made you think he understood what it took to make a person feel whole. It's hard to describe without sounding like a romance novel, but the guy just thought on a different plane than the rest of us. Also, he was a slight bit nuts. You know about the murders around here?" Killing pauses to pick up another weight and I shake my head.

"No, I just transferred in a month ago. It sounds like I missed out on a lot."

"That explains your accent. Well here's the Reader's Digest condensed version. White guys were getting killed, but in ways that were designed to send a message. And those messages were very specific: Someone wanted to even the score from the days of the Klan. Did you know there was an investigative commission report done on Klan activity in 1975 for the areas around Aurora, Joliet and Cicero? The KKK wasn't just a deep South problem. They had a presence around here so the murders seemed like someone finally wanted to get revenge on them."

I realize that Killing is far more vested into this than a mere witness to the North Haven events. He's done research, he's taken the time to back-trail the reasons he and Moller collided. He comes off as a bit of a dumb jock in his mannerisms, but I sense someone fairly intuitive underneath that facade. The question becomes: Why does he want people to think he's less intelligent than he is?

He continues his recap. "It appeared like a group of blacks had set out to make a statement, a very racially motivated statement that may or may not have been triggered by some new white supremacy activity. Maybe the Klan was rebuilding in Illinois, maybe someone just had a long-held grudge. I don't know. But it all blew up. Lynching, mob rule, white supremacy; we had it all. Of course, there is no action without reaction. A few white guys turning up dead in Klan robes tends to make people sit up and notice. And not all those people take it lying down. Suddenly black people had a target on them. It seemed like a group of blacks making an example of a few white guys created an atmosphere where we all started to look at each other cross-ways. When a black guy turned up dead, everyone realized this was not going away soon. A storm was brewing. That's how it seemed, anyway, and the press was happy to run with that line."

He pauses again, distant look in his eyes. I think he's remembering something he'd prefer not to. "Then along comes Geoffrey Moller and his two sons. Says all the right things, does all the right things. He wants to help out, to help soothe the civic anger and stop the madness. Since his 'business' was human relations, diversity and equality, it makes perfect sense. He walks up the street one day and talks me into recruiting my friend Dee Davis to be the face of peace for North Haven. You have to understand, Moller could sell ice to an Eskimo. Since Dee is originally from this area, he had the cred to stand up in front of everyone and plead for peace. He's always been racially aware so it was a natural progression for him to become a spokesman for harmony. Moller tutored him in public speaking, arranged his interviews; he probably even wrote the damn speeches for him."

"Wait," Griff interrupts. "Dee Davis from the Cubs? The third baseman? You know him?"

Oh, Christ.

Killing ignores him, eyes fixed on the five pound plate he now held in his hand. "Turns out we were all being played. Me, Dee, the entire town of North Haven, the media. Moller had a larger agenda. He wanted Dee assassinated, in front of a camera, with a national audience. It was never confirmed, but I think he made all the murders happen, white and black, to set the stage. His idea was to kick off a race war, right here in North Haven, that would coincide with the turn of the millennium. He had some fixation on changing the world at such a momentous time."

I feel uneasy. I mean it's 1999 and this guy's talking about the Ku Klux Klan, mob lynching and race wars. I'm from the south, where racism ran rampant earlier in the century, but even then what I've experienced in my life wasn't anything like this. I just attributed the undercurrent of racial tension to generations of small minds unwilling to leave or expand their horizons. I couldn't reconcile that same cultural trend in a shiny place like North Haven.

"What was this race war supposed to accomplish?" I ask.

Killing shrugs. "Beats me. Never figured it out. I was kind of busy not dying."

"But somehow you managed to stop this thing without understanding it?" I don't mean to sound skeptical, but it's hard.

"It might be more fair to say that I just got in the way, that I mucked up the plan enough to cause some sparks. The true fire came from one of Moller's son. He was the one who crashed the train, by smashing his dad in the throat."

I pause, processing all this. I feel like I'm hearing the plot of some ridiculous novel.

"It was a father-son angst thing." Killing rubs his eyes and for the first time I notice how exhausted he looks. There's more going on with him than he shows and I'm guessing it has to do with his current domestic situation. "Let's just leave it at: None of the Mollers are a threat anymore."

"And when did you say this all happened?"

He gives another short laugh. "Which part? The manipulation, the murders, the riot, or Moller's kid nearly decapitating him."

"I guess the last one. That seems most pertinent to our case."

"About six weeks ago, give or take a few bloody days." He fixes his eyes on me. Now it's his turn. "You still haven't said what the link is between Moller and your case."

I pull out a picture from the murder book and hold it up. It's the image Towney gave us, of a Tahoe taken from the rear angle as it turned into Middle Plains. Despite the slight fuzziness, the plate numbers are clear and legible along with other details. "What can you tell me about this truck?"

Killing just glances at it. "I can tell you it needs a new back window."

"How? You hardly looked." I'd used a magnifying glass to identify a star-shaped crack dead center in the window. It looked like something impacted the glass with significant

138

amount of force.

"Because I'm the one that did it. With a rock."

"Hell of a throw. That rock did some damage."

"When was this taken?" Killing asks as he racks the five-pounder.

I don't know how much I'm allowed to share with a civilian, even if he does have detailed information already. But I can tell my partner's not going to be much help. Griff is staring down at the football, turning it over in his hands. I'm on my own, so I take the bit.

"Last night. At the scene of the Noah Bell homicide."

Killing stares at me and in his eyes I see shades of something haunting flit past. He walks over and collapses on one of the theater room chairs, scrubbing his eyes again. Finally he takes a deep breath and looks up at me. "You have a very big problem."

This captures Griff's attention. "Define problem. Define very big."

THIRTEEN

Rick Killing makes several attempts to clarify, saying a word or two each time, before backtracking. Finally: "I'm not sure I can even explain in a way that makes sense. Mostly because I don't understand it all. There was more to Moller than his plan for a race war in North Haven. It was all part of some larger movement. The problem is, no one knows how large. I got the sense that whatever he was doing was just one piece of a puzzle all designed to culminate at the end of our century. Have you guys heard about the Covenant Church of the New Millennium?"

We both nod and I say, "It came up in an interview earlier today. Sounds like Bell knew about them and was somehow affected by what happened up here."

"Well, think of it as the KKK re-branded for the new century. Bell would have been an opponent of them in every way. One of the black people murdered was a guy named Jerome Carter. He lived down in Chicago. Maybe Bell knew him. Or maybe that connection struck home for him." Killing lets out another long breath. "Anyway, the Covenant. At its core, it's a white supremacy group like any other. They believe in separation, of some kind of social order between whites and minorities, which is anyone's guess what that order is, but you can probably figure it out. Where they differ is in their mission, their methods and their game plan. The Klan marched in the streets wearing white robes, they held community events and conducted very public campaigns using the press. They've died off but now you get groups like Aryan Nation or the Blitzkrieg who exist in the same category. They want the same things as the Klan, yet they couldn't be more different. Those guys get together in the woods around a burn barrel, toss back homemade hooch and bitch about the state of our country. They couldn't plan a two-course meal if you spotted them dessert, much less create something like what happened here."

"But this Covenant group can," I say.

He gives a sharp nod. "Hell, yes. They have a leadership structure more complex than GM, Ford and IBM rolled together. Good luck figuring out who reports to whom, or what powers each title gives. They have a recruitment program that would put Amway to shame. I don't know how they reel their targets in, but they identify young kids who are in some way already leaning towards bigotry. A nudge is all that's required to get them into the fold. They come from all across the country and once a part of the group, a relocation scheme kicks in to isolate them from old friends or family. By removing them from those influences, the Covenant becomes their new support structure. These young, impressionable kids get secreted away in apartment complexes filled with other Covenant recruits, which only serves to deepen their racist thoughts by surrounding them with others who think the same way. If you step back and look from a distance, this group is run like a corporation, with layers of middle management and an internship program."

Killing points to the back of his neck. "Just that instead of a name badge or white hood, you get something more permanent. Vetted members are branded right at the base of their skull with a symbol to indicate their pledge." The gesture stretches the sleeve of his t-shirt and I wonder if he's ever ripped one that way.

"A brand?" Griff lets out a low whistle. "That's got to hurt."

"Yeah. Hard core, right?"

"I'm hearing you state that Moller was their leader in this area. So what happened to them afterwards?" I make a leap in logic, Killing never actually said that. Maybe this is our twenty thousand dollar question. All this information about some white supremacist group hasn't cleared anything up. In fact, it's muddled the picture further. What does a truck associated with this group have to do with our crime scene? Could it be a simple coincidence? Or did they play a role? Maybe I'm putting too much stock in the story of a civilian who very recently endured some traumatic interactions and seems to still carry the effects with him.

There are so many data points floating around now, yet no clarity around the picture they paint. It's like the dusting of stars in a clear night sky. You know there's a constellation buried there somewhere, but until you see lines that connect them, the picture remains hidden.

I want Killing to deliver a statement that

provides me the overlay, that places the lines in order for my constellation to emerge.

He shrugs his shoulders. "Beats me. They all disappeared, faded back into the woodwork. The Covenant might have released them all, but my money is on relocation to another hot spot. Think of them like an army fighting a battle on multiple fronts. They shift resources where they are most needed, or move them out of spots where the fight has died. I provided Warren with the addresses of a couple places where I found them living. He checked each one. Same story: Nothing. No trace. Landlords said the apartments were just abandoned one day, scrubbed clean and emptied. Probably made a mint on deposit fees since no one left a forwarding address."

Something catches in my brain. "Wait. There's this elaborate scheme to incite a race war that will change America, involving lynching and crafted murder scenes, unearthed by you and Warren, yet not one Covenant member was arrested? How does that happen?"

"I didn't say no one got arrested. Some who participated in the riot were tagged, but only with general disturbance infractions. At that time we hadn't put the pieces together yet, so while they were in custody no one knew the right questions to ask. Once released, they faded to the wind. The ones who came to my house..."

"They had to have been arrested, right?"

Killing nods. "Eventually. They're still in the hospital right now."

Griff looks up, surprise on his face. "Still? What did you do to them?"

He smiles, a grim thing that cuts across his face without humor, as he moves back over to the weight room and picks up a twenty-five pound plate. He tosses it up in the air and catches it with his other hand before racking it. "Danced to heavy metal under the pale moonlight."

I note again the size of the stains on the floor. We are all justified in protecting our house from intruders with ill intent, but this guy seems to take a little too much pleasure in the damage he inflicted. His manner screams loose cannon. I think back to Warren's parting comment about him and get a glimpse of what the guy meant. We're catching Killing on a down slide, he's obviously exhausted over something and giving us minimal attention. I can only imagine what kind of a handful he is fully charged.

He glances over at a wall clock. "Look, I don't know what else to tell you and have to get going. Things to do, people to be you know. Get a copy of the file from Warren. It has everything I gave him, plus his interviews with those kids in the hospital. Maybe there's something in there that can help."

Without waiting to see if we were through, or agreeable to being dismissed in such a manner, Killing heads up the stairs. At the front door he turns back as he opens it and holds out a business card. It's got a logo of the local Hyper-Mart on the face and a cell phone number scribbled in pen. I take it. The title under his name states *Loss Prevention Manager*.

"You catch shoplifters? I thought you were a football player."

"I'm in my transition phase, from caterpillar to butterfly." He spreads his arms and flaps them. "Quack."

What a strange guy.

We shake hands, something we never did on meeting, and his grip crushes mine. "If anything else pops up, I'll call you."

We both know we'll never speak again. I hand him my card and exit onto the front porch. Griff pauses, looking like he wants to give Killing a hug. Instead they also shake and my partner mumbles something I can't make out. He holds up the autographed football with a smile, then follows me down the driveway.

It's my turn at the wheel. As we exit Windemere Fields, I look over to Griff. "Did you get the sense he was more in control of that interview than we were?"

Part of me burns thinking about different ways I could have handled things. I should have been more forceful.

Griff stares out the front window with a distant look. "Man, he was huge. Did you see his knuckles? They were like someone stuffed walnuts under his skin."

"Enough with the fan boy stuff. What do you think about his information? How does it all fit?" My tone is sharp and irritated. Griff is an old man with grown kids, too old to be fawning over an arrogant football player with a hobby cop syndrome.

He snaps back into work mode and his stare sharpens. "Everything he said meshes with what I remember happening up here. He just added some local dimension. But yeah, I don't see how it fits either. Truth: A white supremacy group committed crimes up here against people of color."

I take the bit. "Dare: Bell was a champion to people of color, automatically placing himself across the field of war from something like the Covenant, if not directly, then by his actions."

"Truth: We think one or more kids survived the basketball scene and came back to the factory for some reason, perhaps to clean up, to look for any evidence that may have been left behind that could pin them. Rollins caught one of them in the act and they attacked both of you to escape."

"Dare: The Covenant disbanded up here, as far as anyone can tell. Maybe they migrated south. Maybe some of those branded kids came across Bell and his attackers and got involved. Maybe that's why weapon and ammo counts don't match." I look over. "Did Rollins say whether the face he saw was black or white?"

Griff shakes his head. "It was just a flash of movement, a head backlit against the sun coming from behind."

We drive in silence for a bit. I let ideas click and clack in my head, trying to see which ones fit together like cogs in a wheel. It feels like I'm missing the one cog that connects all the others. "Okay, what about two working theories? One: black kids assaulted and killed Bell, gunned down by Johnstone. Two: the Covenant came across the scene and decided to act. But why would they care if Bell was being beaten? I think it's part of white supremacy charter that you applaud anything that harms minorities."

Griff shrugs. "What if they simply leaped at the chance to kill? What if they were the ones to finish off Bell after dealing with the kids? They come back, find out he's still breathing and pummel him for kicks. We know this group is vicious. It might have been an opportune moment for them to act."

I pause at a red light before Jordan Way and see the Hyper-Mart sign ahead. Glancing at Killing's business card, I note, "This is where he works."

Griff glances up at it and mutters, "Big place." He returns to studying the football.

"Let's swing by Warren and grab a copy of the file on the way out."

He nods absently then holds the ball up for me to see. "Does it look like his autograph says 'Mickey Mouse'?"

FOURTEEN

The sun is skimming along the horizon as we exit North Haven and grab the interstate south. Red sunlight streaks the sky in broad swaths, painting trees black on one side, pink on the other. I flip on my headlights and move the cruiser into the fast lane.

Griff's cell phone rings. He glances at it then flips the lid open and answers. "Hey, chief." He listens for a second. "Yeah, hang on."

Pressing a button, he switches it to speaker mode and sets the phone down on top of the binder occupying the seat between us. This is what Warren provided, everything he had on the Covenant. "Okay, we're on. Arch is driving."

Deputy Super Gonzales' voice fills the car. "Where are you both?"

"In the car," Griff says with a wink to me. "I told you, Arch is driving."

"I know that. Where is the car?"

"We're up near the border, sir," I cut in, before Griff can respond with something like: 'Earth.'

A pause. "Is this the truck lead from Towney? North Haven?"

Gonzales is on top of things. The other two detectives must have given him a closing day brief. We will have to do the same. In fact, I'm surprised he hasn't called us before this, pestering for progress. Either he's hands off in his style, or he's giving us plenty of rope to hang ourselves. The latter doesn't fit with what I've observed, or his rep thus far.

I provide a short recap of our trip, taking care to leave out any theories we formed around the Covenant's role. Until we have something solid underpinning those ideas, better to keep the waters clear. I can tell by his replies that he's not thrilled our trip failed to bear fruit but he doesn't dwell on it.

"Well, get back down here before the media figures out where you went. We don't need them connecting dots and creating public theory."

"On our way," I respond, and wait. He didn't call just to ask what we're up to, so unless he's micro-managing the case, there's another motive.

He clears his throat. "I received a call from William Travian a couple of hours ago."

"Did you take it?" Griff says. "There's nothing to report yet and whatever we've discovered isn't for public review."

"When someone like Travian calls, you always answer, detective. However, I informed him that we had no new facts yet to share."

I make a leap. "But that's not the only reason he called, is it?"

"No. He offered the assistance of his security detail for us, to quicken this case along. He's anxious for answers, as are we all."

"Are you talking about that walking fire hydrant Turk?" Griff snaps. "No way, dep. No way in hell. That guy doesn't even have a neck."

"We have it under control," I add.

"Understood, gentlemen. We don't allow civilian partnerships during investigations per policy, but you both know this is an unusual situation. The rules of engagement will be tested. Travian can make all of our lives complicated even if he means well. Keep that in mind as you progress."

"Will do," I respond and Griff stabs the *End* button.

"Jesus H, Arch. If that butt plug Turk so much as darkens my doorway, so help me God..."

"Yeah, yeah. I get it. You're preaching to the choir."

We continue down the Tri-state tollway, wrapped in distinct but related thoughts. I'm the first to break, after twenty minutes of silence.

"Do we dig further into this Covenant group? Try to understand how they are related?"

Griff shakes his head. "The supremacy angle is radioactive, especially with what we've got. A bed-ridden man who, one, may have been involved in a plan to bring on a race war to end the millennium that, two, duped two professional athletes into being his pawns and three, was stopped by one of his own sons. You got to admit that's a crazy story to swallow. If we put that out there, the news hounds - your girlfriend included - will tear into it like piranha going after the hind leg of a goat dropped off the dock in shallow water."

"You like your analogies really specific, don't you?" Before he can respond, I continue, "So we circle around the Rosenfel angle, put together his story and let that lead us deeper?"

"Bell met someone there. Who was that

guy and where is he? What did the bodyguard do? How did he end up on the court? Answers to those questions will bust this thing wide open."

Outside the last rays of sun wink out, giving over the sky to twilight. Now the trees and buildings are black paper cut-outs, stacked and glued to the walls of our own private diorama. I exit off the Tri-state onto I-290 heading towards Chicago.

Griff yawns. "We won't be doing much more tonight. The realty office is closed so we can't interview any of them until tomorrow. We need more info before calling Travian to pick a little more at his role. Plus, he might think we're taking him up on his offer. Let's keep digging into Rosenfel, or whoever that was."

I nod. I feel too wired to sleep, but a yawn crosses my face as well, against my best efforts to contain it. We had an all-nighter, followed by a full day of concussions, chases, power talks and racial plots. Another stretch run will not do either of us any good. And I am beat. Humans are not made for constant acceleration, we all have to ease up and recover at some point. The call of my pillow is strong.

"Drop me off at home, you can take the cruiser. I'll pour through Warren's binder with a glass of Jameson to sharpen my mind. Get me at seven tomorrow morning."

I follow his directions to an address in River Forest. It's a buttoned down area, with precise geometry in the sidewalks, driveways and streets. His house is a small two-story Cape Cod, with an enclosed front porch and a wall of windows. A lot of work has been done to update it. He mumbles a good night through another yawn and shuffles up the concrete driveway. I wait until the front door is slammed shut before backing out.

My plan is to head home but I want to stop at the factory once more. It's as if there's a clue hanging out somewhere around that place, just waiting to be found. Maybe I'll stumble across in the dark what dozens of police and forensics missed in broad daylight. Mostly, I just want to be alone at my first crime scene as a detective and let my mind decompress.

Plus, it's not far off the route I need to take home anyway.

***

The July night is still rife with humidity as I stand there, listening. The ever-present sound of cars along the highway floats over my head, rustling the tree tops. Everything has been removed now. Bell's car, towed. Rollin's squad, absent. The cones and border tape, tossed. Griff couldn't get an extension on patrol watch for Middle Plains, those hours were needed elsewhere. Or Hecker was just being a dick and pulling his officers back.

Johnny Nayaki and his team bagged everything they could find and abandoned the scene. From here, our facts will arise from his lab. Anything left behind is now victim to the progression of nature and humanity. I have no doubt plenty of locals have trampled through the factory, like tourists viewing the last stand of Noah Bell. It's rather surprising no one is around right now, unless they heard me roll up and are hiding.

The heavy clack of train couplers vault over the tree line towards me, from the switch yard to the south. My father worked at a place like that when I was young, before he moved into another industry. But he never lost his love of trains. My brother and I spent many hours in the basement, helping him construct a massive train set. His attention to detail was exacting, down to the color we painted the railroad ties. I loved sitting there with a fine-bristle brush, mixing browns to give the appearance of weathered wood.

Even now the sounds of a train yard are familiar and welcome.

I can see the tops of cars stacked in line beyond the edge of Middle Plains property. The yard lights are bright high up on their poles, bathing the place in artificial daylight. A voice hollers over the yard and I can tell it's a safety inspector - car knocker - yelling about something he found. Sounds like he's not happy about a lash up between two locomotives.

After a bit of listening to the car knocker and a road foreman argue, I turn my attention away. There's nothing here for me. The vibes I'd hoped would come to me like some miraculous vision are missing, frittered away on the breeze of process efficiency. If we'd been able to persuade our brass to preserve the scene just a few days longer, that might have contained the vibes. But our wishes were in direct conflict to theirs. They wanted the scene brought down, to minimize the attention paid to this place where Noah Bell died.

I decide to make my way home. My eyes are heavy, my thought patterns frayed. And my head still hurts.

***

I park the cruiser at the outer edge of my apartment complex lot. It's a mid-70s place, featuring white brick and Tudor styling. I'm sure I've seen uglier styles at some point in my life, but that's not a certainty. However, it's clean and cheap, and close to Anna. That's all I care about.

The door is unlocked. I pause in mid-turn of the knob, realizing it. A quick glance at the planter next to the door reveals it's been moved slightly. It's where I keep my extra key. Not real original, I know, but I'm not that clever.

Pushing the door open I step into the apartment and wait, letting my over-clocked senses attune to the rhythm of the place. Nothing seems out of order. In fact everything is now in order. The living room has been picked up. Through the opening to the kitchen I can see the dishes have been done.

I let out a sigh and walk down the hall to the lone bedroom.

A single lamp burns in the corner, casting a dim glow over the bed. Sheila's dark hair spills across the pillow. She's turned away from me and I can't tell if she's sleeping or not. Part of me thinks I should never have told her where I keep the spare key, but she would have found out anyway. She's smart that way, much sharper than me.

I give a soft knock on the door frame. "You asleep?"

"No," comes the muffled reply. "I'm knitting a scarf."

What is it about me that brings out the smart ass in everyone?

I step into the room and remove my jacket, draping it across the back of a chair parked in one corner. I start loosening my tie. "What are you doing here, Sheila?"

She rolls over onto her back, tucking the comforter up under her chin. It makes her look vulnerable. "It's our daughter's birthday Arch. Can't we celebrate that fact?"

Socks come next, tossed onto the chair. There are other clothes forming a small pile. One of these days I will buy a laundry basket. "We did, earlier today. With ice cream cake. I think you were there."

"But that was cold. Now I need something warm."

I unbutton my shirt and wad it up. It gets added to the pile. "Or are you here to pick at my case?"

"I don't know. Maybe. When can you talk about it?"

"Tomorrow, probably."

She pushes down the covers, revealing her nakedness. The girl has a body to match her looks, skin the shade of light mocha and smooth to touch. Light drifts across the lines of her rib cage, the hollow of her belly, the gentle rounds of her breasts. She is sexy incarnate, and knows it. "It's almost eleven, we have an hour until tomorrow. Let's spend it wisely."

I stand there, taking in the sight of a body I know so well. Many thoughts crowd my mind, but in the end there is only one choice and neither of us can deny it.

Dropping my trousers to the floor, I slide into her.

FIFTEEN

Wednesday, July 14, 1999
3:34am

I jump awake, startled out of exhaustion and slumber. The realization rattles around my brain and I give my head a shake, just to double-check the thought.

Sheila mumbles, something about la vida loca, and snuggles deeper into the covers. She's always been prone to talking in her sleep and I long ago gave up trying to decipher anything. I think it's a song.

The clock on the bedside table shows 3:34am. I bite back a curse, angry with myself for not thinking of this sooner. The blow to my forehead must have really rattled my brain pan; I'd like to think I would normally catch this detail.

I take a few minutes to clean up, staying quiet as possible, and let myself out of my own apartment. The night is hushed, the world settled through the last bits of sleep before rousing for another day. I should be dragging, eyes barely open, but the thought that woke me has energized my body. There's no way I could go back to sleep without checking out my theory.

Re-tracing my route back towards the factory, I bypass the entrance to Middle Plains and continue down Lauren avenue. A dozen blocks farther I come across a driveway leading into the train yard. I spin the steering wheel and enter the parking lot for the yard. It's not a large one, designed only to hold the workers' cars. This is not a place for the general public, or passenger traffic. This yard is behind the scenes, the place where train safety exists to ensure cargo - human or otherwise - arrives safe and whole.

The yard is full to the nuts tonight. Hoppers, flat tops and yard goats sit silently along their tracks, patiently waiting in line for the next run, the next inspection, the next repair.

Switch yards like this run around the clock and I'm counting on that fact. This is one of the larger ones I've seen. Acres of asphalt are given over to semi-trailers, either ready to transport or waiting to unload their cargo. It's a weird sensation, like moving through a prehistoric assembly of creatures all so large that you don't even register on their senses. I see several men standing around an engine coupler. A blue service flag is mounted on the rear, indicating it is safe to work on. All three men turn and watch me as I idle past them, but none give any signs of stopping me. They likely don't see very many non-worker cars coming through here but police cruisers tend to have their own pass.

Towards the rear of the yard I find the tower and park right in front of the door. It's open and unlocked, even at this hour, which tells me someone is inside working.

I find him on the first floor, in a small office along the side wall. He looks up at the sound of my feet, annoyance on his face. He probably thought it was another yard worker with yet another idiotic request. The look changes to uncertainty when I march into his little office. "We're not...um, open. Office hours start tomorrow at seven."

"This can't wait." I flash my tin.

Now his color changes to red. The guy looks like mid-30s. But when he flushes, it drops ten years off his age. "I'm just hub duty, sir. The senior manager will be back in the morn..."

"I need access to your camera room. You do have cameras, right? Security feeds that overlook your yard?"

He stands, mentally off balance. The commercial rail industry has stringent training requirements but I'm guessing there isn't a course for handling young black detectives walking into your place of work in the middle of the night. "I'll have to call my boss. I'm not sure where the keys are to the room."

"Just get me to his office, I can figure it out."

His mouth gapes open and closed, testing responses, trying to catch up with the mash of thoughts undoubtedly banging through his skull. I can almost see him formulating resistance and don't have time for protocol.

"Now," I demand.

He leads me upstairs. All four walls are glass windows, providing a bird's eye view over the full yard during the day. Now, deep in the dark, all I see are our reflections in the glass as he flips on lights.

The manager's office stands in the center of the open rectangle, surrounded by a collection of desks arranged in rows. Most of them look empty. I rifle through the manager's desk until I come across a ring of keys. "Where's the camera room?"

We traverse back downstairs and he mutely points down a hallway to a closed door. It's a closet of a room, barely large enough to hold a flimsy table and single chair. In fact, the door bumps into the chair when I push it open. "I don't know how any of this stuff works, I just switch tapes on a schedule," he says. The tremor in the guy's voice is audible.

I hand him one of my cards. "Relax, you're not in trouble. Please notify your manager that I'm here. If he has any questions, he can call. Also let him know I may be taking a tape or two. Thanks for your help."

He nods and moves away with quick steps. I hear the key tones of his cell phone as he punches in a number, followed by a hushed conversation. I didn't mean for him to call his manager *right now.*

The camera setup is simple and cheap. One monitor displays four images at a time, the screen sectioned into quadrants that rotate through all the different cameras. The rotation is programmed, switching views every minute. I count off the cycle and come up with sixteen cameras. Two tape recorders are stacked to one side of the monitor, humming and blinking *12:00* on the displays.

On the other side of the monitor are stacks of tapes with date ranges written in black marker. I scan labels, doing the math.

They use four tapes per day and rotate them out every week. I pull the tape from last night and shove it in the VCR player. If there is a good angle, and if the rotation of the camera catches that angle at the right time, and if the light is enough...there are a lot of 'ifs'.

My hands are trembling just a bit.

One of the cameras is mounted on the rail yard fence but pointed outward for some reason. The left half of the image captures a portion of the courtyard but I'm not sure if it will show enough to see the attack. I punch buttons on the video controller sitting under the monitor until I figure out how to display a single camera. One eye is on the time tracker. My hands tumble the remote over and over as I scroll through the tape.

When my cell phone rings, I nearly leap out of the chair.

It's Griff. "I wake you?" Normally it would be a pretty stupid question at four in the morning, but we passed that the minute we clipped on our shields.

"No, I couldn't sleep."

"Me neither. Where you at?"

I tap the remote against my palm, impatient. "I'm at the train yard just south of Middle Plains. I might have found a security camera with an angle towards the Bell scene. Long shot, but I'm hoping something turns up."

"Shit, good thinking. There's a part of the yard that backs up to the factory. That would be huge, Arch. I mean, shut-Hecker-the-hell-up huge, you know? See anything yet?"

"I just started."

"Okay, pause for a second. I went through Warren's binder. Does the name Donald Sutton ring a bell?"

"If this is a setup for a pun on Bell's name, I'm punching you in the mouth."

There's a long silence. "Actually, I hadn't even thought of it, but now that you mention it...Anyway, Sutton is a lawyer, corporate entities or some other such shit. His office is located in the same building as Travian's."

"How do you know?"

"I saw his name plate on the directory listing next to the elevator."

I didn't even notice the directory. That makes me feel somewhat stupid. I really need to up my game. "It's a big building. There are probably lots of lawyers hanging a shingle there. I'm not seeing the connection."

"So...Donald Sutton was one of the victims murdered up in North Haven this spring. Remember seeing the report of a guy staked through the eye in Warren's binder? Sutton."

Interesting. "Coincidence?"

"If you're a believer in them. I'm not, so I dug around, trying to connect some dots. Sutton's primary clients? Travian and Radd. There's also a minor on file for him, unlawful assembly in some dinky town down south, about a decade ago. I can request that jacket in the morning."

A little more interesting. I start the camera replay back up. The time resumes in the lower corner, seconds ticking away at a steady pace.

Griff continues. "It gets better though. Sutton has a son Douglas. Douglas is currently pending arrest. Care to guess for what?"

"No, you can just tell me." I push fast forward on the remote. Now the timer starts to move double-pace.

Griff sounds insulted that I don't want to play his guessing game. "Fine. B&E, first degree attempted murder and a slew of other charges, all occurring at the residence of one Rick Johann Killing. Once Douglas is healed up enough to leave the hospital, he'll be charged."

That catches me. The recording is

momentarily forgotten. "Those are a lot of dots, Griff. I don't think I see the picture though."

"Me either. But somehow Travian is central to all of this. His lawyer was killed in a horrific way up north. His lawyer's son was caught attempting to murder a really cool football player, who in turn was being played for a pawn in some scheme to start a race war. The man moving the pawns around is breathing through a tube, yet a month later his truck appears at the scene of a homicide. The victim was meeting an agent arranged through Travian, yet the agent died long before the meet. That's what we know from the Travian angle. How's the picture now?"

"Like Pollack and Escher had a bastard love child. None of this makes sense, Griff. How do the kids from the basketball court come into play? Is it safe to assume Moller and the Suttons are connected through the Covenant Church?"

"We can. But it doesn't get us much. If they are, what does that mean for this case." Griff exhales, loud through the ear speaker. "Lots of questions, not many answers."

"No kidding," I murmur, fiddling with the remote. Motion on the monitor catches my attention. "Hey, hold on. I think I'm getting to the right part."

"Time stamp?"

"8:31. I've got a car pulling up. The shot is fuzzy, but it's Bell."

"No sign of a Tahoe?"

"None. But there's a lot of ground not covered by this camera. I think it's set to capture a back gate to the rail yard. It's the only thing that makes sense."

"I remember doing a report out there several years ago. Kids breaking into freight cars. They probably put up the system after we never solved it."

My attention is focused on the screen, not his words. "Okay, so I see Bell getting out of the car. Bodyguard was driving, he stays put, sitting sideways with an open door. Bell's walking...he's stopped now, facing into the courtyard...maybe talking to someone but I can't tell. Film is too grainy."

"The deceased Rosenfel? That would be a trick."

"Now he's walking further into the courtyard...shit."

"What?" Griff's voice raises an octave. "What happened?"

"He walked off screen. The near building blocks my view. I can see one end with a door but not much else."

"Mother Hubbard." Griff's voice is

dejected.

I feel deflated. I wanted the recording to show something other than what we've been thinking, to show that Noah Bell wasn't the victim of the violence he fought against; to let Chicago know that his life did not end with one terribly ironic act. The man swung a bat in my favor and changed my life, the least I can do is make sure he doesn't become a file jacket stuffed in a drawer somewhere.

This was my best chance at seeing what truly happened.

I scrub my eyes, feeling the adrenaline exit my system like a storm sewer flushing.

Because of that motion, I nearly miss the motion on the tape. When I see it, my eyes goes wide and I jump up out of the chair.

"Holy...fuck!"

"Did you just swear? What? *What?*"

"Griff, we need to forget everything we think about this case."

PART 2

SIXTEEN

Monday, July 12, 1999
8:28pm

Gwendolyn Manner leans back against the wall and draws deep on the makeshift bowl formed out of a discarded beer can. Smoke fills her mouth and she holds it long, before letting it curl out of parted lips. The tangy, burnt corn smell drifts past her nose, welcome and familiar.

The factory sits empty and silent around her, a place no longer needed and now abandoned. At one point in the past it was a place that made industrial plastics, according to her grandmother. Gwen is only twenty and by the time she came along the factory had already been closed for years. Her grandmother once told her the name but she couldn't remember it.

Gwen loved the place. No one else ever comes here, which meant she didn't have to deal with other people or unfamiliar faces. When the occasional vagrant did set up home somewhere inside, the space was so vast she could easily avoid them. Over the last couple of months though, the regulars had disappeared one by one. Whether it's due to the heat of summer - hotter this year than any she can remember - or them finding a better place, she didn't know and didn't care.

Next to her, sitting on the dusty floor of an office, lies a drawing pad. In a while, when the drug takes root and lifts her mind away, she'll put chalk to paper and let the images flow. It didn't matter what she drew, only that she did. The chalk will take a life of its own, creating whatever emerges from her haze. Still life portraits are her favorite: machine parts forgotten on the shop floor, hallway perspective, a chair in a shrouded room.

People are her least favorite. If any show up in her drawings, she leaves their faces blank.

Tonight will be devoted to small scale items. The office she occupies is on the second floor, in a row of offices, each one identical to the other. Windows in the front wall of every office face the main factory area; she imagines a time in the past, with men in ties standing at those windows, while men of grease and sweat worked the machines far below, like the personification of class warfare.

Opposite the front windows, an identical set opens the back wall to the outside. These windows overlook the courtyard between the two buildings. No glass remains in the panes, just shards poking up from the wooden frame. Vandals had targeted them first, long ago when this huge building turned into a ghost.

The sun has just set in the west, but the remaining glow provides sufficient light for Gwen. She doesn't need much, just enough to get the outline started and let her hands do the rest. She twirls a piece of chalk between her fingers, marveling at the texture and smell. The way the dust floats through the air, suspended motes of flat color held aloft by invisible currents, bound for a destination no one knew.

Sounds of a car arriving interrupt Gwen's reverie and pull her mind from the blissful funk she craves. Outside, tires crunch over cracked pavement and gravel.

Gwen sighs and gets up to her knees, peering over the bottom edge of a broken window to see who has arrived. It bothers her to think someone else now shares her private space.

It's a fancy car, gleaming black, reflecting shards of orange light where remnants of the sun poke through gaps in the trees. The driver's door opens. A bulky man swivels to place his feet on the ground but does not exit the car. Another man opens the passenger door and emerges, walking around the back of the vehicle and heading her way.

He's black and dressed in a suit. She doesn't recognize the face, but then again she never does. He most certainly did not belong here. As he walks, he speaks, directing his words to someone out of sight from her vantage point. She's startled to realize someone has been down there.

"...tonight?" The words float in and out of her mind, either taken by the echo chamber effects of the courtyard, or muddled by the state of her mind.

"Good...bit ago. You?"

"Where are...parked?"

"Out back."

Mindful of the glass daggers sticking up from the window frame, Gwen places her hands in between them and leans out, trying to see the other man. There is no real reason behind it, as she'd never know him anyway, but curiosity drives her.

A single post lamp in the courtyard gives off the only light now that the shadows have taken over down there, a concession by whoever still owned the property to provide minimal light. Probably a city requirement. It's not much, but enough to make out detail. Both men have disappeared somewhere below her perch, blocked by the angle and wall design. She can still hear their voices.

They walk back into view, carrying the body language of business. The other man is smaller and white, with thinning hair and a hunched posture. Gwen knows what it means: Some businessman is contemplating the purchase of this old factory. The *For Sale* sign still hung out near the entrance, sun-faded from the years. The black man is a buyer, the white man an agent. His deference makes it obvious.

Gwen's interest starts to flag. If the factory is sold, she will have to find another place to hide away from the world and that saddens her. This one still had so many things to be drawn.

The men pass under her position, the words slowing. An awkward silence emerges and she thinks that the hunched man is doing a pretty terrible job of selling the place. Maybe she won't have to find a new hideaway after all.

Then it happens.

The realty agent slows, a tiny movement that drops him behind the other man's pace. He points to the far side of the courtyard and speaks about something there, directing attention away from him. The black man follows his gesture.

In that instant, the agent kicks the other man's knees from behind, a short powerful strike that tumbles the man down into an awkward heap.

Spinning, the agent whips a gun from his jacket.

The big guy sitting in the car leaps out with a yell, charging towards his companion, when the agent fires two shots. They are quiet but explosive puffs of air. The big man collapses, skidding forward in the dirt, clutching his chest. He does not get up.

Gwen cries out, a clipped gasp of horror and shock that escapes her lips before she can corral it.

From the ground, the agent - the killer - snaps his head around and they lock eyes. It's a snapshot of time, a frozen moment forever branded across her skull. Even at that distance Gwen can see the green of his eyes, like those of a jungle cat padding towards her out of the darkness, glowing with feral light.

She tears away from the window, panic consuming her. The languid nature of her thoughts just moments earlier evaporate in a wink, replaced by a raw instinct for survival. She does not know who the killer is, why he did what he did. She knows only one thing.

He saw her.

SEVENTEEN

Julien Crux spins and strokes the trigger twice. The bodyguard goes down face first, like a charging rhino, and slides into a flaccid heap on the courtyard brick. If he isn't already dead, he has only seconds.

Without pausing in his motion, Julien drops the pistol and whirls back to grab Noah Bell's tie. The crown prince of activism is still on his knees and out of position to prevent the move. As Julien yanks the tie tight around Bell's throat, a scream erupts above and behind him.

He stabs his stare back at the source. There: window on the second floor. He fixes the image in his head.

Young girl, pale skin, dark hair, horrified expression. She has seen his face. Irritation blossoms inside Julien. Complications irritate him. Things need to be neat, to be tidy. He prides himself on killing in a fog, coming in like the mysterious vapor and leaving death behind, but no one the wiser for his presence.

That's his goal and he likes goals.

Bell is struggling, grasping at his throat, desperate to peel the constricting fabric away and open his lungs. It's a primal reaction, survival instinct guiding his actions but blinding him to others. If he would simply stand up and turn, Julien loses leverage and now the chances of living rise. But when you're dying, rational thought is often absent.

Julien watches the light dim in the other man's eyes. A clock ticks in the back of his mind. For every moment he takes to eliminate his target, that's one moment more for his witness to escape.

He should just shoot the man through the back of the skull and be done with it, but his contract spelled out exactly how the murder should appear. The man that hired him represents a larger organization. He's done enough business with them thus far to learn his boundaries. If his sponsors want this death to appear a certain way, he will make it so.

There is a specific motive behind the death of Noah Bell. Julien suspects it revolves around pushing some racial separation agenda, a continuation his contract work up north several months ago. It's the same group, so it's no great stretch to connect the dots.

The bodyguard is a small complication. He had not planned for Bell to arrive with protection, the meeting was not set up that way. Now he'll have to make that man disappear, a simple task. Only one body is to be left as evidence.

But that girl is a risk, one he needs to remove before this comes all undone.

When the last shudder ripples through Bell's body, Julien drops him and retrieves his weapon. He had scouted this location thoroughly, even going to the extreme of removing the natives over the last two months. It pained him to kill homeless people who only sought shelter, but he couldn't risk any of them lingering around when he executed on his contract. It meant he had to make sure they disappeared without a trace, which often meant chopping them into quarters and disposing of the body parts into remote areas where wild animals could feast on them and remove the evidence naturally.

Julien did take care to make their death as painless as possible, using chemical methods or quick shots to the temple. He likes to think he has some level of compassion. For a killer anyway.

It pained him even more to kill for no recompense. He's not a charity.

However, the girl sneaking in here is a gap that he needs to close. He had walked the entire factory before Bell arrived, so somehow she snuck in after he cleared the place.

As a result of his scouting, he knows the layout well. There are only two unlocked doors. Any windows on the first floor are mounted high and horizontal, something he thinks was done for ventilation. She's not going to be able to crawl out of those, so the doors are her escape.

One door is right off the courtyard, a wide service entrance. This building had not held any customer entrances, those belonged to the sister building across the way. This one was all business, devoted solely to plastics production.

He pushes it open with forced care, resisting the urge to leap through the door and start blasting away. The interior is darker than the outside. Dim light filters through the upper floor windows, giving just a hint of definition to the shape and the space.

Julien slows to let his eyes adjust, straining for any sound that might betray her location.

Once adjusted, he moves forward, weaving around the debris littering the floor. Anything made of wood - pallets, crates, shelves - had long since been scavenged for burning by the transient population during winter, but there are still a number of machines, metal drums and other items strewn throughout the factory. Their size, weight or manner of affixation kept scavengers from removing them. These things provide cover as he makes his way towards the only other exit door that isn't chained shut. This is where he suspects the girl will run.

The soft scuff of feet comes to him, confirming his thoughts and Julien picks up his pace.

In the dim light he sees her shape, a tiny rabbit going to ground against the predator. It's almost not fair, he thinks, how little chance she stands. Part of him feels empathy for her plight. Truly a case of wrong time, ever so wrong place. But a larger part of him is annoyed by her presence, creating a variable he has to address; creating potential outcomes that may arise out of his control.

And that is most certainly not acceptable. Everything must be under control.

The far door opens with a creak. The girl is cut in silhouette for a frozen second as faint light from the courtyard spills inside. She turns back at the sound of his running feet, sees him and screams.

Julien brings his Beretta into firing position and strokes the trigger. Sparks flash off the door frame, indicating a miss, and he swears under his breath. Shooting and running have never been his strong suit, he's better from a grounded stance. Using a suppressor only cuts into his accuracy further.

By the time he exits the building, she's scampering through the ragged chain link fence towards the back of the property. He takes a second to center into a firing stance. His next round clips one of the fence posts, sending more sparks into the night. Now his annoyance blossoms into anger, and no small amount of angst. The rabbit has found her way out of the meadow. If she slips into the surrounding neighborhoods, he may lose her forever.

That would mean a witness existed to identify him and his role in Bell's death, which is unacceptable. It would also mean there's a potential leak in the scenario his client wants presented to the public. Their agenda is quite specific and Noah Bell figures prominently into it, or rather the manner of his death. Should contrary stories emerge that cast doubt on how he died, the client could hold him responsible and seek redress.

Julien Crux would be the rabbit then, running from a new predator on the scene.

On the back side of the factory grounds, woods emerge to stake a claim. The trees are thick and hunched close, but they capture the sounds of her frantic flight, giving him direction and speed. His wingtip dress shoes aren't fit for this kind of activity, but there's nothing to be done for that. He had planned to burn all the clothes anyway to eliminate the chance of trace evidence.

Julien tracks her through the woods that surround the factory, to a park several hundred yards away with an old basketball court at the center. He catches up in time to see her collapse against the shoulder of a black kid. Five others cluster close, asking questions, talking over each other. Her body language is frantic, her words equally so, and Julien can tell by the group's expressions that no one can understand what she's saying. Nor do they know how to react.

Pausing just inside the tree line, Julien takes a moment to assess and evaluate. These boys are all young. Half are shirtless, their clothes thrown in little piles around the perimeter of the court. One of them still holds the basketball, attempting to spin it on his finger while the others listen to the girl. There are only six of them and their presence is easy to understand. In her blind panic, the girl disrupted their pickup game. Now she's trying to rely on them for help, trying to make them realize that she's a rabbit in danger.

What she doesn't understand, what she won't understand until it's too late, is that she has run to the wrong place. Now there are just more rabbits around her.

Julien mentally ticks off the remaining rounds in his clip. It's going to be close, he doesn't have much room for error. He formulates an approach to get him within a few feet of everyone before it all goes to hell. This level of calculated action is what sets him apart from other contractors, one of the things that has propelled his rise to a favored station in the world he walks. Too many other contract killers grow complacent in their success, falling into the trap of thinking they are better than stupid law enforcement officers. They start getting sloppy with vetting clients, which often leads to an undercover agent setting them up for a false contract.

The tactical thinking capability and situational reaction dulls from lack of use and before they know it, they are staring across a table in some interrogation room, trying to convince officers of their innocence.

Julien Crux long ago vowed that would never be him. He will stay sharp and cautious, lasting in a vocation that doesn't feature many long time practitioners.

With a deep exhale to clear his mind, the contract killer hired by the Covenant Church of the New Millennium steps out of the woods.

EIGHTEEN

Gwen screams as sparks ignite on the door frame inches from her head. She stumbles out into the night and sprints blindly towards the far edge of the factory grounds. She doesn't know where she's headed, only that the forest on the other side of the fence offers a sense of protection, a haven amongst the tall pines.

The world spins violently around her head as she runs, every breath a ragged cry for help to no one that can hear, every step a violent jarring of her senses. She doesn't understand what's happening, her fogged mind unable to sort through the events to grasp the cause and effect of her situation. All she knows is to run, in any direction that takes her from the faceless man with dead green eyes.

Another spark lights off a metal post as she darts through a hole in the fence. The metal links had long ago been cut and the fence pulled up in one corner to allow passage, whether in or out.

The pinging sound of the bullet hitting metal drives another scream from her mouth and re-directs her as surely as if she'd run into an obstacle. She falls, rolls and scrambles back to her feet, limbs herky-jerky in their movement, making her steps unpredictable.

Ahead, the forest line beckons, a stand of trees spreading their branches wide. Only a few yards now.

It seems like the air swarms with bullets tracing their way to her. That suspense seizes her mind, clamps the panic tight to her teeth, and makes her shoulders hunch in anticipation of a hit.

But no explosive pain flares in her back. Nothing happens to knock her down forever.

Gwen rushes past the thick branches, needles scraping her skin, trunks popping up in random fashion. The denseness of the forest forces a change to her route often. She doesn't have a plan, only a general direction of flight. The sound of cracking comes from underneath her feet as she steps on pine cones and dead branches. It's a trail of sound, marking her passing for anyone to follow but she doesn't think of this.

Without a backward glance to check her safety, Gwen plunges deeper into the trees. She doesn't know what lies on the other side, only that this area of Cicero has a lot of neighborhoods, faceless blocks of identical houses. If she can somehow make her way into them, she can disappear into the anonymity of those streets. There is no plan beyond that, no tactical thought.

Only the next step, the next breath, and the next several feet exist for her.

A crack echoes behind her and she bites down on a scream. He's still chasing her. In the darkness of trees that smother any light, a monster tracks her with singular intent, absent of face, absent of emotion. He is an embodiment of all that she fears.

Gwen slams into the trunk of a large tree, gulping for desperate air, grasping it for support. Just for a second. The bark is rough and it scrapes her palms. Smells of pine sap fill her nose, sticking to her hands. Normally this would be a wonderful scent, something that would keep her in the thickness of the trees, reveling in nature. But now it's been twisted. Her own panicked breath changes the flavor of pine scent to something repugnant.

She cannot get enough oxygen into her lungs. The fire in her chest spreads out through the rest of her body. Maybe she's been shot already and simply doesn't realize it.

The thought occurs that maybe, just maybe, she should slide down and wait for the monster to arrive. She can't run forever. Why fight it? The fog in her mind lifts just a bit at that thought. No more aimless days walking in a world full of strangers, no more scratching out a life in the margins.

No more futile wondering what lies ahead for her, a girl with no skills and no hope.

One shot. She might not even feel pain. It would be like suicide by stranger.

Then another crack rises somewhere behind her and the panic returns. She is too afraid to face the end that way, too weak to make a stance and take control of her fate. In the bends of her mind, if she was a stronger girl, she could stand up and say 'Here', face the monster. But because she's weak and spineless, she takes off running once again.

She knows he can track her by the sounds of her feet. She's not trying to sneak away, she's trying to outrun him.

Through the thickness of the pines and oaks and elms, light filters towards her. A faint glow from somewhere beyond the trees and she turns her flight in that direction.

Gwen busts out of the forest into an old park. Street lamps are lit up around the perimeter, giving light to the boys playing basketball on the court. That's the light she saw.

With dead legs and unsteady feet, she sprints across the grassy perimeter to the protection of others. Her mouth is so dry she can't even form words, and the few that she does are scrambled by the panic in her mind.

They stop playing at her approach, wary young black men looking at a tiny white girl running from the woods towards them.

One young man steps forward and she collapses against him.

"Whoa!" He shouts, grabbing her to keep her from falling. "What the hell...?"

Gwen cries and shouts, trying to tell him about the monster with no face and the death that fills the air back at the factory. She can feel the sweat of his shoulder on her cheek as she clings tight.

"Hold up girl. What's happening?" He tries to peel her away but Gwen grabs him with a strength she never knew she had.

The other boys cluster around and she can hear muttered comments. Some are concerned, some are leering, others dismissive. In fact, one of the boys waves her off and starts back towards the court. He spins the ball on his finger as he walks, practicing.

Before she can calm down enough to speak legibly, Gwen hears words arise from the woods behind her, from the direction she just came. She jerks her head around.

The man in the suit emerges into view. He reaches out one hand as if to call her to him. "Honey, I'm sorry. I didn't mean to say that." Looking at the boy holding her, he says: "My daughter. We had a fight."

Now two other boys grunt and turn away. They want no part of a domestic scene.

Gwen screams and shuffles behind her protector, placing his body between hers and the faceless man who can kill with such dispassion.

The boy stands his ground. "She don't sound like it was no little fight. What you do to her?"

"Son, don't get mixed up in this. You've probably had the same kind of arguments with your parents. Now come on, honey, let's go. Mom's home waiting."

The killer is within a dozen yards now, far too close for her panic. It overwhelms Gwen. She shoves the boy forward and spins, running for the far side of the park, running for the next stage of escape. The trees beckon once again, offering her the same safety their brothers did just a few moments ago.

Come, child. We can hide you.

Gwen stumbles as the blacktop of the court gives way to stubby grass and she smacks her shoulder off a merry-go-round, causing it to lurch a quarter-turn. She regains her balance and circles around it, sprinting for the trees.

Shouts erupt behind her, of the boys, of the man. No longer does he play the remorseful father. She can hear anger in his voice. She can also hear the yell of pain from the boy who stood his ground for her. A darted glance over her shoulder reveals him falling to the ground, clutching his throat, and the killer pointing his gun in her direction.

The other boys are running, in all directions, maybe for safety, maybe for their own weapons stashed under piles of clothes.

Gwen veers her direction, trying to keep playground equipment between her and the killer. The sense of dread blooms once again between her shoulder blades, waiting for that intense pain to signal a direct hit. But nothing happens as she runs into the protection of the tree trunks.

Gunfire flares up. At least one boy had managed to grab a weapon. Several shots are fired. Then silence.

She doesn't spare a thought for what that means. Her world narrows down to the immediate path, to the gaps between trunks that signal a way forward. Now she can hear the sounds of traffic, of civilization. It must be Lauren avenue, she thinks somewhere in the back of her mind. That brings a sense of orientation. The haven of houses lies just to the other side of that four lane road.

Gwen's vision narrows even more with this thought, the idea that she might actually escape. Once in the cluster of houses, she can hide. Then she'll have time to figure out what to do next, how to survive tomorrow and all the tomorrows after that.

So focused on those houses is Gwen, that she sees nothing else.

She bursts out of the trees and leaps across the sidewalk. The cars whizzing by are twinkles in her peripheral vision, all that matters is those houses she can now see on the other side.

Safe haven.

The sound of screaming tires does not distract her as she darts across the road. The headlights play in the night, dancing just above the pavement, an endless race back and forth from traffic going both ways.

Gwen doesn't think to time her dash, she fixes her vision on one house like a beacon. It's well-lit, bright with hope, like a gateway back into anonymity. She runs into the road, tunneled on that hope.

There comes a loud squeal of braking tires, a horn, a sensation of impact. She feels suddenly weightless as her world lifts up and spins wildly through the air.

Then the rough asphalt is against her cheek. More horns blare. Engines roar. More squealing tires.

Her vision narrows down to a point. The beacon dims, receding to the distant end of the tunnel until it winks out of sight.

Darkness. Black.

NINETEEN

"Son, don't get mixed up in this. You've probably had the same kind of arguments with your parents. Now come on, honey, let's go. Mom's home waiting."

Julien keeps his feet moving forward. Half the boys on the court want nothing to do with him and his "daughter" and whatever spat is going on, so they start moving away.

The young protector stands his ground though, squaring his chin. Tension solidifies the hot July air. Of all the punks in Cicero, why did he have to come across this guy? Why couldn't the kid have shrugged his shoulders and gone back to his basketball game? He chose this moment to take a stand in the name of another and now it's going to get messy.

Messy means more variables, more complications. And more free work.

Julien is already drawing down with his weapon when the girl breaks. She shoves the boy forward with a scream and takes off running straight for the other side of the park. The kid stumbles, directly in his sight line. Julien strokes the trigger with a muttered curse, punching a 9mm round through the boy's throat.

He's only going to get one more shot before things get hairy, so he step-slides left to clear his line. He shifts the muzzle and centers the sights on her fleeing back.

However, the boy doesn't go down as he'd anticipated. Instead, the kid grabs at his damaged throat with a garbled cry, lurching to one side, once again blocking Julien's line. What are the odds of that? With no clear shot, Julien holds off sending another round through the kid's head. He's going to need everything in his clip.

Even though Julien has a suppressor attached to his Beretta, it's not silent. The explosions of compressed air are loud in the park. At his first shot, the remaining boys all react with the sudden moves of people to whom guns are no stranger. Each one dives in a different direction, some towards their pile of clothes where Julien assumes they've stashed their own weapons. Two of the boys leap off the court and run towards the woods.

Those come first. He cannot let them escape. It's one thing to have a single petrified female running loose with his face imprinted on her memory, he's not going to expand the problem by allowing two young punks to live.

Deep breath, stroke the trigger, re-align aim, fire again. Cradle the Beretta close to his chest, two handed grip. Move from the spot, turn the body sideways and tuck low to present a smaller target.

All this runs through his mind even as Julien moves, but they are not conscious thoughts requiring him to listen. His actions are practiced and reflexive.

This is where he has the leverage. There's a difference in being familiar with guns, and familiarity with gun play. Julien's experience gives him a strategic advantage. He thinks tactically about the moves, the angles and the priorities. These punks have handled guns, they may even have shot at people, but until you've engaged in numerous firefights, you are a novice. You fall into the "duck and spray" shooting style, which only works in Hollywood.

Julien is counting on this, and he is

rewarded.

Even before the young protector has fallen all the way down, the two fleeing boys are stumbling face first, mortal wounds punching through their backs to major organs. Three down, three to go.

The girl has disappeared into the trees, increasing his frustration. Now he will be forced to track her further. And the presence of houses across Lauren Avenue means she may run for help. He will have to alter his pursuit structure.

Julien slides to his right, crouching down, Beretta still in a combat grip. As with most young gang-banger types, the three remaining boys try to run backward while shooting. It's an odd dichotomy that Julien's never understood. The gun gives power, but the boys react with fear. Fear of getting shot, fear of the anticipated pain.

A shot rings out in his general direction. Julien has no idea where it actually goes, certainly not near enough for him to hear that familiar buzz.

He centers his weight and fires two rounds into the chest of the shooter.

In the same movement, he drops down and crabs back to his left. A tall slim boy struggles with his weapon. It's snagged in the pocket of the warm-up pants he left on the ground. Julien takes him through the temple.

That leaves one last boy, a young-looking kid with two bright earrings. He freezes in the process of pulling out his gun from under a sweatshirt. Fear widens his eyes as Julien stalks towards him. He drops his weapon and holds up his hands in a warding gesture.

"Please...don't," he says, tears forming.

Julien stops in front of him. "How old are you?"

"Sixteen."

"Shame, really." One slug punches through the kid's forehead and he flops backward without another sound. "The teen years suck. Life gets so much better at twenty."

Julien does a quick scan of the area. Cicero hears gunshots often enough that he feels certain no one is running for their phone to call 911. Still, someone will, at some point. He's got a finite amount of time. His mind processes alternate scenarios and he realizes that there's not enough time to find the girl again and still complete the requirements of his contract.

However, there is a way to further the Covenant's agenda. This may help alleviate the pressure he'll be under to find the girl before she reveals what she witnessed. He's got to move though.

One of the boys he shot squirms on the ground; the entry wound is visible on his back. Julien's aim was off just a bit, missing the spine by an inch but likely punching through a lung. He kneels over the kid, assessing his chances of survival. He wants the kid to live for a while longer, but needs to make sure he can't get up and finish escaping.

The boy rolls over and looks at him with blood streaming from his mouth. Julien thinks he asks for help, but isn't sure. The kid's whisper is too soft.

Moving with economy, Julien Crux sprints back towards the factory. He's got a lot to do and little time in which to do it.

***

It's fully dark when Julien finishes staging the scene. He stops and stares down at the dying kid long enough to be certain he will not live. The movements are now feeble and blood bubbles from his mouth, growing smaller in size. There's maybe another ten minutes of life left in him. By the time first responders arrive, he'll have blown his last bubble.

Time to find the girl. This task will be a little harder.

Julien enters the woods, moving in the same direction he saw her head. He moves with planned steps, watching for signs of her passing. In the dark it's difficult to see anything, but he guesses that her panic drove her in a blind run towards safety, wherever she thought safety existed. He's had enough experience with victims to understand their primal needs when death begins to stalk them. They rush forward, trying to put as much distance between them and danger, without thought of how to truly avoid the threat. That's what this girl did, like so many others: Run. Run in one direction because it takes her away from the place where Julien stands.

A smirk crosses his face. People can be stupid. Never give into primal reflex, always think your way through the problem.

After fifteen minutes of tracking her last known direction, Julien emerges on the west side of Lauren Avenue. A police squad car sits just to the other side of the median, a block south, lights flashing. An ambulance pulls up in front of the squad as Julien watches from the trees. That tells him it has nothing to do with his activity in the park. More like a pedestrian hit by a passing car going the other way. Still, it's too close for comfort. They are practically on top of the scene already.

Julien assesses his options. There's no sign of the girl, unsurprisingly. She's had enough time to flee into the neighborhoods across the road. The fact that he doesn't hear any approaching sirens means she hasn't called the police, for whatever reason. If she was hanging out at the factory, there's a chance she doesn't want to interact with cops. She may be running from something else, like outstanding warrants of her own. That presents him with different opportunities, allows him the grace to compartmentalize his efforts.

First things first, comply with the contract requirements.

He exits the trees and finds a pay phone in the parking lot of a gas station several blocks north of the park entrance. Julien calls in the basketball court scene. That's the one he wants found first. He places an anonymous 911 call, adopting the voice tones of a resident resigned to the fact of life that in Cicero, gunshots are reported with little expectation of anyone being found guilty of them. He imagines he's a father in one of those houses across Lauren, annoyed at being interrupted from watching his favorite TV show.

After giving a general location to the 911 operator, he enters the neighborhoods across from the park, trying to imagine the direction her panicked flight took her. The girl has a big lead on him. She won't be anywhere near this place but maybe he'll get lucky and find some indication of her flight. It's a futile thought, he knows. In any event, Julien Crux is a thorough man, so though he expects no reward for his efforts, he trots along the sidewalks, watchful for anything that could provide a clue.

The girl has changed his plans. Now he will have to return to the factory, to ensure nothing remains that might lead police to track her, or worse, him. He won't be able to do it any more tonight. Once the cops realize what they have at the scene, it will be clogged with detectives. He can't risk rummaging through the building on the chance his movement is discovered. In full dark he'd need a flashlight that would be easy to spot.

That means waiting until morning light, with no certainty that the scene will be any more accessible. Damn that girl.

***

Twenty minutes later he's sweating, irritated and feeling the start of a blister on his right heel. Running around in dress shoes will do that.

As suspected, she ghosted. In fact, there's no sign of any life on the streets. Houses are lit up and he catches glimpses of families living their lives, but no one ventures outside. Maybe that's just the way Cicero is: Lock yourself inside at night and pray for the best.

Julien turns up the block, aiming his feet back towards the park area. The sounds of police sirens fill the air. It likely took one officer some time to come across the basketball court and call out every available squad. He can imagine the looks on their faces as they take in the scene.

What the hell happened here?

He finds a different pay phone attached to the side of an auto repair garage and calls in the Bell murder, using designed words and statements provided to him by the Covenant Church. The police will be stretched thin by the park, adding Bell onto their plate could break them.

Julien decides to retrieve his car and take one more cruise through the streets that now echo with police response units. Driving will allow him a larger search radius, even though he doesn't think much will come from it. Maybe he will even return to the park, bury himself in the crowds that are sure to gather, and see if she re-surfaces there. If she does, he's not sure what his actions will be, but he'll think of something.

He always does.

TWENTY

Tuesday, July 13, 1999
9:12am

Gwen opens her eyes, slow and hesitant. The soft beeping of monitors floats towards her. Harsh white light fills her vision, providing further insight. She's in a hospital room, lying warm and comfortable in a bed. Everything in her body aches and throbs, especially her left hip and shoulder.

It takes a few moments for her vision to clear. In that time she cycles through the memories in her head. The panic of last night's events swarm back, but she battles it down with rapid, deep breaths.

The killer's eyes come back to her, those haunting green things, but even as she tries to affix them in her mind, the memory image blurs and twists. She watched him kill two men, he probably killed more on the basketball court, and she realizes she will never recognize him again.

There could be no worse witness to a murder than Gwen.

He came after her, not only at the factory, but through the woods and into the park. He engaged in a gunfight with those kids.

He's going to keep coming. Like a relentless shadow following her through the darkness of her own disability, he will be hovering in the background, waiting for the right time to pounce. This reality hits her like a brick dropped from above.

She can't stay. If he saw the accident, it wouldn't take him long to figure out which hospital she was taken to.

A glance out the window shows bright sun. How long has she been here?

A TV sits on top of a drawer chest in the corner, tuned to a local news station. A dark-haired female reporter stands at the entrance to a park and Gwen recognizes Paluski Park. Just visible in the distant background is the basketball court. People are still moving around the scene, writing in notebooks, talking with each other, taking pictures.

The clock on the wall shows 9:14.

Her clothes have been set in a neat stack

on a chair by the dresser. Gwen sits up, wincing in pain. She pulls the IV out of her arm and curses the slowness of her movements as she pulls on her pants and shirt.

She cracks the door open. Out in the hallway nurses, doctors and patients move to the pace of their individual need. No one pays attention to her as she slips out and lets the door close behind her. At least, no one does until she rounds the nearest corner and runs directly into a large-bodied nurse, nearly getting knocked down.

The nurse grabs and holds her upright. "Oh, lord. I'm so sorry..." Her eyes flick from apology to alarm.

"Hey, you're in 212. You can't be out of bed!" The nurse turns to yell to the desk at the far end of the hall.

Gwen takes that distraction to shove her aside and dart down the closest cross-hall. Unlike the movies, no alarm sounds, no packs of roving security guards fill the floor seeking her. It's just her and the almost empty hallway.

Pushing open an exit door, Gwen follows the stairs down to the first floor. The silence follows her, confirming lack of pursuit. Like everyone else in her life, no one gave enough of a shit to care whether she lived or died.

At the bottom, she emerges out into the

large lobby. People are cluttered everywhere: on waiting room couches, pacing the space, reading, staring out the large plate windows. Gwen moves to the side of the door frame, scanning everyone in her view, looking for him. It's a futile gesture. She'd never recognize the guy until he got close enough for her to make out his death-green eyes. He could be staring at her from across the lobby even now, waiting like a wolf outside a rabbit warren.

Gwen needs the help and security of others.

She doesn't really have any friends. Her dislike of being in crowds keeps her isolated, dampens any desire she's ever had of integrating into normal society. Now that isolation has come home to roost.

There's no question about going home to the basement apartment in her grandmother's house. That would be the first place for anyone to look for her. Plus it might put her grandma in danger from the dead-eyed man. No, she needs someone who trades in harder edges, someone not unaware of the seedy part of the world.

She thinks of her dealer, Dwight Weldon Smith. Street name: Dweldon D.

The small deals she runs for him keep them in regular contact, gives her a little spending money and ensures that her own supply never runs low. He's always been nice to her, plus he hangs with two other guys who always pack. They are tough guys, maybe tougher than the kids at the park, so it will give her a sense of security.

The morning sun blinds her as Gwen steps out of the lobby onto the sidewalk. She has no idea which hospital she's at until she cranes her head around to look at the sign. Cook County Health Center. She came in as a Jane Doe, with no ID or insurance card. This place is where cases like hers get sent, it's only a few miles away from her destination. There's loose change in her jeans pockets, not enough for bus fare. She'll have to hoof it.

She shrinks back against the building, leaning on the wall. People stream past on the sidewalk. No one pays attention and for her part, Gwen avoids eye contact as well. Her senses are hyper-aware like a deer's, scanning the area for someone fitting the general description of the killer.

Keeping her head down, Gwen heads east. Her vision swims in and out of focus under the piercing sunlight; she bounces off arms and shoulders of a crowd moving in the opposite direction. It occurs to her she might be suffering a concussion.

After a couple of blocks the crush of foot traffic overwhelms her. Gwen wants to look up into each face that passes by, yet is afraid to, and the strain of those two conflicting desires wears her down. The thought that the killer could be walking a few steps behind her only adds to the apprehension seizing her guts. She needs to get off the streets.

It seems counterintuitive, abandoning the protection of others for desolate neighborhoods but it makes perfect sense to her. Crowds hid her nightmare. Empty streets offer little cover for wolves.

Fighting back the nausea roiling in her stomach, Gwen Manner makes a slow, circuitous route through the fractured roads.

***

She stops at the intersection of LeMoyne Street and Rockwell Avenue. Two blocks away her grandmother's house sits on the left side of the road. The foot traffic is light here, the neighborhood quiet. Two young girls ride their bikes around in loops, going from driveway to sidewalk and back again. At the far end of the block two women stand chatting, their leashed dogs sniffing at each other.

It's a typical scene, like any other weekday in the summer. Nothing seems out of place.

It's tempting to sneak around back and into her apartment, but Gwen resists the urge. This sense of normalcy can disappear in a second with the arrival of a killer and she doesn't want to put anyone at risk who can't handle it. At least Dweldon and his guys carry. They offer some level of protection.

Backtracking to a side street, she heads east towards the heart of Wicker Park. Dweldon has a place somewhere on Damen Avenue, but she doesn't know where exactly. He's never brought her there. Their interaction always starts with a call from a specific pay phone. That's where she directs her feet.

Their interactions also include other activities and she steels herself for that reality.

The sidewalks along Damen are busier. She pauses in the shadow of a church at the corner, staring intently north along the road. There are no obvious signs of danger, not that she'd know what they are anyway. But no one who fits the general description of the killer is in sight. Gwen looks farther ahead, to where the Chicago Transit Authority rail line passes over the street. Every few minutes a train rattles to a stop on the elevated track, either headed out towards O-Hare airport or in towards the city.

Most of Wicker Park is nice and clean,

home to young hip people. But in the area of the CTA line, there's darkness under those elevated tracks. It's both literal - from blocked sunlight - and figurative. Something about that short span exudes an aura of seedy jobs and undesirable citizens. Gwen knows it's a silly notion, but she can't help it. Despite being an occasional participant in what many would call criminal activities, she's never counted herself among those people and dislikes being there.

But that's where she has to go.

A phone booth sits directly under the tracks, butted up against one of the massive support columns. An alley with a construction fence blocks part of the sidewalk, forcing pedestrians closer to the booth. The fence is six feet high, made of corrugated metal and defaced with graffiti. She doesn't know what's on the other side and has no interest in finding out. To her, it's like peeking under the bed late at night. There's probably nothing, but if there were, she'd be an easy mark.

And that, perhaps, sums up Gwen's overall philosophy about her life: She is prey, moving through the world in small increments so the true predators don't notice her.

Unfortunately, last night she made eye contact with a wolf in the midst of his kill.

With careful steps, Gwen falls in behind a group of three ladies strolling north on Damen, coffee cups in hand, mouths running non-stop. She doesn't know what they're talking about and wants to keep it that way. She tries to remain aware of everyone around her. People walking towards them are forced to the edges of the sidewalk by the oblivious women, and Gwen cuts discrete glances at each one, shading her body away just in case.

The women decide to cross the street, gabbing away about pastry rolls. This leaves Gwen exposed to other passerby, but there's nothing to do for that. Her destination is one block straight ahead. She keeps her momentum, darting glances all around. No one pays her attention.

The phone booth is empty as she nears. It usually is. More and more people have cell phones now, eliminating the need for public phones. Gwen, who has no phone of any kind, relies on these exclusively. It's mere good fortune that she rarely has need to call anyone.

There's enough change in her pocket for a local call so she punches in a number committed to memory. Dweldon has this phone booth number memorized. He answers after three rings. He doesn't say anything, his normal response to a call from this phone.

"Dweldon, it's Gwen. Gwen Manner."

"Yeah." His voice is steady and controlled, neither a question nor a statement.

"I need your help."

"If this about you needing more leaf, I ain't gotcha. You loaded up last week." His voice is curt, dismissive.

"No, it's not about any drugs. I need a place to hideout, just for a little while."

"You got something domestic brewing, little Gwen? I want none of that."

"Please, Dweldon. I don't have anywhere else to turn."

There's silence on the other end for a few moments, during which Gwen can hear murmured conversation. He's asking his two buddies, Jimmy and Deandre. She knows what will be coming from that quarter and it's the price she'll have to pay.

"Stay put. Be there in five." The line goes dead.

TWENTY ONE

Gwen hangs up the phone, looking through the scratched and battered glass of the booth. People are everywhere, singles walking to catch the train stop overhead; couples leaning against the window of a pawn shop chatting; triples sitting at sidewalk tables outside the coffee shop.

She's surrounded by the denizens of Wicker Park, yet Gwen has never felt more alone. None of the faces have familiar looks to them, no one emerges from the fog of recognition to smile or say hello. This is always how it has been for her, how she knows it will always be.

Exiting the phone booth, Gwen shrinks back against the brick wall of the music store under the rail line. She keeps her spine aligned with the corner so she can run in either direction at the first sign of danger. To anyone passing by, she looks like just another lost soul on the fringes of society, a small dark-haired girl with her head down.

A man in a black suit makes his way along the sidewalk towards her, a cell phone pressed to his ear. He's medium height, lean of build, with a thinning layer of light hair atop his head. He has glasses on.

Gwen doesn't know if this is killer. It could be. Her memory of the man's face gets mixed up with the features of the man approaching her now. She feels her back tense, her leg muscles tighten with the urge to run. She strains to see the color of his eyes but he keeps his head down as he speaks into the phone.

A CTA train rattles into the stop on the overhead rail, creating a cacophony of metallic sounds. The man presses a finger to his other ear and for one second his eyes flick up to meet hers. Gwen freezes, uncertainty seizing her reflexes and clamping them in a vise.

Is it him?

Are those the predator eyes she never thought she'd forget? She doesn't know. They could be green, but the shadows of the overhead rail line mute the color.

The man stops directly under the tracks and pulls his phone away from his ear, looking at it like he doesn't understand why it won't work. He speaks back into it but the words are lost to the racket of the CTA train. Snapping it shut in irritation, he looks around and spies the phone booth. With quick steps he walks closer to Gwen, eyes fixed on her. His eyes are light colored. Suddenly she's no longer sure of the color.

She darts her gaze around, seeking an escape. He's too near now. Whatever way she flees, he can easily cut off her route. With wide eyes she watches him reach into his suit jacket. Everything in her body trembles.

"Excuse me. Break a buck?" He extracts a wallet from his jacket, pulling out a dollar.

Gwen doesn't respond, paralyzed by the fear of what this encounter could have been. She just stares at him, eyes tearing up at the corners.

"Hey, you hear me?" The man waggles the bill at her. She's afraid to respond, to reach out for the dollar, as if that would break the fragile membrane separating them and transform her fear to reality.

"Yo!" A deep voice rolls down the street to them. Dweldon comes into view, trailed by two tall figures. "What's up?"

Dweldon she recognizes. His short fat frame and the bright red Bulls sweatshirt that he always wore no matter what the temperature; the timbre of his voice. His Afro shock puffs up, nappy black air looking like a globe around his head. She thinks Jimmy and Deandre are behind him, but she's not sure. It could be two other friends.

The man looks over and immediately takes a step back. "Just seeing if she could change out a buck for the phone." He raises his hands, reacting to the presence of Dweldon and what it infers. "Not looking for trouble."

"Then you best turn around." Dweldon steps in front, blocking the direct line between the man and her.

With a shake of his head, the man retreats and crosses the street, disappearing inside a small convenience market.

Dweldon puts a protective hand on Gwen's shoulder and steers her down the block, followed by his two shadows. They enter a local bar called *Dave's Hangout*. Inside a guy sweeps the floor with rhythmic motion, working the broom under booths and tables. He looks up at their approach, expression of protest on his face since the place wasn't yet open for business. But when he sees Dweldon, he returns to his task, studiously avoiding further eye contact.

Gwen can sense him tracking their winding movement among tables to the back storeroom.

Dweldon ushers her in, standing outside the door for a second to watch their trail. The room is small and smells of mildew. Boxes are stacked along one wall, with a rack of shelves occupying the adjacent wall. A standard refrigerator sits at the end of the shelving, next to a small built-in freezer. There's an emergency exit door on the far wall, leading out to the alley behind the building. Several bulbs are burned out, turning the sign to 'EX'. The room is dim, light provided by a single bulb hanging from a pull cord.

Now that they are closely packed together, Gwen can identify Deandre by the cologne he always wore, and Jimmy by the tattoos running down his left arm. His pale skin provides a contrasting background to the dark ink.

"What's got you spooked, little bird?" Dweldon says as he closes the storeroom door behind him with a soft click. "You forget what your grand-mama looks like again?" His tone is soft, mocking, but in way that makes it seem like they share a secret known only to them.

Gwen shakes her head. "I'm in trouble. I

need to hide out a while. Someone is after me."

"Who?"

"It was down in Cicero, by that old factory near the train yard..."

He interrupts her. "Oh, shit. Woman, you was there in Paluski Park? A whole slew of Two Two Boyz got themselves nicked. Probably 'cuz they was hooping near Latin King hoods. Been all over the news today. Damn."

This confuses Gwen. "I was there, but what about the two businessmen, over by the factory?"

"What men? I ain't heard nothing 'bout that, just the Boyz. If they starting up shit again, don't worry. None of them would come up here chasing on you. You good with me."

"No, you don't understand, Dweldon. It wasn't a gang thing. One guy did it all. He killed two guys at the factory and then chased me through the woods to Paluski. He's the one who shot up the park. He wants to kill me because I saw what he did."

"What he look like?"

"I don't know. White, not very tall, skinny, blond hair cut real short or balding. Older, like 30s or 40s."

Dweldon stays silent but when Gwen says nothing more, his eyebrows raise. "That it?

Some dude trying to kill you and that all you got?"

Before she can protest and remind him how she doesn't do faces well, he goes on. "Who the men at the factory?"

"I don't know, but they came in a fancy car, a Mercedes I think. One was wearing a suit and I thought they were doing a business deal to buy the place. The guy chasing me played the part of a real estate agent."

At that, Dweldon laughs and looks over her head to his two boys. "Ain't selling much when you kill off your clients."

Jimmy gives a snort; of humor or derision, she doesn't know. Deandre says nothing, he rarely does. He's stick-thin and tall, keeping his own counsel and words tight to the vest.

"What makes you think he'll track you up here?" Dweldon asks, reaching to twirl some of her raven hair between his fingers.

"He killed six boys to get at me. I saw his eyes up close, Dweldon. He's not going to quit, I just know it. Can you hide me out? Just until things die down and the cops find him?"

He gives a tug on the strands of hair wrapped around his fingers, yanking her head to one side. She winces.

"You want me to step on some guy that can take out six Two Twos? That ain't no small thing. Those boys know heat and always pack."

"No, just get me out of here to someplace no one would think to look. Can you do that? I can't go home because he'd find me there."

In the dim glow of the single bulb lighting the storeroom, Dweldon's face is cloaked in shadow. She sees him look over her head again at his boys and some unheard message passes between them.

"I do this, little bird, it ain't for free. Ain't nothing for free in this world. I got to think if you scared enough, you willing to make deals."

Gwen feels something crumble inside her. He's going to help, but not from the kindness of his heart. Well, not fully. He's going to extract a price and she knows what it will be.

It won't be the first time.

There's nothing more to say. She looks down as Jimmy and Deandre crowd closer from behind. She feels hands rubbing up her rib cage, around front, unbuttoning her shirt. She's not wearing a bra so when the shirt comes off, Dweldon's hands immediately grab her breasts, rough and strong.

Someone grabs her right hand and places it against his zipper. She feels his excitement. Someone else begins to work at the button of her jeans. She doesn't put up resistance, but neither does she help. When you're prey to the world, kindness from the predators is rare and you have to accept it in whatever form.

As her pants are yanked down, Gwen closes her eyes and lets the three boys have their way in the dank storeroom.

TWENTY TWO

Tuesday, July 13, 1999
8:38am

Julien Crux kneels on the dusty floor in the Middle Plains factory. The office space around him is silent and so is he. Outside, down at the edge of the courtyard, a uniformed officer stands next to his vehicle, guarding the scene. Bell's body has been removed, but the Mercedes, crime scene tape and evidence markers are still in place.

It took him thirty minutes to work his way into this place, keeping as silent as possible to avoid alerting the cop below.

He's been at it for an hour now, sifting through the shadowed factory in search of anything that might reveal the identity of the girl. His time is drying up.

Julien knows the forensics group will

come back out at some point this morning to do a more thorough sweep of the scene. With someone of Bell's stature, protocol will be followed to the letter. He cannot be present when they arrive, on the chance that they decide to explore inside the building.

The morning sun burns through the open windows and gaps in the roof, barely giving him enough light to conduct his search.

Moving with soft feet, he works through the second floor, checking each office. Most of them are littered with items from the time when this building held life, perhaps an old desk or chair, some with metal file cabinets silently rusted into place. During the decades after it closed, homeless people had moved in and made over the offices to their living situation. The leftover detritus of their stay now dominates each space: blankets, wrappers and food cans, cigarette butts, one office even had a set of children's drawings hung on the wall. When he'd swept this building last month and removed the inhabitants, he was glad the creators of those drawings were no longer around. He disliked killing kids, they made so much noise.

He enters the last office in the row, standing back from the window to check the angle against what he remembered of the girl's sighting. This might be it.

The position of the office could not be worse. He's now nearer to the cop in the courtyard and all the windows are empty of glass. One simple misstep could send up sound easily heard from below.

Julien slows his movement down to a crawl, testing each step with care before putting full weight down.

An abandoned desk has papers arranged randomly across the top. On the floor a canvas bag lies half open, disgorging pieces of chalk. He kneels down and picks through them, noting that they have all been used. Some are little more than nubs, others still have life and length. Several drawing pads litter the floor next to an old blanket. He flips through them. The girl is talented. He recognizes several pieces of equipment from the factory, items he came to know during his scouting. He doesn't understand the lack of faces on pictures of people, shrugging it off as some weird artist thing.

None of this helps him identify her, though. He doesn't want to stalk the streets clutching chalk drawings until he comes across someone who recognizes the artist style. Those are a lot of uncompensated deaths.

Upending the bag, Julien spills the rest of

the chalk pieces, pencils, erasers and other items across the floor. There has to be something in here. He picks through the pile until a small slip of paper is unearthed like a fossil buried in chalk dust.

He tilts his head to catch a beam of light streaming over his shoulder.

Dweldon D is written on top. *Damen & Pierce* below it. *2:30_*double-underlined at the bottom.

"Hello there, you," he says to himself. Julien is familiar with Chicago's geography. Damen is a north-south route several miles away. Pierce is likely a cross street somewhere. He's guessing Dweldon D is a person, it sounds like one of those stupid gang names.

This is not his first rodeo. The target position has been identified. He knows what his next steps will be. Time to sleuth and peel apart the layers of her name, location and habits.

Julien stands, feeling the thrill of the chase surge through him. Contract killing pays well and can be fun, but nothing beats tracking a scared human down and watching the fear overtake them as they realize there is nowhere left to run.

He dislikes uncompensated work, but if there's something he has to do for free, it would be hunting and tracking.

In his haste and preoccupation, Julien gets sloppy, just for a microsecond. He slips on the bits of chalk scattered across the floor and loses his balance. He tumbles against the desk, creating a loud bang and squeal of metal leg against the floor.

He freezes, curses himself in the silence of his own mind.

No sound comes from the courtyard below, no holler from the cop stationed there. Julien is not afraid of the cop arresting him, but he is under strict orders not to eliminate any law officers. That would only draw increased attention to the case, attention of the wrong kind. This case has to maintain the appearance of something else and dead cops turning up will defray that image.

After a few seconds, Julien moves again, sliding over to the window. He didn't get to his status level by leaving things to chance; better to check whether the cop is on alert before stealing away through the far door at the other end of the building.

He peeks out.

The officer stands by his cruiser, eyes scanning the building face. He spies Julien's face and lets out a yell. He sprints towards the closest entrance.

Julien shakes his head and slips out a curse.

He has to be careful now. Gliding on silent feet, he moves to the first office at the top of the stairs, tucking in behind the partially opened door.

The sound of feet bounding up the metal steps fills the vast interior space.

His timing will have to be perfect. He sinks to a crouch, coiled and lethal.

***

Mid-morning sun burns the top of his balding head as Julien pauses near the intersection of Damen and Schiller. He handled his business at the factory, escaping without being caught and leaving no dead bodies.

To his right the triangle-shaped park of Wicker Park fame resounds with activity of people walking, running and kids' laughter. He pays no attention to the noise or passersby as he walks with measured steps north along the sidewalk.

Up ahead he can see the street sign for Pierce. It's the meet place, for whatever deals the girl had with this Dweldon D person. He guesses it's for sex or drugs. No matter how manicured and upscale any place appears, those two elements exist underneath the veneer.

A glance at his watch reveals it is check-in time. 11am every day. He specifies structured, but minimal, contact during an engagement. Many clients want to know what's happening in real-time but he's found over the years that doing so only makes his life harder. It also increases his chances of being caught. Should the client balk, they might have currency in the way of information on his activities or location, enough to sell the police. Keeping calls to once per day provides him the freedom he needs and gives a time buffer in case he has to escape a bad situation.

Julien veers off the sidewalk and through the fenced entrance to the park, finding an isolated spot under a vast oak tree. To anyone else, he's just another guy in a dress shirt and slacks making a phone call. He presses the speed dial for the only number programmed into his cell phone. It's picked up before the first ring ends.

"We're hearing rumors," the voice growls. "What the hell happened last night?"

Julien debates lying and quickly dismisses the idea. He doesn't know what sources his client has within the police department, but the ties are deep. If he's caught in his lie, that could lead to unpleasant results.

"There are always variables in any contract. I'm paid to handle them."

"No, you're paid to execute a scene according to our requirements. Every detective on the west side is being pulled in to investigate the largest mass killing since Al Capone went nuts on St. Valentine's Day."

That pauses Julien. "Really?" *Cool.*

"Listen, asshole. Your contract specified a single target..."

"With contingencies as they arose," he interrupts.

"Yeah, contingencies. Removing potential witnesses, creating a scenario that befits the picture we want. It did not include slaughtering a gang of nigger kids. That park is a quarter mile away, how did they pose a threat?"

Julien knows his client doesn't care about the death of the thugs. In fact, that probably makes him happy. No, it's the risk it creates for undermining Bell's murder that has him angry. Well, that emotion is about to increase.

"There was a witness at the factory. She ran to them for protection."

Silence for a moment. Then, a deep command: "Details."

Julien uses precisely one minute to recap the events of last night, giving only basic information, enough to satisfy his client. He leaves out the details of his recent actions back at the factory. It will come out eventually, but he doesn't want to deal with it now.

"You're positive she's run to ground?"

"I tracked police movement all night. There was no activity from a witness appearance and she never showed up at the station. For whatever reason, she hasn't reported it."

"She's probably a criminal on her own," his client ruminates. "What is your task item now?"

"Find her. Close the loop."

"You have twenty-four hours. The police did not release Bell's name this morning, but it's probable that they will tomorrow morning. There can be no gaps when that announcement comes. The scene must present itself precisely as we described. A witness roaming free can derail that and must not happen. Tell me your plan to find her."

Julien feels his hackles rise. This crosses the boundaries of their agreement. "Only if you tell me the scope of your plan. What piece does Bell's death play?"

"That is none of your business. You are

just one part of a larger puzzle and on a need to know basis."

"Exactly what I wanted to hear. We now have an understanding," Julien retorts. "You only need to know that I will handle my end of things."

It's a reaction that he knows irritates the client but takes a calculated risk. He cannot have someone looking over his shoulder, second-guessing his efforts.

"Watch your mouth, Crux. Understand who you are dealing with. The Covenant has more influence than you think, and other contractors."

"That sounds like a threat."

The client is silent for a moment. When he speaks, his tone is conciliatory. "Look, we're partners in this. You were hired not only for your track record, but because you also share some of the same goals that we do. America is being dragged down by certain elements of society. The fucking Democrats are allowing this country to swirl the drain by coddling an entire class of welfare monkeys. We're raising a generation of darkies that think they deserve to live like kings sucking off the government teat. They're parasites like any other, eroding the strength of what was once the greatest superpower on Earth. The only way to rebuild our country is to control those parasites. Once we teach them their place and put the leashes on, all our lives will be better."

Julien recognizes the manipulation. He feels somewhat insulted. Did the client really think he'd fall for some canned speech? But he says nothing to counter the words. Let the Covenant dogs think he's part of their grand mission. It's not worth disproving them.

In fact, he doesn't care one bit for racism. He believes everyone should get a chance to live the way they want to, surround themselves with similar-minded people if they chose. If this contract hadn't paid so well, he would have passed it up on principle alone.

"Talk at our next check-in," is all he says, and clicks off the call.

A football bounces near his position, an overthrow by a young boy of elementary age. Julien picks it up and winks at the kid who failed to catch it. "Go long."

The boy's teeth shine white against his dark skin as he smiles and turns to sprint in the opposite direction. Julien counts to ten and lets it fly. It's a perfect spiral and the boy hauls it in without breaking stride. He tumbles into a somersault and bounces up to his feet, brandishing the ball overhead in triumph. Great catch.

"Again!" Both boys yell.

Julien waves them off. "Sorry guys. I'm on the clock." He exits the park and turns his feet towards Pierce Avenue.

TWENTY THREE

He starts at the nearest business. Julien Crux understands the way things work just below the surface of a newly-shined place like Wicker Park. The gloss never matters, there will always be those types who lurk just outside the lines, who trade in the elements that society doesn't want to encompass but can never ignore.

Despite the bright nature of Wicker Park - the trimmed lawns, the neatly arranged houses, the hip urban image - Julien knows who Dweldon D is and what he represents. He just needs to find him.

The first stop is a payday advance business. The mere existence of this place is a symptom, a clue that there is a substrate of citizens who require desperate relief from financial exigency. That need usually comes from the same sources: lack of employment, lack of money management, or pressing urges to satisfy some fixation. Drugs, sex, booze, gambling; the usual culprits.

Julien guesses that this Dweldon person traffics in one or all of them.

Pushing open the glass door, he adopts a hunched-shoulder posture, keeping his eyes down. He wants to project a furtive nature, someone who's desperate but embarrassed, afraid of getting caught in his weakness. With the creased slacks and pressed shirt, maybe he's an office worker who needs a woman, or overshot on the horses last week. Julien takes pride in his ability to transform his appearance simply by taking on a different persona. It's one reason his presence goes unnoticed by potential witnesses. Later, when police question them, they might recall a man who fits his general description, but it's the character they describe, not the specifics of his features.

He kills in a fog and this is one way he creates that fog.

A large black lady sits behind a thick glass wall, protected from those who see this business as an easy mark. She's got a cell phone cradled between her ear and shoulder as she picks at her long fake fingernails. There's no one else present in the store.

Julien leans forward and taps at the glass. A small pass-through has been cut out from the bottom. This is where cash and documents get exchanged. When she doesn't acknowledge him, he tilts his head down towards the gap.

"Hey."

She raises a hand to him, indicating that he needs to wait.

"Hey!"

A sigh. "Girl, hang on." She pulls the phone away from her ear and fixes a bored stare on him. "What?"

"I'm looking for Dweldon D." Julien darts his gaze around, avoiding her eyes, using those glances to take in details of his surroundings. A security camera is mounted high above the glass cage, pointed downward over her shoulder. He keeps his body tilted forward so the angle catches his forehead and crown, rather than a clear shot of his face.

"Ain't know no Dweldon.

"He's supposed to be around here. You seen him today?"

She scratches deep behind one of her thick braids and inspects the nail, picking something out and flicking it away. "You got business I can help you with? If not, get along." Without waiting for his response, she picks the phone back up and resumes her conversation. "No, naw. Just some guy..."

Julien stares at her for a few seconds. Customer service is a forgotten art. His character wants to grab her through the window opening.

"Bitch," is all he says and shuffles away.

Outside, he straightens up and moves to the next shop. Three ladies walking and talking with their steaming coffee nearly run him over. He moves quickly out of their way and enters the store, a record and CD shop. Behind the counter a young long-haired kid eats a candy bar as he stares at a vinyl album cover. Headphones are draped around his neck.

Now Julien is a concerned father. "Hey, buddy. Help me out here. I'm looking for my daughter. She's a few years younger than you. Hangs with some guy named Dweldon, something like that." His stare is direct, an executive look that says he's used to directing people around.

The kid looks up, eyes glassy. "What's a dweldon?"

Julien exits the shop a few minutes later, shaking his head. What the hell is wrong with kids nowadays? Can't string two sentences together, can't answer the most basic of questions.

He tries a dry-cleaning store then a coffee shop, leaving with some concoction that's more hot chocolate than anything else. Tossing it in the nearest trash container, he pauses. Doubt starts to creep in. Maybe Dweldon isn't a person after all. No one has shown the slightest flicker of recognition at his name.

Then again, Julien has only checked a few businesses on one side of the street. It's a small sampling. There's no need to cut short his search yet, not until he's come up against enough rejections that change his approach.

Overhead the CTA train rolls into the Damen Avenue stop, accepting passengers. The noise of the rail line is incredibly loud as it rattles eastward, bound for downtown Chicago. Julien watches it depart, reflecting on possibilities and actions.

Across the street a few more establishments occupy the block. He cuts across between traffic and picks the farthest one, figuring to start there and work his way back.

The sign on the door of *Dave's Hangout* states it's currently closed. Julien tries the knob and finds it unlocked, so he steps in. The sound of the door slapping closed echoes through the empty place. He decides to return to the concerned father persona. "Hey, hello? Anyone here? Need some help out front."

A man with several days' worth of beard emerges from the back, closing the door with care. Shelves and supplies are visible in the brief glimpse of the storeroom on the other side.

"We're closed. Open at noon." He's carrying two bottles of liquor. Jameson Irish whiskey. Julien is more of a vodka guy.

"Just need your help, pal. My daughter, I'm trying to find her. She supposedly hangs with a guy named Dweldon. You know him?"

The man shakes his head, turning his back to Julien as he places the bottles behind the bar. "Can't help you there." He starts to touch the others along the shelf, adjusting each one a fraction of an inch as if the placement matters.

Julien glances around the bar. Tables are arranged in a haphazard manner, like they were never moved back after last night's crowd. None of the chairs have been pushed back into place. There's a row of booths against the side wall. One booth contains three bottles of Miller Lite, in various states of emptiness.

This guy is not a neat-freak. His focus on lining up the liquor bottles is covering something.

"She's young, just turned nineteen. Dark hair, tiny, pale skin," Julien states, pressing on.

"I said I can't help you. Never heard of the guy. Sorry." The man's eyes flick up to the mirror backing the bar, meeting Julien's in the reflection.

He's lying. And they both know it.

Julien turns to the entrance door and places his hand on the knob. Reaches up and twists the dead bolt into the locked position. Swings back to the man.

"Let's try that again."

***

Julien lets himself out the back door of the storeroom into an alley behind the bar. Aprons hang off a hook next to the door and he grabs one as the door swings closed. It's full of stains and smells of old beer. He drapes it over himself to cover up the blood stains on his shirt.

In the alley a cinder block sits up against the wall, presumably to prop the door open for deliveries. He uses it to smash off the doorknob. With the front door locked, there's no easy way in for those regular customers desperate to get their *Hangout* fix. That should buy him some time before the body is found.

Exiting from the alley into sidewalk traffic,

Julien heads south towards West Schiller Street. At the northwest corner of the intersection between Schiller and Damen a tall apartment building soars over the park across the street. He had walked past it on the way here. This was the place identified as Dweldon's residence, although the bartender didn't know the apartment number. If he did know, he would have given it. He begged to die at the end, so Julien is confident he got all the information he could.

Behind the building, a flat lawn holds some trees, standing like a sparse gathering of strangers. Julien parks himself at a picnic table under one of the trees, seeking shade from the hot July sun. He's irritated. Another kill done for no compensation and his new shirt is ruined.

He pulls out his cell phone and makes a call.

"You're breaking protocol," his client says.

"This can't wait until tomorrow."

"Sit-rep." The order is barked out.

Julien shakes his head. Once military always military, apparently. He decides to respond in kind.

"Situation report, sir: Clues to quarry uncovered. Team has tracked her to the bunker and plans to infiltrate. ETA unknown but soon to be known."

There's a pause on the other end. "Why the hell are you talking like that?"

"Never mind. I need information."

"For what?"

"Contingency. In case this proves more problematic than I foresee." Julien picks at something dry and crusty on the apron front, not wanting to know what it is.

"That doesn't give me confidence that you're on track."

"It's not about confidence. This is about risk mitigation and making sure I cover the variables."

"What do you need?"

"The lead detective for Bell, who is it?" His client has hooks deep into the city's elders. Their access to information is significant.

"Young guy, Aramis White. Partnered with Griffin Toms."

Julien feels a surprised expression cross his face, involuntary and reactive. "The one who sued the city earlier this year? Didn't Bell grease those skids for him?"

"Yes and yes."

That's a public relations godsend or nightmare. Julien can't decide which. On one hand you have a rookie detective working the most high profile murder in years. The risk of him screwing up is significant. Yet, who better than to chase the killer of beloved Noah Bell than the man who owes him everything in his career? The Chicago PD can use White as the fall guy if things go south and still save some face by pointing to that relationship.

"Get me something. I need weaknesses, flaws, cracks in the armor. How good is your dossier on him?"

"Very good. We know everything. Would you like to hear about his daughter?"

Julien doesn't want to speculate how they know so much about a guy who just arrived in Chicago. He doesn't care. "Not now. Pull it together in a packet and have one of your people meet me at the drop spot."

"Can do. I'll send Todd."

Julien clicks off the call and shifts his position on the wooden picnic bench. His stomach grumbles with hunger but he can't leave any time soon. He just missed Dweldon by thirty minutes, he won't risk that again.

So Julien resigns himself to stakeout mode.

It turns out he doesn't have to wait long.

Twenty minutes later a car pulls into the lot next to the back lawn. It fits the description provided by the helpful man at *Dave's:* an old Impala sedan with skinny tires, sitting low to the ground.

Julien recognizes Dweldon by the description. The rotund size, the bright red Bulls sweatshirt. He doesn't understand how the guy can wear something like that in this weather. It's hot even in the shade.

There's no one else with Dweldon. He gets out alone and waddles towards the building entrance. Julien takes that to mean his two buddies have the girl somewhere else. Now he'll have to conduct some more information gathering. The realization annoys him, but his emotion is held in check by the fact that he enjoys causing other people pain. Call it a perk of the job. Someone like Dweldon looks like he can withstand a lot of punishment before breaking. The layers of fat alone will take a long time to get through.

Julien gets up and jogs across the yard, following Dweldon's path, thinking about the next task. It will be worth skipping lunch.

He smiles with anticipation as he enters the building lobby.

PART 3

TWENTY FOUR

Wednesday, July 14, 1999
6:05am

A girl named Stephanie Joyner plays the tape forward at half speed. She's part of Nayaki's team, specializing in video forensics. After I rousted Johnny out of bed to meet with us, he did the same to her. Normally Evidence Services holds regular business hours but even they have to strap up when something like Noah Bell comes rolling down the pike.

Now Johnny, Griff and I hover, peering over her shoulder at the monitor on the desk.

The angle shows one end of the Middle Plains east building. A single door is set into the expanse of wall, with a row of large windows higher up. To the far right of the

257

video frame sits the Mercedes, empty save for Guy Johnstone sitting sideways in the driver's seat. Bell is removed from view, blocked by the building.

I place my finger on the screen, over the car. "Now watch again. See the bodyguard just sitting there?"

"It's still fuzzy," Griff says. "You sure you can't tighten it up any further?"

Stephanie shakes her head. "I tried before you got here. These tapes get used over and over. Places like that rail yard have them more as a feel good measure, not as actual archival material. They never plan on viewing the video, so they really don't care how many times it's recorded over. After a while, the media degradation is too much even for our equipment. This is as good as I can get it."

"You could have just said 'No'."

On screen the bodyguard suddenly leaps up and starts running forward. He gets five yards before he too is blocked by the building. "Pause it. Does it look like he falls forward?" I jab at the screen, as if that will jar the picture to a wider angle.

"Large men are clumsy," Johnny notes, deadpan.

No one responds. We all stare at the screen, at the frozen moment. The distance and lack of definition make it hard to tell what happened.

Griff breaks the silence first. "He went down with two to the chest. If that's where he got them, how did he end up in the park?"

"Good question, but that's not the money shot. Stephanie, can you fast forward to 8:36, around the 20 second mark? Guys, focus on the exit door."

She nods. Only her and I have seen this part. I lean back to watch my partner's reaction.

Nothing moves on screen. The bodyguard and Bell are out of sight, the car's overhead dome light creates a pinpoint spot of brightness against the fading daylight.

At 8:36:28, it happens.

The single door slams open. This end of the building is closer to the train yard camera. Because the distance is less, the resolution is a little better.

A girl leaps out of the opening, stumbling, but her legs never stop churning. She has dark hair, pale skin, slim build, and I get the impression she's young. There's not much else to see. She's nearly a blur.

Griff lets loose a swear word. Johnny says nothing. It's the first time either of them have seen the raw footage.

"Just wait," I caution.

The girl tears across the yard, making straight for the trees and the park beyond that. Two seconds later a man emerges from the doorway and draws down on her. The resolution isn't enough to see any weapon, but we all know a firing stance when we see it. His hair looks light, maybe blond, and he doesn't seem to be much taller than the girl. Three winks of light come from his gun, in rapid succession.

By now the girl has disappeared off screen.

"Before you ask, we did walk those woods as part of a wider search," Johnny adds. "There was no body." His tone is smug.

"A goddamn witness, Arch. We got a witness!" Griff sounds out of breath. He looks at me. "You're right, we do need to push reset on this case. It's all different now."

"We don't have visual evidence of interaction between Bell and the shooter." I'm not saying it to negate what we've just seen, but rather to keep things level.

"No, but seriously, Arch. That door is less than fifty feet from where Bell died. There is no coincidence that big." To Stephanie he says, "One more run."

We watch the entire scene once more, then twice, each of us formulating thoughts and theories. "Watch how he reacts afterwards,"

Griff says.

The shooter straightens up after he fires his three rounds and begins to jog in pursuit. His gait is relaxed, almost casual, as he disappears off screen at the same point as the girl. His blood has to be pumping, adrenaline charging, especially if the implications of his presence and actions mean what I think they do, yet his body language doesn't reflect any of that. That concerns me. "Either he knows she went down, so he's going to fetch her body."

"Or..." Johnny says.

"Or, that is one cool customer," Griff states before I do.

I finish. "Meaning, he's professional." That quiets the room as we all try to process the implications of such a statement. Even Stephanie looks like she's pondering something, although I suspect she's merely waiting for someone to talk.

It's Griff who does, of course. With a profanity.

He grabs Johnny. "Oh, shit. The factory! Yesterday...second floor, office...!" He sputters, trying to say twenty words at once.

"Slow down, breathe." The Evidence Tech lead holds up his hands and lowers them in a calming gesture. "We processed quite a bit from there yesterday. What are you referring to?"

Griff grabs him by the arm and starts dragging Johnny towards the door. "Come on, guys. I know who our witness is."

***

"You're going to be so impressed," my partner says as he walks us to the evidence room entrance. He punches in a five digit code to the lock and opens it. The room is long and narrow; shelving racks bursting with boxes of evidence are arranged in rows. Hard florescent lights bleach out the color of everything. A single desk near the front serves as the clerk station. At six in the morning there's no one on duty yet.

Johnny looks over his shoulder at me and whispers. "You probably won't be impressed but it makes him feel better if you pretend." He walks down the rows of shelving, returning with a box. Griff goes through the bar code scanning procedure to log his action of opening evidence. It's a cumbersome process, but necessary to maintain our chain of custody trail. Many cases have failed in court when it's revealed that evidence had been opened without recording who did it.

He pulls out a drawing pad encased in a plastic bag. Serial numbers are written across the face of the bag. It's one of those heavy paper pads, spiral bound across the top, smudged with charcoal on the cover.

"Ta-da!" He says, brandishing it like a prize.

"Okay," I say. "What am I looking at?"

"This is the possession of one Gwendolyn Manner, my friend. Small time runner, young, lost and a compulsive sketcher."

"This is where he wants you to be impressed," Johnny says, low, as if keeping it a secret from Griff. My partner is standing right next to him.

"How do you know it's hers?"

"Because," he flips it open. "I'm a genius."

"No, he's not," the evidence tech counters. "He's barely literate. And old."

"It could be anyone's Griff. I see those things in places like Target."

"Every artist has a signature." He flips a couple of pages and turns it to me. It's a sketch of someone sitting on an outside bench, drawn from an angle straight across. The setting is somewhere in a park. People fill the background, walking, holdings hands, pushing kids on swings. The figure is wearing a suit and tie, lunch bag crumpled up next to him, head thrown back as if watching a plane fly overhead.

The rendering is actually quite good, with the exception of one common item.

"No one has faces," I note. Where there should be eyes, a nose, mouth, there is only blank space. On everyone. It's kind of creepy.

"And that is her signature. I've come across Gwen on several occasions. She lives in the basement of her grandmother's house up in Wicker Park, but leads a transient lifestyle. She runs weed for some small time operators. In return they keep her supplied. She'll smoke a bowl, hole up somewhere and spend the day drawing whatever is in front of her."

I take the pad from him, flipping through the pages. "And the faces?"

"She's got some rare condition, something that keeps her from recognizing facial features, so her drawings reflect that. I think she called it face blindness."

"The clinical term you want is Prosopagnosia," Johnny states. "Greek origins. 'Prosopon' for face, 'agnosia' for not knowing. It is an acquired or congenital condition associated with an area of the brain called the fusiform gyrus. Visual processing is impaired while other intellectual functioning remains intact and commensurate with the age of the afflicted person."

"Is that even English?" I feel exasperated, like they're running a long form joke on me.

Griff sighs. "Arch, trust me, it's her. We recovered this drawing pad from a second floor office overlooking the courtyard, which places her at the scene. The video recording confirms her presence at the right time."

I take a moment to process. "So, you're telling me our star witness in the death of Noah Bell, the one person who can reveal how he died and perhaps also what happened on the basketball court; she will not be able to recognize the face of the guy who committed the crime because of some weird medical condition? Is this a cosmic prank?"

Johnny nods, a look of dawning irony behind his spectacles. "Well, when you put it that way, it does seem rather humorous."

Neither Griff nor I laugh.

"So why hasn't she come forward? If she's running for her life, why not seek protection?" The logic doesn't match up for me.

Griff shrugs. "She's got outstanding warrants. Class C misdemeanor for Schedule 2 possession, I think. Nothing serious but maybe enough to keep her away."

My partner glances up at a wall clock. "First things first. We've got briefing in sixty minutes. That tape needs to be shown so we can square these cases. Hecker's eyes are going to bleed."

That makes us all smile.

"After that," he continues. "We'll check up with Gwen's grandmother. It's not unusual for those two to go weeks without seeing each other. You have an old lady who never leaves the house, and a young girl who never comes home. If that doesn't pan out, we'll track down a guy named Dwight Weldon Smith, Dweldon D on the streets. He's her primary source and about the only person who keeps track of her."

I feel somewhat numb. A breakthrough like this and it involves a girl who may be useless. I've never heard of such an affliction like face blindness and wouldn't have believed it was a real thing if someone tried to describe it. Thoughts tumble unchecked through my head as I distantly watch Griff and Johnny log the evidence back in and replace the box.

My cell phone rings as I walk up the stairs ahead of the other two. It's Sheila.

"Where did you sneak off to?"

"I forgot to check a lead and it just hit me while I slept."

"You promised me information. What am I going to hear at this morning's press?"

"You can't wait, Sheila? It's only a few

hours away. Go back to sleep."

"If anyone deserves this scoop, I do. Especially after what I let you do to me last night. Don't expect that often."

She makes it sound like sleepovers are going to become a thing. She's also bartering against them. That type of manipulation doesn't sit well with me.

When I don't respond right away, she forges ahead. "Rumors are already flying. It's Noah Bell isn't it? I know you guys have been trying to keep it under wraps, even going so far as to cover the plates on the Mercedes at the scene so no one could trace the license." There's accusation in her tone, at me, at due process. I don't take it personal. Over the years we've had many opposing agendas, personally and professionally. As she said: *This is us*.

I pause, debating internally, then relent. "Yes, Noah Bell. Beaten and strangled with his own tie."

"Oh God, honey. I'm so sorry. I know what he meant to you," her tone truly is apologetic. She has empathy for those things that cause us pain, but is too controlled to let it get in the way of a good story. She can turn it on and off as needed. Case in point: "This is huge. Is there a connection to the basketball court homicides?"

Suddenly it comes clear to me how Sheila can be useful in her role. I think about how the two cases have been classed so far, about the agenda of some in the district. There may be a way to blunt that angle.

"Off the record."

She pauses. "Sure. Record off. Why?"

"I have an anonymous tip for you."

TWENTY FIVE

Griff was right. Hecker's eyes don't literally bleed, but they sure do go red along with the rest of his face. "You have to be shitting me. White supremacy? William Travian? A blind witness?"

It's barely ten minutes into my briefing and things have already gone off the rails. But we knew they would and I resist the urge to protest back.

"Not blind," Griff says, in his most helpful voice. "Face blind. There's a difference. Imagine throwing a bunch of Scrabble tiles on the floor. Somewhere in that jumble is your name, but you have to visually pick through the tiles to assemble it. Sometimes the letters are close to each other, making it easy to identify, other times they aren't. She's the same way, just with your facial features."

Hecker pins his red glare on me. "There's no evidence of the actual crime. This long-distance video shot is circumstantial and you're drawing all kinds of inferences from it. That's not the approach a seasoned officer would take." He turns to Gonzales. "Are you going to hang your badge on this guy's theory? We don't even know if she's still alive. The shooter could have tagged her and taken the body."

The Deputy Chief hesitates. Off to one side of the briefing room a TV sits on a rolling cart. The video of the man shooting after a fleeing Gwen Manner loops over and over, courtesy of some splicing efforts by Stephanie. She knows how to stage things for effect. Everyone else in the room stares at the screen as if transfixed.

"You're right, it doesn't show the crime. This could be a domestic violence situation for all we know." Gonzales holds up a hand to forestall me as I open my mouth to protest.

"However, it's disingenuous to think the two events are unrelated. The bodyguard died from gunshot wounds. This video places him in the vicinity of a suspect willing to fire his weapon. There is no sign of any gang kids conducting a beating. We cannot ignore the math, no matter how simple it may be to run with the random assault theory."

Hecker gaps open his mouth as he searches for the words to argue with.

Stewart clears his throat and stands up. "I don't know whether White and Toms are onto something, but we've also got gaps. The bodyguard has dirt on him that traces back to the factory courtyard. Nayaki's crew found blood that had been covered, like someone kicked dirt over it."

"DNA matching?" Gonzales asks.

"Minimum six weeks, even with you clearing us to the head of the line. That's all the lab would give." We use an independent lab and our priority is not always theirs. At the response nod, Stewart continues. "None of the Two Twos' hands show any sign of violence. If they beat Bell, it wasn't by punching him."

"Unless they had friends we don't know about," Hecker says. "I think there's a lot of credence to the idea that White and Rollins were attacked at the factory yesterday by some punk coming back to clean up his tracks. Someone doesn't attack two badged and identified officers unless they are desperate. Who was there and what were they doing? We need to look into that angle."

No one responds. Gonzales looks at Stewart. "Ballistics?"

"Supposedly today, but it should just confirm what we already know: There's a mismatch. Not only are there weapons missing, but we've got mismatched calibers, too. They could be from the missing guns, but if first pass is any indication, nearly everyone suffered at least one round from the same weapon."

"Further evidence that there were others present who scurried back into their holes. Like the Latin Kings. Maybe they grabbed their illegal guns and disappeared." Hecker fixes Stewart with a glare, as if making his eyes hard will convince the detective.

Gonzales taps his pen on the file jacket of Gwen Manner, staring down. "Six weeks until DNA..."

"We don't have six weeks, Hector. We have two hours. We got away without naming Bell yesterday, but that won't last. The media is smelling something. Do you know I got a call less than an hour ago from that new girl over at FOX? The Walters one...Sharon, Susan..."

"Sheila," Griff offers. "Sheila Walters. I hear she's pretty good. Beautiful, too." He doesn't make eye contact with me. "Whoever her man is, he's a lucky guy."

Jerk.

"Yeah whatever, Toms. She called to confirm a rumor she'd heard that Bell's death was not random, that the two scenes are not related. Not even Charlie over at NBC knows that, or he would have called first. There's only one way she found out: Someone is leaking information. We have to get in front of this. The gang angle makes all the sense in the world. Bell was an unfortunate victim of the war between the Two Two Boyz and Latin Kings. We put it out as one of several leads we're chasing. That will buy us time to vet all this." Hecker waves to the loop of Gwen and her unknown attacker.

Gonzales stares at the television monitor, tapping his pen in staccato. He pulls his eyes from the loop and lets them skim around, making contact with everyone. There are fewer beat officers present today, squads released to help with other work. Still, a dozen of us fill the room. "My position remains. We must do right by this case, by Noah Bell. He meant much to this city and to the people who needed his hope the most. This is more than losing a great man, it's about losing a symbol for those who clung to the promise he brought."

He takes a deep breath and no one

interrupts him, not even Hecker. "We're going to be at the center of the maelstrom when we publish his name. The heat will be greater than anything we've ever felt, there will be no room for error. We get one chance to do things right. If the white supremacy information slips out wrongly, it could bring the FBI knocking. None of us want to field any calls from federal area codes. If the events of North Haven taught us anything, it's that no one is off limits, not even the crown prince of Chicago. If it turns out there's more to this than a series of unfortunate events, we need to make sure we're wrapped tight to protocol."

He looks over to me, holding my gaze to the edge of uncomfortable silence. "This is your case, Arch. By luck or by fate, you were standing next in line when this came up. There's a public relations angle to this now. People will quickly assume we assigned you to it due to your history with Bell; that you will work harder than any other detective because of such history. I'm willing to allow that assumption some breathing room if it gives us grace."

"You're also wearing the target," Hecker adds, not without certain smugness to his tone.

"I apologize for putting you in the vise," Gonzales says. "It's not the way anyone should start their career, but this is the new reality of our world. Everything is up for public review." Expanding his attention to Griff, he states: "Find the girl. First and foremost, we need to find her, if she's alive. Start unwrapping the truth to the death of Noah Bell. David is right, though. We need to buy time and including the basketball court in our statement about Bell will give the impression of a connection. We will not explicitly say so, we'll let the media process the theory."

"I've got a home address, dep. We sent a car already, but no answer. We'll follow up personally and track down a couple other known connections," Griff says.

Gonzales points to the monitor. "If this is what it appears to be on the surface, if she survived those gunshots, there's a twenty year old girl out there scared to death, running for her life from a killer she can't recognize. Beyond learning the fate of Bell, we have to save her."

***

We break briefing thirty minutes later after hashing through details of both cases. Listening to Stewart's evidence, I come away convinced those kids on the court were collateral, victims caught up in something they didn't know. If the shooter on video was part of the Covenant and killed Bell, maybe he had friends who took out anyone nearby who could identify them. Maybe this was more than a crime of opportunity. Maybe the aborted events of North Haven have spilled over to my new stomping grounds, a wave of white hate washing towards Chicago's newest black detective.

Hecker is right: I have the target on me, in more ways than one.

Both he and Gonzales depart the room, to provide their boss an update on the case. Instead of progress, they will have to report less understanding of the events today than they had yesterday. That's not progress and I can tell neither is relishing the fact. We all have our pressures.

The rest of us remain, exchanging notes and side commentary best kept from the brass. I'm anxious to get going, but Griff is deep in discussion with Towney and based on the gestures, I know they're talking about ballistics.

Rollins catches my eye from across the room and nods. I nod back. We have a budding kinship, forged in the cauldron of Middle Plains. Being attacked by the same person can bring that type of brotherhood. He's got it a bit worse than me, though. We're both rookies, young bucks heading up a new wave of youth into the next millennium. I come with the burden of court orders, he comes with a more traditional cross of bumbling mistakes. In the span of twelve hours he had hit a pedestrian less than a few blocks away from an active scene, been assigned babysitting duty at said scene, gotten jumped by someone who had crept into the very scene he was supposed to protect, and choked out by said someone. It really was a comedy of errors.

Then something clicks. Adrenaline surges through me.

I leap across the room and grab his arm. "The pedestrian! Exactly where did it happen?"

His face colors and he yanks his arm free. "What?"

"The night of Bell's murder. The person you hit with your car. When and where?"

The rest of the room drops quiet, turning their attention our way.

"Screw you, White. It was an accident." I'm guessing the guy has taken plenty of ribbing for it and is a little sensitive. Then, realization flushes across his ruddy features and he goes pale. His eyes dart to the monitor. "Shit. I didn't even make the connection. I only saw her lying on the pavement."

Griff hollers. "Are you fucking kidding me? You ran over our star witness?"

The room breaks out in shouts and laughter, though it's no laughing matter. Rollins' life just took a turn for the worse. If he thought the hazing he'd gotten yesterday was bad, wait until this one races through the station. I almost feel sorry for the guy.

I tear out of the briefing room, followed quickly by Griff. "Someone get me the hospital address and have dispatch send it!" He shouts over his shoulder.

At last glance, Rollins is still standing there, shocked gaze across his face, staring at the loop of Gwendolyn Manner fleeing her attacker. At that moment in her life she probably never thought she'd escape one threat only to be taken down by the very thing that could protect her. Is that the definition of irony?

***

"What do you mean?" I shout into my cell phone as Griff guns the car forward through an intersection, lights flashing from behind the radiator grill. He's driving fast and sure-handed, look of intense concentration on his normally jovial face.

The nurse replies in a calm voice. "We

aren't a prison hospital, officer. She left yesterday, knocking down one of our other nurses in the process. If she's going to flee, there's little we can do. But when you find her, we need information for billing purposes."

"You didn't get any identification? A name or address?"

"She came in under Jane Doe. No ID."

I click off the call with a frustrated growl. "You can slow down and cut the lights. She left."

"Seriously?" He barks. The racing engine drops in volume. I lower my window, feeling deflated. There was a sense of pride at the intuitive leap and I wanted it to pay off immediately.

"But the description of her matched what we saw on tape, so I'm thinking it was Gwen. Which means she's alive. She probably escaped because she's scared out of her wits." I don't bother to state it, but the cop part of me wonders why she hasn't come to us if she fears for her life. The other side of me knows why: In this area, there's significant mistrust of the law. Cicero has bad guys and they wear a uniform, according to some residents.

"All right," Griff grunts. "Back to the original plan. Let's go wake up the grandmother and have a chat."

He turns the car north. Looking back, it was a symbolic turn, the moment when everything else turned, the moment when our lives pivoted from the paths we'd put them on. But neither of us could have guessed. Given hindsight, I'm not so sure we'd have made different choices even then.

Not even with the way it all turned out.

TWENTY SIX

Sheila calls me before we've traveled two blocks. "Well?"

"It worked. Hecker's all riled up and focused on damage control. Thanks."

"You're welcome. Now tit for tat. My tits, just for you. What are they worth?" Her voice is jaunty. She's in a good mood, flirting.

"You mean money?"

"Never mind. You're terrible at this. Let's talk about your theory. Give me something."

"Hang on." I cup my hand over the mouthpiece and look over at my partner. "How much should we say?"

"On the record: We have a lead on a witness. Nothing more. Off: Whatever you want. I trust she won't burn you."

I pull my hand away and start to repeat his comments.

"Tell Toms I would never burn you." She fires back before I get three words out. The girl has good ears. "Now, spill."

"There's video of the aftermath at Middle Plains. We have pretty good certainty on the identity. It's a girl and we're on the way to her place now. But she may not be of much use, even though she saw everything up close."

Sheila gives a distracted hum in response and I know she's writing this down. "You don't think she'll cooperate?"

"No, I don't think she can. Maybe that's why she ran."

"Hey, Dr. Seuss, how about plain talk?"

I scrub the bridge of my nose. "It's something called face blindness. I don't recall the clinical term."

"Prosopagnosia," Griff says from his seat, eavesdropping.

"Proso...are you kidding me?" Sheila exclaims. Like I said, she's got good ears. "Arch, remember that investigative series I did back in 96? The one down in Charleston?"

I don't but want to avoid saying so. That admission will come back to haunt me, as in: *You never pay attention to my work.* "You did a lot of good reports. Be more specific."

"It was about a clinical program designed to help people with rare conditions, such as prosopagnosia, synesthesia, Cotard's delusion, Stone Man syndrome, that sort of thing. I interviewed a guy down there who was face blind."

Now she has my attention. I have no idea what those other conditions are and don't really care. "Anything that could help?"

"Give me the witness. Just a name."

"No, not yet. If she's out there running, it could hurt more than help by releasing her name. Especially if there's a gunman still hunting her. Right now, our best weapon is stealth."

"Fine, but when you can, you tell me first."

"Promise, now help me out here."

There's a long silence and I know she's organizing her thoughts. Sheila has incredible recall, which is great for her, not so much for me at times.

"A person diagnosed with prosopagnosia struggles to recognize facial features in context. It's often partnered up with other recognition impairments, like places, events, emotions and such. The affliction can range from needing a couple seconds to place someone's features, all the way to not recognizing their own face in a mirror. That's obviously an extreme case. It's hard to pin down numbers since we all forget someone from time to time but I saw somewhere it said up to 2% of the world's population." She takes a quick breath. "It's often acquired via some kind of brain trauma, although there are many documented cases of inherent prosopagnosia. The different types are broken down into genetic, pre-experiential, and post-experiential."

"Sheila, I don't need a psychology lecture. I just need to know how to deal with someone who has it."

"Do you even know what psychology means?" Her tone is miffed, but if I didn't stop her, I'd end up listening to a repeat of her on-air script. "Prosopagnosiacs rely on coping mechanisms to deal with other people. They use hair style, voice, physical build, movement habits. However these things aren't as reliable as facial recognition. Someone can lose weight, change haircuts, or sound different from a cold. That throws everything off then. To this girl, you will be a stranger, now and every time afterwards. She's living in a state of perpetual uncertainty and confusion, never sure who she's talking to, of what she may have already said to a person she doesn't realize is the same one from a few moments ago."

"That's got to be hard," I mutter, trying to

place myself in her shoes.

"Imagine going to a party. You're introduced to a person and have a conversation with them. Maybe you talk about a movie, or Sunday's game. It's interesting and you're engaged. You excuse yourself to get a drink and on your way back are introduced to someone else. They might resemble the last person you met, similar in build or clothing, but you aren't sure and don't want to ask if you've already met. Imagine how self-conscious that would make you."

I think about the video snippet of the shooter. He looked of average build and color, with a generic haircut. He might be a guy anyone would have trouble remembering, so for her it's a potential nightmare. But on the plus side, I'm completely opposite of him, so when we catch up to her hopefully she can tell the difference.

If she's still alive and breathing, that is.

"What are they like to deal with? Do you have speak in a special way or handle them carefully?"

"Good god, Arch. It's not cerebral palsy or manic depression. Everyone is different, obviously, but there are some common traits and habits. They tend to avoid interactions with others, especially in groups. It's a condition that breeds hesitation and introverted actions. As a result, many of them slide to the fringes of society, to the disenfranchised corners where they can control the faces coming at them."

Or they seek solace in abandoned locations, marijuana and charcoal sketches.

I can't conceive of a life like that, the day to day difficulties. When we find Gwen - and I'm thinking positive here, she's still alive - I'm not sure what my approach will be. She narrowly escaped a killer, she got hit by a car, a police car no less, escaped a hospital by assaulting the staff and is possibly wandering the streets. Every face that passes by could be the blond man and she wouldn't know it until too late. My guess is she's avoiding everyone and everything, burrowing down into her hole, wherever that may be. The fear and tension must be crippling.

"Okay, anything else?"

"Well, there's a ton more, Arch, but you're not willing to hear it all. You have a job to do that doesn't take into account her status in life. I get that, but don't forget this girl is a pawn. She never asked for any of this and certainly doesn't deserve to die over it. Remember that. Have compassion."

I mumble something back and click off the

call.

A copy of Gwen's file jacket is sitting on the seat between us. I pick it up and look at it again, for the hundredth time since we first made copies. Gwen's most recent mug shot is stapled to the cover.

She's got the look of a waif, like a softer version of the actress Winona Ryder. Her hair is just as dark, but longer and wavy. In the photo, her eyes are dark, smudged liner underneath, as if she'd been crying. It's the stare that gets me though. My first impression of the photo had been to categorize her as someone high out of their mind.

But now, with my newfound knowledge, the image takes on a new tone.

Her eyes are glassy, slightly unfocused, the irises light. I see an expression of faint confusion, as if she doesn't fully trust what she's seeing. Her gaze is aimed just to one side of the lens, so I'm guessing she was looking at the photographer, studying his or her features for any signs that she might recognize. There's a sense of lost desperation in her expression, as if she knows it's futile to try but holds out hope there will be some kind of clue that says: *This time, it will be different.*

"So, you said you've dealt with her before?" I ask Griff.

He signals and changes lanes without checking, passing a slower car. "Busted her twice, talked to her a few other times. I've been working this district forever and after a while you know everyone. Some of them stick out more than others. She's really a good kid, not hurting anyone. She just wants to be left alone to do her thing, but her thing is against the law, unfortunately."

Leaning against the door panel and rubbing his chin, Griff continues. "It's weird. Every time I come across her, she says nothing until I identify myself by name. Even then, she acts like she doesn't believe me and I could turn out to be someone else. She never smiles either. Not like she's stern or angry, but like she's forgotten how. She admitted during a psych eval that she's face blind; that she'd done a bunch of research on it and was convinced. They followed up and confirmed the symptoms, if not the condition. So I guess that's as official a diagnosis as we're going to get. She'll never go to the right doctor and find out."

"Maybe she's faking to play the sympathy card? Maybe she can finger the guy after all?" I'm grasping at straws, praying there's a pitcher's chance in this case.

Griff laughs. "Yeah, if she's faking, I'm

George Clooney. When you talk with her, you'll get it."

"So then what about this Dwight guy?" I flip Gwen's file back to the seat, selecting the one underneath it. Dwight Weldon Smith stares back at me from his mug shot. Unlike Gwen, his expression is completely formed, and it's hostile. His DOB puts him at twenty-six but he looks younger, almost boyish. His fat features stare back at the lens as if he can intimidate the camera. I've seen the tough guy look for years and his face can't carry it. The glint of one gold tooth peeks out from a slight curl in his upper lip. The collar of his red hooded sweatshirt is tight across his neck. A thick gold chain rests outside the collar. I'm guessing it has a large pendant or some other thing hanging from it, but it's cut off by the bottom frame. If only this Dwight kid realized how much he perpetuated the stereotype of a young black thug...then again, he probably doesn't care about social perception and racial understanding.

"Dweldon D. Low level pusher up in Wicker Park, which is how I'm guessing he and Gwen crossed. He runs consistently with two guys: Jimmy Tiller and Deandre Hall. If you want racial harmony, these guys can give it to you. Two black gangster thugs tight with a white trash castoff and none of them care about color."

"I'm not sure that was Bell's ultimate vision, but it's a start. I bet he would be proud." I can be sarcastic too, but it's harder for me.

"He operates out of an apartment building in a pretty nice area, working mainly pot, coke and prescription. We've got him on possession with intent to sell, but have had the DA cut deals, so the kid hasn't ever really served serious time. He's smarter than that fat fuck face would lead you to believe."

"How so?" He doesn't look smart. In fact, he looks like a petulant child acting tough.

"He keeps traffic away from his place, using local businesses that he props up with investments. He donates time and money to visible causes."

"Visible?"

"Yeah, like if there's a fund-raising event for a sick girl from the neighborhood, he'll be the first to throw into the money bucket, and no small amount either. Because of stuff like that, people around the area who know what he does accept it and stay mum. The guy isn't evil, just self-serving. He's like a thousand others who didn't make the right turn and ended up down the wrong lane. He once confided that he wished he'd become a teacher."

I shake my head. We all are a collection of our choices. What will mine say about me when it's all over?

TWENTY SEVEN

Griff crosses West Division Street and waves to indicate our surroundings. "Wicker Park is a pretty small area. We just crossed over the southern boundary. Ashland Avenue is the eastern edge, Bloomingdale to the north and Western Avenue on the west side. Back in the mid-century everyone who lived here either spoke Polish or was related to someone who did. Just like Ukranian Village to the south, people immigrate to the culture they know. My dad said back in the day you could drive along North Avenue for miles and know exactly where you were by the accents. By the 70s it had become largely Hispanic and Wicker had some rough times with gangs, like the Spanish Lords and Maniac Latin Disciples. I never worked this district, but heard enough stories."

I look out the window. The houses and shops lining Ashland speak to a revitalized economy. I don't see a lot of gang tags. Street signs, telephone poles, sidewalk garbage cans; none of them bear the telltale graffiti signs that mark territories. Of course, the alleys and backs of buildings could be a different story, but from what I can tell this is not an area where citizens cower in fear of crime. There's a posture in the body language of people moving along the sidewalk that says: *Life is good and only getting better.*

The whole country is soaring on the wave of Internet explosion, every day another web site goes live selling some product that you'd never think would be its own store. Our current millennium is receding at full throttle, soon to be a memory, and the new one is shaping up to increase that acceleration. Who knows what things will look like on January 1, but one thing I do know: The Covenant shouldn't have a say in painting that picture.

"You know," Griff continues. "I grew up in the lower west side and remember when the major highways weren't even built up here yet. When the city threw down the Kennedy Expressway, it really split this area up.

Hispanics moved out from the city, it seemed like overnight. Bet you didn't know Wicker Park was the original home to the Latin Kings."

"I didn't."

"Yeah. Huge Puerto Rican population. But back then, gangs worked differently. The LKs worked with local groups and conducted peace marches, sit-ins and other things to make this a better place. They abided by process and persuasion to make changes, not violence. It didn't work though. Construction slowed, people started drifting away; there were a series of arsons that many thought were intended to move out businesses so other kinds could move in. Things went to hell quickly. North Avenue became hooker row and the gangs turned dark. When it was happening, no one really knew what to do, but looking back now, it all seems so clear. Hindsight, I guess."

"Apparently it all turned out for the better," I comment as Ashland splits into lanes separated by a flower garden exploding with color.

"Oh yeah, place shaped up real nice. Lots of artsy-fartsy culture now, hippie and yuppie types living side by side. Needs to stay that way." He turns onto Le Moyne Avenue. "Okay, the lady's name is Olivia, Olivia Manner. Her house is around the twenty-one, twenty-two hundred block. I've only been there once but I'll recognize it."

Le Moyne features low apartment buildings and two-flats pushed up against the sidewalk. In Chicago, especially the post-war development areas, I've noticed many of the residential blocks are cleaved in half by an alley that runs behind the houses. Garages are stacked along this alley, allowing home owners to keep their cars off the street. Where I grew up, most houses didn't have garages. We also didn't have the rigid grid of streets like Chicago. The blocks here are even and square, east-west are avenues, north-south are streets. It speaks to controlled civil planning back in the days when Chicago stretched her wings out from the shoreline of Lake Michigan.

Griff slows the car to a crawl in front of a small, bright blue house on the north side of Le Moyne. A set of steps flanked by wrought iron handrails lead up to the front door from the sidewalk. A plate glass window dominates the front exterior. The curtains are drawn.

At some point in the past, the front yard had been excavated, creating a sunken courtyard surrounded by more iron rail. I can see a set of stairs that lead down and guess that there's a basement apartment with a separate entrance.

Griff pulls the cruiser ahead a few spaces and parks next to the curb. We exit and start back toward the house. At this time of the morning - just past 8:30 - on a sleepy side street, there's not a lot of pedestrian traffic, even fewer vehicles. The only person in my field of vision is an old man at the west end of the block, leash in hand, waiting for the light to change so he can cross. A little Corgi barks at his legs, urging him to move, but he ignores it.

Out of the blue, Griff spouts, "Colored folk like you scare old people so I should do the talking."

I look at him and don't try to stifle the look of shock. "'Colored folk'?" *What. The. Hell.*

He smiles. "Busting on you. This whole racial Covenant angle makes me think more about stuff like that. But seriously, I should do the talking. Olivia is sweet, and a bit loony. I think she's got some Alzheimer's disease going on. She gets lost in her memories sometimes, sometimes her memories lose her."

I shake my head. "Christ, what a family. Girl can't recognize anyone, grandma can't remember anyone she does recognize."

"Conversations are a riot: 'Do I know you'? 'I don't remember. Who are you?'"

Despite myself, I laugh. Griff can be

annoying with his flippant nature, but every now and then he gets one through.

We mount the stairs and knock on the door. It's early, but not so early that I think we're disruptive. Plus, it's a matter of life and death, literally.

"No one answered the phone when dispatch called?" I ask, looking over the rail to the sunken courtyard. From here it's a good fifteen foot drop. I avert my eyes. Again, heights and I: not friends.

"No, straight to the answering machine."

There's no response from inside the house. I can hear the TV playing a morning news show, volume turned loud. Olivia Manner, in addition to not remembering anything, also seems to have bad hearing. If she walks with a cane, that's the trifecta right there.

Steeling myself against the drop down to the courtyard, I lean over the railing and place my hand against the plate window, shading my eyes. There's a gap in the curtains. The front living room is small. A love seat is the only couch. Bookshelves line two of the walls. An old console TV sits on the floor; it's the source of the news show volume. Beyond the living room a narrow hallway leads back to a dining area. From my angle I can see what appears to be part of a shoulder or back.

"It looks like she's sitting at a table back in the kitchen. Probably can't hear you knocking over the TV."

Griff nods. We retreat back down the steps and around the side. The house is pressed so close to the one next door that his jacket snags on the rough brick. "I guess property line setbacks weren't a thing when these were built," he grumbles as he pulls the fabric free. He does so rather carefully. Like me, he only has a couple different jackets to wear on the job. They can get expensive.

"It's not a problem for me. Suck in that belly, old man."

"I am, can't you tell?"

Out back is the single-car garage that I expect to see. A slim sidewalk leads from it to the rear of the house. Flowers line the walk, neatly tended and bright. There's a lot of care and pride evident here.

As Griff pauses at the bottom of the rear stairs to inspect his jacket, I bound up the steps and give the door a loud rap, announcing myself, shield ready in case Griff was right about old folk and colored people. The top half of the door is window pane, like the standard kitchen doors I grew up with. In my hometown, women decorated this door, because this is where friends and family entered the house. Front doors were for deliveries and salesmen.

Olivia's door could fit right in back home. The window is sectioned into six panes separated by wooden muntins. The glass within each pane is colored in bright tones, abstract in design and result. I wonder if Gwen had anything to do with the artwork. The paint coating the glass is fairly opaque, allowing some visibility through, but the curtain hanging on the inside of the door reduces that small amount of visibility to zero.

"Is she hard of hearing too?" I ask. I knock again.

"All old people are," Griff replies as he shrugs back into his jacket. "Can't wait until my hearing goes so I can block out idiots. Try the knob."

I peek through a gap in the paint and curtain, trying to see if there's movement, but my angle is all wrong. I can only see the side wall and part of the sink. The knob is loose and I turn it. There's a deadbolt but it's not thrown.

I hold up my badge and push open the door into Olivia Manner's kitchen.

And let out a shout to my partner.

TWENTY EIGHT

Olivia Manner is slumped over the small table, head flat on the surface, arms hanging limp. A broken cup lies on the linoleum floor amid a puddle of coffee and ceramic shards. Her face is turned away from me and I circle around as Griff rushes up the steps.

"Oh, shit," he says as he enters. He draws his weapon and I follow suit. "Clear the house first."

I take the lead. Even though I'd seen the empty living room through the front window, I still take precautions. If someone is in here, they could have moved in the time it took us to get around back. With everything as strange as it is in this case, I'm not taking chances.

The living room is still empty. Across from it are two bedrooms. One shows signs of recent use. The bed is unmade, rumpled as if someone had just slept there. Books stack both side tables and dresser top. The closet stands open. This is Olivia's room. The one next to it is set up as a sewing room and empty as well. Everything is neatly laid out, spools of thread lined up in rows, fabric swatches draped over a hanging rod. There's no dust or clutter.

Where I would expect to see basement stairs, there is only a wall covered with pictures. I tap it with the muzzle of my weapon. "Looks like this got closed up as part of a remodel to create a separate apartment downstairs."

Griff grunts distractedly and snaps on a pair of latex gloves. He presses his fingers against Olivia's neck. After a few seconds of silence: "No pulse."

I holster my weapon and pull on my own set of gloves. We usually carry spares, a practice Griff instilled in me from day one. On the kitchen table a brown prescription bottle lies on its side. I don't know what the medication is, but the label indicates it's to aid sleeping. A few pills are scattered on the table surface.

Griff takes the container when I hand it to him. He has to hold the bottle at arm's length to read the label. "For the love of Pete. A suicide? Really? This is such bullshit."

Neither of us buys the suicide. I don't need to know Olivia to dismiss that possibility. There's too much coincidence in the timing. Somehow the killer has been here. The man who impersonated Rosenfel found out Gwen's identity and tracked her, doing it faster.

"How did he beat us?"

Griff doesn't need me to explain who I'm talking about. We're in tune. He stares at Olivia's face, frown across his brow. "We didn't interrupt his search for Gwen's identity at the factory. We interrupted his departure. That has to be it. She never carries an ID so there had to be something in her stacks of drawings and notepads that told him how to find her."

"He's one step ahead," I say, taking the bottle back and setting it down where it originally lay.

"One?" Griff shoots back. "How about ten? We don't know who he is, where he is, what he's doing or who he's doing it with. All we know is that he isn't Rosenfel. That buys us shit. Further, we don't have anything in the way of leads to get all that information, other than questioning one of the most powerful men in town. And I doubt we'd ever get clearance from the top to haul Travian in for a sit down. We're chasing a ghost who's chasing a shadow. He may already have caught up to Gwen for all we know and there goes our case. Poof."

"Are you always this optimistic?"

He grunts out a bitter laugh. "We need to check out that basement. I want to do it before calling this in. I'm half afraid we're going to find Gwen there, but I'm more afraid we won't. Once we call in the death of a relation to our key witness, we're going to lose control real fast. Gonzales, Hecker, hell maybe even Jacobs will all start banging down our door for updates."

I nod as Griff lifts Olivia's head and inspects the down side cheek. "If I had to guess, she received a visit last night. Rigor has set in, but I don't see much livor mortis. Let's go."

We exit the kitchen to the back yard. The neat sidewalk with its border of bright color now takes on a different aspect. There's much care and attention inherent in the arrangement of flowers and it saddens me to think that it will all end now. The future of this house is blown wide open and who knows what tomorrow will bring for it.

Griff stands there for a second, staring back at the garage. He looks over to me and I understand the question. I nod.

We move down the sidewalk, splitting to each side as we circle around to the front. There's a service door on my side and I test the knob. It's locked. The overhead garage door is also locked. We have no way in unless we break down the door. I peer inside. A dark Ford sedan occupies the single stall, clean and shiny. Olivia takes care of her possessions.

"Anything?" Griff stands with his back to the wall, watching outward, trusting me to look inward.

"No. Closed up tight. Let's sweep the basement."

Off to one side of the back stoop a door opens to reveal stairs heading down. I take the lead. The hinges emit a soft groan.

"That's a bad sign," Griff says and pulls out his weapon again. "Old people lock everything."

"Have you been down there?"

He shakes his head. "Never been inside either place, just outside on the front steps."

The stairwell is dank and tight. Light filters in from the morning sun to reveal a set of wooden steps and a door at the bottom.

We move down with care. I make an effort to keep my steps quiet but Griff sounds like a bowling ball bouncing down a pile of pallets. He grunts and groans, old knees protesting the movement. I give a look over my shoulder at him but he just shrugs.

The door at the bottom of the stairs is also unlocked. I turn the knob and push it open, stepping back and off to one side. The stairwell is so narrow that there's no cover, the move is more mental than protective.

After a second with no reaction from inside, I breach the threshold and move into the apartment, stepping off to one side of the door.

The layout is identical to upstairs. We're in the kitchen at the back. A small round table sits against the near wall. Dishes are piled up across the counter and sink. Gwen seems to favor saltine crackers. There are empty cracker sleeves and boxes strewn everywhere, on top of the table, on the floor. A small set of shelves serves as an open pantry and more boxes occupy them.

"What's up with all the crackers?" Griff wonders aloud.

We move forward into the hallway connecting kitchen to living room. That space is just as cluttered, with clothes thrown on a beat-up futon sofa. There's no TV, just a stereo with CDs stacked everywhere. If Olivia passed on anything to Gwen, it was a collector mentality. The grandmother had hundreds of books, Gwen has thousands of CDs. I'm betting more than a few are stolen from stores. The cases litter the floor and one cracks under Griff's foot.

"I can't tell if this place has been tossed or just needs a cleaning," he says and kicks the case aside.

Both bedrooms are clear. We stop outside the bathroom and glance inside. It's small like every other room, a shower stall, toilet and pedestal sink.

I notice there's no mirror above the sink. A portrait of a cat in a grassy field on a bright summer day hangs in a frame. Likewise, the dresser in the bedroom had no mirror on it. This must be a side effect of her face blindness. Maybe she didn't like seeing a stranger in the reflection every morning.

There's a thickness in the bathroom air, different than the rest of the apartment. I've been a number of crime scenes in my career, usually as a beat cop, so I know what I'm smelling.

Old blood.

I nudge Griff and nod my head towards the shower. The curtain is pulled closed.

He looks at me. "Seriously? Arch, this place is so small we'd be able to hear the heartbeat of anyone hiding."

"Let's just clear it."

My partner sighs and steps into the bathroom. With a look of exaggerated show, he reaches out and flips the curtain open.

TWENTY NINE

My first impression, the thing that will stick with me long after all this is over, is red.

Red, pooled up in the shower basin.

Splashed along the walls.

Sheeting down the slick fiberglass surface. In many spots, it has started to harden and turn brown, making the visual more grotesque, as if that's possible.

Both Griff and I take a step back. Neither of us says a word.

A torso has been propped up against the corner of the shower. The legs are stumps at mid-thigh. The torso still has a sweatshirt on, soaked throughout with blood and the sleeves hang limp, indicating no arms attached to the shoulder.

The head is missing, sawed off at the top of the neck.

Gristle, organ or whatever the hell else comes out of a body hacked up like this has clogged the drain, a small pile of meaty bits, creating a pool of blood. It nearly overflows the lip of the shower.

"Mother of God," Griff breathes and lets out a hacking cough.

We retreat out into the living room, as if there is not enough oxygen for both of us. The smell is stronger with the curtain open.

I stand there, staring at the gruesome scene. Whoever it once was, was fat. I can't tell male or female. "This person has been here a while." I point out the drying blood. In some spots it's already cracked.

"This person is Dweldon D." Griff's voice is ragged and hoarse.

"How do you know? There's nothing left."

"The size of the torso and that stupid Bulls sweatshirt. Guy wore the thing all the time, even in summer. Someone told me he had one for every day of the week."

"So where's the rest of him?"

"I'm almost afraid to find out."

I think back to Rick Killing's words: *You've got a very big problem.*

I'd say this fits that description. If it truly

was the work of the Covenant, they've escalated the violence factor to whole new levels. This is a work of savagery married to clinical precision. The straight-edged cuts on the neck and thighs tell me a sharp blade was used with no small amount of expertise. And experience.

Most of my homicide experience has been in the role of the Dick Alberts' of the world. I'd respond to a call, find the deceased and secure the scene. Sometimes I'd man the log book, other times I'd help investigators canvas for potential witnesses. As a uni your role can change based on case need. No two scenes were alike, but similar themes and actions ran through them all. Detectives work to uncover motive, opportunity and identity. Forensics work to establish manner of death, using an array to tools and techniques when it's not patently obvious. I don't pretend to be versed in those ways, but I don't need to be an expert to see how it was done. Dweldon was cut apart by someone with a goal, and it's no stretch to figure out that goal.

"What the hell are we dealing with here?" I ask, rhetorically. I don't expect my partner to have an answer.

Griff runs one hand through the thinning gray hair atop his head and plops down on the futon. Suddenly the precise rules of crime scene handling seem secondary to the overwhelming nature of what we're seeing.

"Arch, I've got thirty years into this badge, pretty much my entire working life. All of it has been spent in the same area. Cicero, Berwyn, Oak Park...they were the places I knew growing up and where I watched everyone else grow up. I know those blocks like I know my own kids. It's always been about the crime, the domestic violence, senseless drive-by shootings or other gang murders, drugs, prostitution. They were never ending, but at the root you knew what the motivations were. People needed an escape, they needed a family, they needed the next fix. Those needs drove them to join a gang, or steal to fund a habit, or sell their body because it was the only thing they had of value. I arrested them, but I understood the Why."

"This..." he motions to the bathroom with a short wave. "This I don't know. I don't think I can understand the Why."

For once my partner is dead serious and I find it's a side of him that makes me uncomfortable. The Griffin Toms I've come to know is sarcastic, irreverent and willing to tweak authority. As I stare down at him now, I'm seeing an old man looking into the depths of his own limitations. He suddenly has realized he may not be enough for this case.

"We both know the Why, Griff. Dweldon was tortured for information on Gwen. Whoever is chasing her connected the dots in the same way we did, faster than we did. If Dweldon knew where she was, I hope he took that knowledge with him, but we have to assume otherwise. Who wouldn't break under those conditions?"

Griff doesn't respond. His haunted eyes stare at the corpse. A multitude of thoughts flit across his face and I can only imagine what they are. He's so close to his retirement, is he wondering whether he stayed on a little too long? Or is he worried about making it to the finish line?

"Are we in over our heads?" This is me opening up Pandora's box.

Since I set foot in this town, carrying a suitcase and new stuffed animal for Anna, all of me had been focused on earning the right to my tin. After the lawsuit and all the legal wrangling that befriends such activities, I wanted to make sure I worked my butt off to prove it was all worthwhile. Some guys might have throttled back, thinking the hard part was done and now that they're in the door, they just have to avoid screwing up.

That's not my way. I will do whatever it takes to show I was a great get, regardless of my methods.

Now, standing here in the middle of a basement in Wicker Park, I'm opening the door a crack to say 'I may not be able to handle this.' It sticks in my craw, but I know when to say when. More importantly, I'm afraid to do something wrong by the case, due to lack of experience or knowledge. Tossing my career to the curb by breaking rules is not part of the game plan. This job is critical to staying with Anna in Chicago, so I cannot put my job status at risk no matter what.

Griff nods, a slow and controlled motion. In that gesture is the confirmation of surrender. Under his flip and casual manner is a guy with pride equal to my own, just sourced from a different place. He matches my energy and determination with his experience and skill. We're a good pairing that way. I know acknowledging our limitations needles him as much as it does me.

"This is serial killer level shit, Arch. Way out of our league. Toss the hate crime aspect of the Covenant on top of this bonfire and you're talking task force territory."

Which is the very thing Gonzales wanted to avoid. Bringing in federal resources means matters will be taken out of our hands. It also means we publicly admit our own lack of confidence that we can solve this.

"So, what do we do? Call in the FBI?"

"First things first. Let's secure this scene and get it reported. Once the scene is cased, Hecker is going to have a field day with you. Be prepared for the public relations angle on this. You'll be forced to defend yourself against whatever he dredges up, regardless of how true it is. We'll need to huddle with Gonzales and get his weight behind us. He's going to be our best ally, as long as he believes we did the right thing. Are you prepared for that?"

I feel pressure on my shoulders, a spike centered on my spine. It has a name, this feeling: Failure. There are no words in me to answer his question. I'm scared, scared that my failure here will signal yet another upheaval in Anna's life, trigger another change in scenery. I can't move her to a different facility; we went through hell to get her into this one. The thought of starting over clenches my jaw tight.

But the thought of failing to do the right thing freezes me even more. It's who I am. It's that one core item for which I know my daughter would beam with pride if she knew. Someday she'll understand everything and when that day comes I want her to be proud of me.

Griff accepts my silence as acceptance. He pats his jacket pockets. "Okay, buddy, let's do this. You got your radio? I left mine in the car."

"No. I'll get it." I turn for the front door.

"Hey," Griff stops me. "Pull the cruiser around back to the garage. Once the party starts here, they'll shut down the entire block. I want to be able get away. Hopefully we won't need a sudden escape, but I don't want to be caught out if we do."

I pause at the door, hand on the knob. "Just curious. If we weren't going to hand this over, what would be our next steps?"

"I'd find Dweldon's two boys: Tiller and Hall. If Dweldon knew about her, then they will too. Those guys shared everything."

I nod without replying and exit the apartment through the front. The morning sun is angled just right to blast the sunken courtyard with stifling heat. Along one side a small wrought iron table and two chairs sit, rusting in place. Potted plants line the other walls, browned and wilting. I wonder if it's Gwen's job to take care of these or Olivia's.

It feels like every step up to the sidewalk echoes with the consequences of my decision but I remain firm. If we are but the result of our choices, then I have to believe my actions are right and true.

The car is already hot on the inside and I roll down the window as I guide it out from the curb and up the street. The old man walking his dog is long gone, perhaps already home. The block is still quiet. I cut down the cross street and then into the narrow alley behind the row of houses. Trash cans, old bikes, pallets and other junk crowds the alley, forcing me to navigate slowly. It feels like the sides of the cruiser will scrape at any second. I coast the vehicle down the alley, glancing between the structures until I spot Olivia's back door. I pull the car into the space in front her garage.

Getting out, I'm several steps away before I remember the radios.

Jesus, Arch. Get your mind in the game. I'm so focused on what's going to happen with this case even the simplest of tasks slip past. My mother had a saying for me when I was young. I'd zero in on one thing I wanted to the exclusion of anything else, forgetting to eat or worse - in her eyes - neglecting my chores. When those situations happened, she'd say: *Boy, if your head wasn't attached to your shoulders, you'd forget it somewhere.*

I lean in through the open window. Both of our radios are sitting on top of Gwen's file jacket. I'm reaching for one of them when I hear the distinct sound of a gun being cocked right behind my ear. A warm muzzle presses against the bone of my skull.

"Hello, Detective Aramis White. I understand you've been looking for me."

THIRTY

I freeze, panic and uncertainty seizing my limbs. A slew of words come to my mind, but none seem to fit the magnitude of this moment. What would Griff say?

"Is that a gun or are you happy to see me?"

Oh, good god.

A moment of silence behind me. Then: "Did I hear what I just think I heard?"

Unfortunately, yes. But I don't say anything. The barrel is still against the base of my skull. He's positioned directly behind me, negating the advantage of a sudden move. I don't know what kind of move I'd make anyway. This has never happened before.

He sighs. "Hand me the radio and kneel down, ankle crossed. Fingers clasped on your head. You know the drill. There you go. Good cop."

I follow his instructions and feel my head pushed forward until it's leaning against the car door. My mind is racing and I can't corral the thoughts. I should be thinking my way out of this, yet thoughts of Anna fill my mind. I'm not afraid to die, but I am petrified to think of her without me. What will Anna think when she no longer hears my voice? How will Sheila cope? I can't clear my mind.

"Did you hear me?" The man behind me says and pushes the barrel harder against my skull.

"What?"

"I said: 'Where's your weapon?' Are you distracted? At a time like this?"

"Shoulder holster, left side."

"Left hand, fingers only. Set it down on the ground."

I start to follow his orders but pause, forcing myself to slow this moment down so I can think through it. "Do you know what you're doing here? How many charges you're bringing?"

He chuckles. "Um, yeah. I researched it very thoroughly, Detective White. I'm up to seven infractions so far, would you like me to rattle them off?"

I don't actually know if he's right or not. With that simple reply he undercut my efforts to mentally regroup. I'm completely off balance and unable to think of anything else. I follow his directive, knowing I'm violating every policy on weapon protocol. With my left hand I awkwardly pull out the gun.

It drops to the ground with a metallic clank and I hear him pick it up. "Let's keep this friendly. I'm not here to hurt you."

"Like you're not here to hurt Olivia or Dweldon?"

"That's not fair. I purposely let her down easy. She passed in peace."

Incredible, he actually sounds offended. "Generous of you."

"It was. She just happened to be a piece of the puzzle that I couldn't leave lying around afterwards. Unfortunate. Lovely lady, although I think her mind was going."

"Dweldon wasn't lovely? What you did to him is beyond sick."

A grunt. "He was a thug, a drug dealer poisoning kids' minds. Your life is better with him off the streets. This place is better off. I was his karma."

This guy is talking like we're having a simple difference of opinion. I find that more frightening than if he were raving and reciting his personal manifesto against our government. "What do you want with me?"

"For starters, I need you to walk ever so nicely back into the basement apartment. We need to initiate a transaction."

I have no idea how to react, other than complying with his directions. Something will come to me, some action that will end this little scenario. It has to. My mind flips through a thousand memories of the academy, other situations, even movies and TV shows. But nothing surfaces that remotely resembles a practical plan.

On autopilot, I gain my feet and stand up. In the reflection of the cruiser's back window I see his face. Thin blond hair, pale complexion, medium build, medium look. From a distance he could resemble the younger brother of Jerold Rosenfel, but in actuality, he's a guy I could pass a hundred times and never recognize. His bland features melt him into a crowd, one of the faceless passersby.

"Do you remember me?" He asks.

"No. Should I?"

"The basketball court. I stood there and watched you. We even made eye contact. You looked sad."

It comes back to me. The small white guy set apart from the rest of the crowd. I worried that he would be vulnerable if things got ugly. His reflection doesn't bear much resemblance to the face I remember seeing.

"It doesn't matter. We've got surveillance video on you. Chasing after Gwen from Middle Plains."

In the reflection, I see his features go still. The eyebrows, slightly darker than the hair on his head, knit together in frown. "I kill in a fog," is all he says. I have no idea what that means.

His expression clears. "Well, I hope you got my good side. For the record, it's my left. Now, let's make our friendly way to the house."

He steps back, just out of reach so I can't attempt a counter move to disarm or wrestle him to the ground. In the movies bad guys never think of that.

"When we walk in, call out to your partner in a normal way. This is what you will say: 'You still here?' Just like that, no code words, no alarmed tone in your voice. Well, you can use his name if that's your thing. Use only your left hand to open the door."

We descend the stairs to the basement. I'm racking my brain for details on the layout. I know the kitchen is on the other side of the door, but just how close was the table to the door? Could I use it to throw this guy off? What about the angle to the hallway? Is there cover?

I put my left hand on the knob and turn, letting the door swing open. "You still here, Griff?" It's hard to keep my tone normal.

"It's seven hundred square feet, Arch. Where would I go? I've got belts larger than this place." His voice comes from the living room, out of sight from my position.

I don't respond, hoping that my lack of reply tips him off to something strange. There will be a split second when I'm visible in the hallway but the killer won't be. If I can block the sight line just a bit, that might give us a chance. To do what, I'm not sure, but better than nothing.

Sweat beads across my forehead as I enter the short hallway. Griff is still standing in front of the bathroom, staring in at the corpse of Dweldon. He doesn't spare a glance at me. I open my mouth to shout a warning.

The killer kicks me in the back, sending me tumbling forward. In the same motion he fires. The sound comes out as an aggressive bark and I realize that he has a suppressor. It doesn't silence the gun completely, but it does dampen the sound enough.

Griff lets out a grunt and clutches at his

right thigh. He stumbles back, crashing into the futon before falling to the floor. A roar escapes his lips, half surprised, half pained, all confused. "Arch! What the fuc...?"

His mouth clamps shut as he sees the killer.

The blond man steps into the living room, retraining his gun on me before I can get back to my feet. We're alone in a darkened living room, us and the gruesome remains of a street dealer. He reaches in and snags Griff's gun from the belt holster before my partner can react, tucking it into his waistband.

"You said you wouldn't hurt anyone," I growl through clenched teeth. *Think Arch, think.* But my mind still swirls, uncontrolled.

"Actually, I said I wasn't here to hurt *you*. Words are an important facet of human interaction. Take time to ensure you listen and understand what's being said."

"You got blindsided by an English teacher?" Griff says, expression flaring red in pain. He's grabbing his thigh, squeezing his leg. There's no gushing of blood, so the femoral artery didn't get hit. This is one time when my partner's excess fat came in handy.

The killer gives a laugh, a real one. "Oh my, you are funny, Detective Toms. I'd heard that about you. Now, crawl over and tie up your partner. Left wrist to right belt loop." He tosses a riot cuff on the floor in front of Griff. It's not much more than a thicker, longer zip tie.

"Screw that, asshole. I'm not doing anything. You'll have to shoot me."

After a second, the killer gives a shrug. He lifts the gun and aims. "Okay."

He pulls the trigger.

THIRTY ONE

Griff rolls over, grunting in pain, clutching his right thigh now in two places. "Jesus mother Mary...fuck!" He yells through gritted teeth.

"We didn't get off to a good start," the killer states calmly, as if he hasn't just shot an officer of the law. "Blame it on my manners..."

He pauses, eyes growing unfocused for a second. "Ha. Get it? 'My manners'," he waves his arms to encompass the apartment. "Gwen Manners. I didn't even mean to do that."

"Anyway, we didn't do introductions. You won't know me long, but for the time you do, I'm Julien Crux. Don't bother responding since I already know both of you, Aramis White and Griffin Toms. Please accept my apologies for lacking in basic social skills. I don't often interact with other people."

I can't believe what I'm hearing. His tone is the same as if we were at a dinner party. The guy just shot a cop, twice. *Twice.*

"Let's push reset," Crux says, gesturing loosely with his weapon. "Detective Toms, please tie your partner up as instructed. For every refusal, I will be forced to respond 9mm at a time. Trust me, it's not a fun game."

After a moment, I say, "Just do it, Griff. Don't be a hero."

"I know that gun. There are only ten rounds in the clip. He's down to eight." But he crawls over with pained grunts and cuffs my wrist to my belt anyway. Sweat sheets his forehead and blood stains his pant leg in two places. He's huffing by the time he finishes.

"Tighter. And I have nine left. You forgot one in the chamber. Plus, I've relieved you of both your weapons. I'd do the math there, but I'm an English teacher, remember?" He gives a small laugh.

I'm at a loss for anything that resembles coherent thought. This is the most surreal experience of my life. We could be dead already, but it's obvious this Crux guy wants us alive for something. His nonchalant air and casual comments paint the scene off-kilter.

After Griff finishes, he rolls onto his back, breathing heavily. Crux relaxes his stance and crouches down in front of us. "You both know my name, but do you really know who I am?"

Griff throws an arm over his eyes. "Christ, Arch. We've just landed in the middle of an action movie, where the bad guy gives his speech. I need popcorn for this. Wake me when it's over."

The killer looks at me with a puzzled expression. "Is he always like this?"

I skip the answer. "You killed Noah Bell. That's who you are. I told you, we have video. Other than that, we now know your name."

He stares at Griff for a second then shrugs and turns his attention back to me. "And that's all you will ever know. This already has a defined ending and nothing you do will change that. We are bound by a shared goal and until that's done, consider us friends. For the sake of our partnership, please call me Julien. I'm not big on that last name stuff. Too macho for me."

"My friends don't shoot me," Griff spouts. "Well, except for that one guy at the neighborhood block party."

I don't know why he keeps firing off the comments, but I suspect it's a coping mechanism for fear. He has to be afraid. I know I am. Petrified, in fact. Anna's face keeps flashing across my vision. Just yesterday she turned six.

"Where are the rest of you?" I ask.

"Rest?" Julien's face grows confused. "There is no rest. I kill in a fog. What exactly does that video show?"

My heart thuds. "You took out all those kids in the park?" We've been operating on the assumption that there were a group of attackers. The thought that one man eliminated six armed gang bangers escalates the danger potential by many degrees.

This guy is a vanilla wafer with TNT filling.

Instead of pride at such a triumph, Julien's face falls a bit. "Unfortunate, but yes. Not because of the deaths. Let's face it, they were thugs with little productive value to society. But it was not the scenario I had planned and I dislike when plans go awry."

"And what plan is that?"

"If I told you, I'd have to kill you. Literally. Again, we have a shared goal, albeit with different intentions. I have exhausted my sources. Mr. Dweldon in there turned out to have an honorable core. He acknowledged that little miss Gwen came to him but would not divulge her whereabouts. Who would have thought a drug dealer possessed ethics? It's a surprising world. He ended up dying on that honor."

"So you want me to find her for you? Why would I do that?"

"Because we all have something to lose. It's just that you have much more." He looks over to Griff who is now leaning on one elbow, staring at him. Despite the obvious pain, my partner has enough gumption to raise his middle finger to Julien. The killer merely winks back at him.

I decide to take a chance. "Or, maybe I'll just crack wide open your little Covenant scheme with the help of Gwen. Then where will you be? From what I understand of that group, you'll disappear from the face of the earth."

That widens Julien's eyes. "Oh my, you both have been busy. Impressive. I heard you visited North Haven. Hey, can I ask you something?" He leans closer. "Did you read the report about the guy hung from the tree in shackles? What did you think? Pretty good huh? That's a lot harder to do than you think, especially alone. Dead bodies are heavy."

Did he just confess to one of the North Haven murders?

That means there is a direct connection

between Bell and what happened up there. More importantly, it means someone is orchestrating and manipulating events for some undefinable reason. I think about what Killing said regarding the Covenant, about their approach, planning, and care that far exceeded typical white supremacy movements. It looks like he might have been right. It also confirms the fact that Griff and I are in way over our heads. How big is this scheme?

Without pausing, Julien switches topics. "I'm assuming you spoke with the police up there, probably also Rick Killing to get his take. That guy. Now there's a wild card. I told everyone we should just put him down."

"Sounds like no one listened to you," Griff taunts. "You obviously don't have a wife, or you'd know what that's like."

Julien shakes his head, picking at the grip of his weapon. Who knows what's stuck in the cross-cut pattern. "Geoffrey had this grand plan and just had to make it work. He wouldn't entertain the thought that things could turn out differently. Smart guy, brilliant really, but blinded by his own intelligence."

"Not a problem you have," Griff shoots.

"And look where that got him." Julien gives a disgusted sound. "They feed him through a tube in his stomach. Have you ever seen what collects in that thing between feedings? They have to rinse it back into his gut. Gross."

This, coming from a guy who dismembered another man and left his torso in a shower. Who knows what he did with the limbs and head, but if he was responsible for the real Rosenfel's murder - and that now seems completely plausible - I'm guessing arms and legs will start turning up around the area.

I try to conceal my internal emotions. Julien has the jump on us and has been one step ahead the whole time. How could he know we went up to North Haven? Who leaked? From our end, only Gonzales and a couple of the dispatchers knew yesterday. Everyone else tied into this investigation found out at briefing this morning. Could it have been someone from the room? There was plenty of time to make a call after we broke.

Or is it from the other end? Someone from North Haven?

He continues, as if needing to explain himself. "I do want to make one thing clear. I am not a branded member of the Covenant. If you ask me they're all a little nuts deep down, what with their plans for the new millennium and all that. I'm more of what you'd call a death consultant. They hire me to complete a project and I've never failed an assignment. I won't start now."

Julien flips a glance at his watch. "Time is fleeting. I'd love to stay and chat, but we're all on someone's clock. From here, what would be your next step to finding Gwen?"

"Arresting you," Griff spouts. "Charging you as a pedophile and throwing you down in Joliet where you can meet Big Jose whose child suffered molestation. He can serve you his favorite meal: franks and beans. Watch the dessert though. Lots of cream."

Julien shakes his head and steps on Griff's leg, eliciting a groan. "How do you put up with this guy, Arch?"

I need to buy some time, to think. "Why would we help you? Now that we know, you'll kill us after you kill Gwen. You can't just assault cops, confess, and expect to walk away."

"You'd be surprised what I can do. But no, you are not in danger. I'm not allowed to kill officers. It brings too much scrutiny, given my methods." He waves dismissively towards the bathroom. "I was hoping Olivia's manner of passing showed I can be discrete. We'll see."

"Okay, okay. Let up on his leg." To Griff: "Where should we look for Tiller and Hall?"

Julien only presses harder with his foot. Griff's voice is ragged. "Check down in Archer Heights, house on Kedvale avenue. Big green awning on a corner lot."

I look at Julien. "There you go. Check it out and we'll wait here. You can even use our car." Spending a month with Griff has exposed me to his humor and I'm a good student.

Julien laughs. "Well done, detective. I have a better plan though."

He clears his throat and makes sounds like a musician getting ready to sing. He pulls our police radio from where it's clipped to his belt and keys the mike.

"Officer down, officer down! My partner just shot me. White is shooting everyone. Wicker Park, all units respond!" His imitation of Griff's voice is spot-on.

With a smile, Julien stares at me. "That should stir up the hornet's nest. I'll keep company with Detective Smart-ass while you run your race. You have two hours. Call his phone when you have Gwen. Ready, set, go!"

THIRTY TWO

I yank the wheel over and bounce into the parking lot of a hardware store, parking to the far side. I rifle through the glove box, pulling out a map and Leatherman tool. I don't know where Archer Heights is, much less Kedvale Avenue.

The radio squawks over and over from units responding to Julien's fake distress call as I saw through the riot cuff. It's awkward and I slice my finger. In the distance I can hear the sound of converging sirens, all screaming this way.

A first year detective, less than two months into the job, charged with going rogue and shooting his partner. Especially when that young detective sued his way onto the force, making many enemies in the process. Can there be any worse scenario?

I'm not naive. Justice is one thing. Court of public opinion is another. Regardless of how this all turns out, the Heckers of the world have just been handed incredible leverage against me. I pound my hands against the dashboard and allow myself a few moments to rage at the cosmic prank being played on me.

Dammit, dammit, dammit. How can this be happening? I lean my head against the steering wheel and close my eyes, expunging my thoughts of rage and negativity. Julien funneled me into his desired course of action. I'm pinned on all sides and the only way out is through him. Somewhere along that course I will need to flip the tables on him. To do that, I need clarity of focus. I squeeze my eyes shut.

Game face, Arch.

Swiping at the band of sweat on my forehead, I unfold the map. My fingers are trembling as I trace along the roads. I think Archer Heights is somewhere down by Cicero, but it's a small area, meaning small letters. I don't have time to hunt down six-point fonts.

There. Near Midway airport.

I fix the route in my mind and throw the car back into gear. The whoop of police sirens has increased, in proximity, volume, and number. More have joined in the chase.

Thousands of scenarios play across my vision as I gun my way down Western Avenue. I don't know what I'm going to do once I find Gwen. Handing her over to Julien is a death sentence I'm not willing to abide. Nor am I going to let Griff dangle from his twisted fingers one second longer than necessary.

Julien doesn't know about Gwen's face blind condition. He doesn't know that she's unable to identify him. Is there an angle I can play up there?

On the heels of that thought I let out a disgusted sound. What the hell am I thinking? There's no bargaining with a killer. I don't believe his words about killing cops. He wants to clean up his trail, that much is clear from his obsession at finding Gwen. Anyone who has crossed his path is also collateral he cannot afford, especially two law officers. Once he has us three together, we'll be his victims.

I can't go to my district. There are very few friends waiting me there. Even if someone was willing to break ranks and side with me, due process for sorting out my story would suck up time. There would be interviews with Internal Affairs, hearings on my action, testimony from others involved in the events. All the while I'd be held until they came to a determination or cleared me of the shooting. By the time they find Griff, he'd be a corpse. Of that I have no doubt.

I need a wild card, someone outside the law structure who will ally with me.

Problem is, I don't really know anyone else. Sheila, Griff, the caregivers at Anna's residence...meeting new people hasn't been high on my priority list since moving up here. I am on my own.

The light at Cermak flips to red and I pull to a stop, the lead car in a group of five. I debate running my own lights, but that would draw too much attention. Someone might notice I'm heading in the other direction from the rest of the squad cars and take note. Better to stay low profile.

My phone buzzes at my hip, it's done that a dozen times in the last fifteen minutes. I ignore it, as I did each other time. No doubt it's someone from my own district trying to reach out; perhaps they are even treating me under a hostage scenario and want to begin the rapport-building process.

I open the map back up and scan the streets again, trying to get a sense where I should turn onto Kedvale. I want to start at one end and work my way along it, rather than going back and forth.

So engrossed am I in the grid work of Chicago suburbia that I don't notice the squad car until it's too late.

It's one from District 11, running with lights but no siren. I fail to see him until he turns left directly in front of me. Our eyes meet through the open window as he passes and the shock is plain on his face. My own probably looks the same.

Without a second thought, I gun the accelerator, narrowly missing the rear end of a delivery van crossing the intersection. The roar of the sedan's V-8 rolls through my window and I hear the call-out on the radio. I've met that particular officer and remember seeing him around the station. Unfortunately, he also remembers me.

In my rear view mirror I see him pull a smoking U-turn. His sirens blare to life. Cars try to move out of his way, but the alarm caused by his sudden actions makes their panicked reactions worse. More than one driver tries to get out of his way, misinterpreting his direction, and turns into his path. They effectively block him. I hear his horn, long and frustrated.

It won't last. He just has to reverse to swing around the cluster of cars. I've only got minutes.

I have to shake this guy before he can identify my intended direction. We're close enough to the Odgen Avenue station that all remaining cars will flood the streets in pursuit. If they pull in air support, I'm screwed.

Over the radio I hear Hecker's voice yelling instructions to other units. He's taking a personal stake in this, throwing his badge into the mix. Guys at his level don't usually get involved in pursuits.

Guess I've got a new classification now: Suspect.

The cruiser tires squeal in protest as I take a hard right without slowing. There's a Firestone garage just ahead and I sling the car behind the building, to the area where other vehicles are staged for service work. I'm familiar with these places since my car is junk and in the shop far too often. A spark ignites in my brain.

I run through the back repair bays with my tin in plain sight, clutching the map and radio. Mechanics look at me with dumbfounded expressions. They have no idea what to do or say. The training they receive to change oil or replace brakes doesn't cover this type of situation.

"Police emergency!" I yell as I push into the front desk area, shoving my shield towards the first shirt logo I see. As I say that, the pursuing cop roars past the shop, lights and siren blasting. I point at the departing car through the plate glass window, as if it's proof of my statement. "I need a car!"

The two customers sitting in the lobby stare at me with expressions identical to the mechanics. No one says anything.

Without waiting, I snatch a set of keys off the counter. This place handles their orders like many others I've seen: The keys sit on top of an invoice, waiting for the car's owner to come back and pay.

Running out the front door, I glance at the key ring. The blue and white checker design tells me I picked a BMW.

There's only in the lot, parked off to the side where all the other finished service jobs sit. It's a mid-90s 5-series, deep blue in color, freshly washed. I get in and discover that it's a six speed. The engine roars with aftermarket pipes and a V-8 bass.

I leave a cloud of smoke from the rear tires as I re-merge onto Western and continue south.

I've bought myself a few minutes, so I need to use them wisely. No doubt the garage is even now calling 911 to report my actions. They have to in order to justify losing a customer car. I need to be long gone from this area before dispatch has a make, model and plate to broadcast.

I jam the shifter into third and the German horse leaps forward. Its acceleration puts the cruiser to shame and the exhaust bangs off the nearby buildings. No sneaking up on anyone in this beast. I should have taken a Toyota.

Weaving in and out of traffic, I work the pedals like a man desperate, which is the most accurate description of me right now. Several times the lowered suspension bottoms out with loud clunks. Horns blaring at my sudden moves become a constant sound and the smell of burnt rubber filters through the open window.

It takes me another fifteen minutes of navigating the side roads to reach Archer Avenue and follow it to Kedvale. Less than three blocks south on Kedvale I see a small brick house with a bright green awning sitting on a corner lot.

I pass it and pull over to the curb halfway down the block.

One deep breath to center myself. I'm without my weapon, walking into a house of known drug runners. All I have is my badge and my authority.

Time to rock, Arch. I shove open the car door and run towards the house.

THIRTY THREE

The block is quiet. Many of the houses are well-kept. Some have toys littering the yard, others feature American flags proudly displayed on poles poking skyward. This is an area of working people. They leave in the morning and return at night, expecting things to remain the same.

I hope my arrival isn't a rock dropped into a small pond, rippling outward with change.

The yard is small and in need of a mowing. It has the aura of a place abandoned. A path has been worn through the yard from the side street, which means there's regular foot traffic. Instead of abandoned, I revise my impression to that of a house neglected. Cars are stacked along the curb and I wonder if they represent owners inside the house. If so, that's a lot of people.

Time to square up.

There's no time for due process. Those formalities evaporated the second Julien keyed Griff's radio. I give the front door one rap with a knuckle and twist the knob, not waiting for any response. Hopefully no one's on the other side holding a weapon.

The living room is trashed. No furniture other than a couple of folding chairs. Beer cans and Styrofoam food containers are strewn about, and the burnt smell of marijuana fills the air. From the basement I hear the muffled thump of music. I follow the sound through the kitchen to the rear stairs and start down, badge held out like a chip of armor.

"Chicago police," I say, but the music is so loud that anyone down there could not hear me.

Carpet remnants have been thrown down on the concrete floor at the bottom of the stairs. In the far corner a makeshift bar has been set up. Bottles, ashtrays, and cans litter the top. The place stinks of stale beer. No one is in this area.

I circle around the stairs to the other half of the basement. At some point in the past someone started to finish it off into living space. A wall has been stood up, drywall unfinished and faded. Instead of a proper door, the opening is covered with a yellowed sheet. On the other side is the source of music.

Taking one deep breath, I hold it to center myself then yank the sheet to one side.

Two mattresses occupy the center of the ad-hoc room. A dozen black men encircle them, all unclothed to some degree. No one notices me; their attention is focused on the mattresses. Between the sweating bodies I get a glimpse of what's going on.

I've found Gwen.

She's naked, flat on her back. A young black guy is on top of her, thrusting with loud grunts. Another kneels near her head, forcing himself into her mouth. A third fondles her breasts.

Gwen's eyes are closed, her body limp. This is not the reaction of a girl participating, she's drugged out of her mind and these guys are running a train. Heat flushes through my veins, anger erupting in a kick to the stereo equipment on a card table next to the wall opening. The crash is loud and the music winks off as the cord yanks from the outlet.

Stand up for yourself, stand up for someone else.

Everyone whips around at this intrusion.

Several try to cover themselves, but others stand there fully revealed and aggressive. They're the ones I need to mind.

"The fuck is you?" The lead dog demands, a guy around my age, built like a powerlifter. His belly protrudes but everything is thick on him. He's got his dick in his right hand and doesn't let go as he steps forward.

I jab my badge out for all to see. "Chicago PD. I'm here for her."

"Don't give a fuck 'bout no tin man. Po po. Mother fucking five-oh." He rattles off a host of derogatory slang names for police. I've never heard half of them.

The kid on top of Gwen lifts himself off and stands up. Her knees flop to one side, head rolling away.

I'm not engaging in a debate here. The quickest way out is through them. "Deandre Hall, Jimmy Tiller. Are they here?"

The powerlifter glances over his shoulder then back at me. A skinny kid with shiny diamonds in his ears and cornrows is the target of his look.

"So what if they are?"

"Then they're dead men walking. Dweldon already is."

At that voices erupt, shouting, at me, at each other. The powerlifter lets go of his member. "You better come clean, law dog. Dweldon be my homeboy."

I look over to the skinny kid. "You Deandre?"

He looks away for a brief moment, avoiding my eyes. "Yeah, man."

"Then you have an idea what's going on. Why did Dweldon have you take Gwen?"

He shrugs. "She called him in a panic. Something about trouble. Something about the shootings over in Cicero the other night."

"That's right. She came to you guys for help, for protection. And this is what you do." I flap a hand towards her and shake my head with disgust. "Now you're the ones who need protection. We found Dweldon this morning. Whoever did him is coming for her. Trust me, you don't want to be around."

Deandre's eyes go wide. "What happened? Where is he?"

"Part of him is in Wicker Park. I don't know where the rest is."

This silences the group. Shock and awe. These guys have been around death, of that I have no doubt, but their world is dash and grab, shoot and run, drive by and fire. It's held at arm's length, targets through the sites. There's very little up close and personal. Methodical dismemberment is not on the menu, most don't have the stomach for it.

Gwen makes a muffled sound and throws an arm over her eyes. It sounds like she's crying.

"Now, I'm going to take her." I move forward. "She's under police protection."

No one responds, not until powerlifter grunts. "Fuck that. We ain't done with her. No crackhead killer gonna scare us off. He steps foot in here, we'll mow him down like the bitch he is."

He's shorter than me by several inches, but also heavier. I'm lean to his bulk. I've seen this guy before. Maybe he had a different name, different place, but the personality is the same. He's fronting for his boys, throwing up attitude to show them he's the Alpha. The badge didn't buy me a pass, only a few moments of grace.

I don't have time for this.

Taking one step forward, I slip his compact job and thrown an elbow into his face. Never use your fists, not if you want to hold anything afterwards. The knuckles will swell and stiffen quickly. Elbows are better, they smash with intent and are harder to defend. You can disguise an elbow strike. Most guys react like it's a punch, moving their head away from the fist, and that leaves them in good position for the elbow to follow through.

His nose cracks with a thick, wet sound, dropping him to the concrete floor. He rolls over, holding his face. The worst thing about breaking noses isn't the pain, it's the eyes. They water up so much, you can't see.

No one says anything else as they stand aside. Either my skill impressed them or - more likely - they're processing the fact of Dweldon's death. Gang bangers are human too, susceptible to dismay at the loss of a friend.

Gwen's eyes flutter open when I kneel down and call her name. They are glazed and unfocused, but she tries to hone in on me. I take off my jacket and cover her up as she gains her feet. Her balance is shot and I need to steady her.

She stares up at me as I help her across the room, a creature entirely dependent on the compassion of others. She's in the wrong place for that. Rage re-ignites in me and I kick the powerlifter in the kidney as we pass. "I ever come across you again, it will be years before you see sunlight."

I look over my shoulder, including everyone in my warning. Only Deandre nods, eyes red, face blank.

Together, we exit the basement.

THIRTY FOUR

"Gwen, my name is Detective White." I look down at her as we emerge onto the main floor of the house. I'm half carrying her.

She keeps staring at me, the gaze of an infant exploring a face, trying to imprint the features for the first time. Her eye makeup is smeared across her cheeks, her black hair mussed and tangled.

"Do you know why I'm here? Can you understand me?"

"I'm high, not stupid." Her words are slurred, the tone small and defeated.

"Then you know why I've come for you."

She nods and mumbles something, leaning heavily into me.

"Why didn't you come to the police for help? Why Dweldon?"

"Only cops I know don't help. Worse than criminals," she replies softly, rubbing at her eyes. "Don't count on them."

The words are choppy, barely understandable through her haze, but I hear the sentiment. I came across the same attitude far too often as a beat cop and tried my best to overcome it. Sometimes I won, sometimes I lost. Maybe it speaks to my naiveté, but I always wanted to know I made a positive impact on someone's life.

Maybe that someone has finally crossed my path.

I stabilize her so she can stand. The coat slips off one shoulder, exposing her nudity. I tug it back up.

"We need to get you away. Those guys down there are pulling on their clothes and figuring out what to do. I don't want to be here when a plan comes together."

"Me either," she slurs. "I'm sore."

I open the front door onto the porch and peek out. Down the street sits a police cruiser, full light rack swirling red and blue in the midday sun, silent but colorful. It's parked alongside the BMW and I can see a cop bent over the windshield, peering at the VIN plate.

How did they find me so fast?

I move Gwen towards the railing and

place her hands on it so she can stand. "Wait until I call for you." Her head is tilted down, hair covering her face and I don't know if she heard me.

Without pausing for an answer, I leap off the porch and sprint up the sidewalk. The cop is Danny Rollins, I can see his shock of red hair. He is so intent on reading off the 17-digit Vehicle Identification Number into his radio that he doesn't notice me until it's too late. When he does, his reaction is delayed.

I vault onto the trunk of his squad, using that to launch myself at him. I catch him flush as he backpedals and we tumble into a front yard stuffed to the brim with flower beds, rock beds and ornamentation. It's really overdone.

He strikes a small concrete statue of a boy looking like he's peeing. Water flows from his pretend penis into a shallow birdbath. A loud grunt of pain explodes from Rollins' mouth on impact, followed by an unintelligible curse.

"Sorry, Danny," I say as I club him in the back of the head. "I owe you."

His radio flies across the grass as he goes limp. I snap his cuffs around his wrists, looping them around the base of the birdbath, then throw the key away. It lands in a flowerbed near the house.

"Come on," I holler to Gwen. She's already

moving towards me, with the gait of someone trading the enemy you know for one you don't. And also someone high out of their gourd. Her feet are light and hesitant on the pavement, her movements uncoordinated, her path wandering. "Hurry!"

I usher her into the squad. Rounding the front of it to the driver's side, I catch a glimpse of the rear passenger window on the BMW. A Lo-Jack sticker is plastered in one corner. That's how Rollins found me. God bless technology. I bet when he woke this morning, he never imagined that he'd be attacked by one of his own, knocked unconscious, strapped with his own cuffs in a yard full of begonias, daffodils and lawn ornaments.

At least the little statue boy isn't peeing on him.

We peel away in a cloud of tire smoke. In the rear view I see neighbors emerging from their houses, disturbed by the sound. Several stand in the street, watching our departure. One moves to help Rollins.

I don't have much time. The disruption of his transmission won't trigger immediate alarm. Radio chatter is often sporadic. But once the first 911 call comes in, all available units will be on their way. I've got to get out of their line of intercept.

Flipping off the light rack, I look over to Gwen. She stares at me with wide eyes. The adrenaline is starting to burn through her high, I think. There's not a lot of clarity in her gaze, but I can see thoughts clicking into place.

"You just attacked another cop," is all she says.

"I've had better days."

I spin the wheel and head down a side block, getting out of view of any bystanders so they can't pinpoint a direction to responding officers. "Gwen, I have to ask you some questions. We don't have a lot of time and these are incredibly important, so focus on me please. Try to hold it together and think. Can you do that?"

She nods, eyes still fixed on my face. It's unnerving how she stares. Her light-colored eyes bore into me like she's looking past my features and seeking something else.

"Did you witness a homicide the other night at Middle Plains Plastics?"

Gwen sighs and runs her hands through her hair, attempting to untangle it. The move causes the jacket to slip off again. She makes no move to recover it. "Yes. One man was shot. The other strangled."

I keep my eyes averted from her naked breasts. So the bodyguard did die there, shot

357

by Julien. That meant he hauled the guy to the basketball court and staged the scene. I don't know whether to be impressed at his determination, or dismayed at his level of tactical thinking.

"Do you know who the strangled man was?"

"Noah Bell."

"Could you identify the killer if we placed him before you?"

She shakes her head. "No, I'm not good with faces. I mean, really not good."

"I know about your condition, about the face blindness. I'm not going to pretend I understand anything about it, but just how bad is it? Can you recognize anyone?"

"I can't even tell you what my mom or dad looks like. They moved away years ago and when I look at their picture, I'm looking at two strangers." She sniffs and I realize she's crying.

God, that has to be horrible. I wonder if that's what Anna sees deep down: A man she doesn't recognize but who comes around often. Does she think about who I am? Does she wonder why I keep coming around? My mind leaps to a thousand instances of moments spent with my daughter, a silent photo reel playing before my eyes.

Focus, Arch, focus.

"How did you know I wasn't the killer then?"

"You're tall. And black. I'm not overall blind." She gives a hacking cough and wipes her mouth with my jacket sleeve. "I can still tell people apart by their hair, height, the way they walk. I look at eyes and listen to voices mostly."

"Then how did you know it was Noah Bell that night?"

"I didn't. Dweldon told me."

The rock that's been sitting in my gut since Wicker Park grows. I've been chasing a witness with no real value, on behalf of a killer who doesn't realize it. Her testimony will be useless and without that, I can't tie Julien to Bell. Unless he left DNA all over the scene. If that's the case, I can hope for forensics matches in the CODIS database. But that will take weeks, maybe months.

I have one hour left.

THIRTY FIVE

My cell phone display shows dozens of calls over the last hour, with nearly that many voice mails.

Sheila's number appears multiple times. So do a handful of local numbers I don't recognize, but I'm guessing are from the precinct. There's nothing from Griff's phone, which I can take to be good news, or the worst news. I choose to be positive.

I play all the messages as we wind through the streets from Archer Heights in the general direction of Wicker Park. There's no plan and I need to think, to devise one. Gwen's gaze is stuck to me and I can't let her know what I'm thinking, not yet.

One after another, the theme of the messages is the same: *What the hell are you doing?*

Two of the local numbers belong to Gonzales, both his personal cell and office phone. He's left me six messages, the tone shifting across the spectrum from asking to call him, to demands for my immediate surrender. He's been my biggest, most fair, supporter since I joined the force, aside from Noah Bell. If ever I needed his backing, it's now.

He answers before the first ring finishes and skips the greeting. "White?! What is going on? Where's Toms? Get yourself to the station now."

"Can't do that, sir. Not yet. That 'officer down' call from Griff was fake. He was still alive when I left him, although he took two rounds to the thigh."

"What do you mean 'left'? Left where? Who shot him?"

I take a beat, arranging my thoughts. I'm only going to get one chance to set this table in a way that can be explained once the hounds have cornered me. "This is about the Bell murder. Forget the basketball court. Forget about escaped gang bangers on the loose. That scene was a setup. It's a single killer, an assassin, the one from the tape. He put out the fake distress call. He has Griff even as we speak. I have to bring him the witness for a trade."

At that, Gwen's eyes go wide and she opens her mouth to say something. I forestall her with a hand and a shake of my head. One finger goes up in the universal signal for 'Hang on and I'll explain'.

"This is not Hollywood, detective. You are not some rogue cop righting the day. If it's truly a hostage situation, it needs to be handled by the right team. Come in so we can pull together the rescue and negotiation team. We'll apprehend this suspect together." Gonzales' voice is calming, measured. I'm being handled. Whether he believes my story or not is immaterial, he's proceeding by the book.

He's treating me as a potential suspect.

If I follow his directive, there will be hours of debrief, meetings, fact gathering, assembling a task force...Griff will be long dead before anyone is through their second cup of coffee.

"Can't do that. This guy is not kidding around, I've seen the evidence of his intent. He may be working with some very powerful people in this city and has had the drop on us from square one. If he thinks I'm pulling an end around, Griff's life is forfeit. He has a radio, so watch transmissions."

There's silence on the other end. He's

muted me and is probably talking to others in the room with him. They could be pulling a trace as we speak, although I know those aren't instantaneous.

He comes back on the line. "I have reports that you attacked Officer Rollins." And there's the 911 call I expected. It took less than ten minutes. That means they can still triangulate on my location, using distance, speed and directional vectors. I'm going to need someplace to stash this car.

"Yes, sir. I needed his car." That will tell them what patrol unit to look for, if they didn't already know. No sense holding back that information; it doesn't buy me much.

"These are serious charges you're incurring, White. Career impacting decisions. Think about what you're doing. Think about everything you went through to get here. Do you really want to throw it all away?"

I glance over at Gwen. She's staring out the front window, a thousand yard stare. Dried tears on her cheeks. I have no idea what she's thinking, just that she's petrified. She ran from a killer, into the arms of a drug dealer who lent her out to his train-running crew, only to be rescued by a rogue cop talking about hostage barter.

Reaching over, I pull back up the jacket

and squeeze her shoulder, trying to reaffirm. This is what it all boils down to.

When today ends, I may not have a job. I may not have a future in law enforcement, no matter how Griff's testimony shakes out. I may not even have freedom, staring at my immediate future through the bars of a jail cell. Due process and government policy doesn't abide personal extremity. The hearing officers won't care that I tried to save both Griff and Gwen, while apprehending Julien. They will hear that I assaulted officers, that I broke nearly every damn code of conduct in the handbook while rampaging through the suburbs. My intensity towards resolving the death of Noah Bell will pale against the infractions on written policy statements.

My primary goal in life is to find safe haven for Anna, a place where she can receive the best care affordable to Sheila and me. Now I stand at the precipice of tossing it all away over a lost girl and a partner just months from retirement.

My will wavers. Maybe I should give Gwen over to the force, let someone more experienced take over, throw myself on the mercy of process. Maybe I'm not so far down the rabbit hole that I can salvage something yet. The thought is tempting.

When I was a teenage boy working a minimum wage job, I once heard my boss say: *Managers do things right, but leaders do the right thing*. At the time it was a stupid saying with no context.

Then, as I stayed longer, it surfaced itself in my boss, in the way he ran his life. It didn't matter that he was a low-paid supervisor in a bottom feeder business. He carried himself above the fray and weighed decisions against that mantra. I can do no less.

Turning Gwen over is what I should do. But what then?

Julien will kill Griff. Of that I have no doubt, and it will be a gruesome end, not a simple round to the temple. We may never find his remains. The assassin will fade back into the woodwork. Bell's murder will go unsolved. At some point, Gwen will be cast back out into the wild when she no longer has use. If this Julien guy is half what I suspect he is, he'll be waiting. Waiting to tie up a loose end even if it no longer matters to anyone except him.

I have to do the right thing. I'd like to think Anna, if she could comprehend my actions within the prison of her mind, would approve.

I'd like to think my daughter would be proud of me. Proud of her father.

"White...Arch," Gonzales continues. He's going off script, no longer sounding like he's handling me but speaking man to man. Or it could be a subtle tactic. "Let the Chicago PD help you. We have experienced officers who can help find the witness, who can..."

"I have her already."

More silence. Then: "You have Gwen Manners? She can confirm that Noah Bell was murdered by a single man and not a gang mugging gone wrong?" There's weight to his words, subtext that's escaping me.

"I do. Not only that, but the reasons behind the murder - the assassination, if we're to speak plainly - are part of something far bigger than all of us. It includes people far bigger than all of us, like Travian big and the Covenant Church of the New Millennium. North Haven was not isolated, sir."

"Then what was it?"

"The beginning."

THIRTY SIX

Julien stares at Detective Griffin Toms. The old man is sweating, grunting each time he shifts his weight. His face is pale from pain and blood oozes out through the holes in his trouser material. It's dark and quiet in the living room of Gwendolyn Manner's apartment, and cool.

"This heat is really something, isn't it?" Julien remarks in a conversational tone. "I don't understand weather."

"Fuck off," the detective responds. "Wait until we bring the heat to you, then you will understand, peckerhead."

Julien smiles. "There's no need for us to be confrontational. This is little more than a transaction between seller and buyer. The currency is your life. You like your life, right?

Be a shame to lose it over something silly like a little lost waif who just happened to see something she shouldn't have."

"Still, fuck off."

"Griff, can I call you that?" Without waiting for a response, Julien continues. "You amuse me. Where did you get such a great sense of humor? I'd think this job, the life of a cop in a crappy place like Cicero, would make you cynical and angry. I get irritated just with slow drivers, I can't imagine having to deal with the stuff you do."

"What can I say? Guys like you come along to brighten my day and suddenly everything is better." He shifts again on the floor, placing his back up against the wall outside of the bathroom. Over his shoulder the drying blood of Dweldon D stains the shower walls brown. "Can I sit on the couch at least? My fat ass isn't meant for this. I might be denting the floor."

At that moment, the detective's phone rings. It buzzes against the surface of the tiny coffee table. Julien reaches for it while shaking his head. "You can stay right there. I have a feeling we'll be moving soon."

The phone screen shows detective White's name, so he snaps it open and answers. "Dunkin' Donuts." He winks to detective Toms.

A pause. "I have her, Julien. Let's do this." In the background there's the rush of air and cars streaming by. It's obvious he's calling from a moving vehicle.

"For the record, detective, I realize you will try to thwart me. You won't simply hand over an innocent girl to me, knowing my goal. Understand that I cannot allow that to happen, so whatever you want to try, don't. Otherwise everyone will end up dead. And you're such a good-looking young man with a bright future. It would be shameful to piss that away."

"Whatever. I need to get out of the city. There's too much heat down here thanks to you. I'm heading for a place up in the northwest suburbs called Rollins Savanna. It's isolated. We can do the exchange there."

"Interesting choice. Why there?"

"Because then I can shoot you through the eyeball and leave your carcass to rot. Less paperwork for me."

Julien smiles. "Not bad, but you still need practice to be as witty as your partner. I know Rollins. What part of it?"

"There's a little park off End Run road. Couple of tennis courts, basketball court. Meet there at one-thirty."

"That's a long way from now."

"Like I said, there's a lot of heat down here

for me. I have to stay away from major roads, so it will take me longer."

"Or you could be lining up some kind of ambush, pulling in your district to capture me."

"Well, if every cop in the city wasn't hunting for me, I might be able to do that. But you obviously don't understand police procedure. I'm wanted for questioning right now. No one knows what's going on, only that my partner relayed a distress call and has disappeared. Whether they believe or understand what's going on, they need to debrief me and detail out the response. That all takes time. If I go to my captain for help, it will be November before anyone is satisfied with my explanation of events. By then Griff will have eaten his own arm."

Julien stays silent, assessing the weight of the detective's words. That does give him time to get there, scout and set up. He decides the risk is minimal.

"One-thirty it is. Keep it straight or you're going to have to drag your partner home in a bag. I don't think you want that, the guy must weigh three hundred pounds."

A click is all that Julien receives in reply. He looks over at the wounded detective. "Your partner needs a lesson in manners."

"Well, I taught him how to wash his hands after pissing. Anything else is up to you."

Julien gives a laugh as he pulls his own phone out and scrolls to the contacts log. "I'm going to regret killing you, Griff. I'd like to grab a beer one day and just talk. You seem like a great guy to hang out with."

"You are nuts."

Julien calls his client. "In control," he says when the call is picked up. "The detective has our witness and will do the exchange."

"When and where?"

Julien recites the information as he spins Griff's phone in circles on the coffee table.

"You don't truly believe this detective will just hand over the girl, do you? That's naive."

"No, I think he will try to play the hero. He's backed into a corner and the only way out is through me. If he can arrest me, bring me in and have the girl testify, he probably thinks that will clear his name and resolve the case, all in one."

"It would."

"Well...yes, maybe. But Bell will still be dead. His efforts will be washed away, his name relegated to an honor roll somewhere."

The client growls in frustration. "That's not the point. This was never about stopping Bell from doing his work. We didn't care about that. There's a larger play here, one that you don't see, but it needs Bell to have died in service to his cause. The public needs to think he fell victim to his own niggers, that these people eat their own."

"Well, what about the detectives? I can't just let them waltz away. They've seen me."

"Do not kill them. Leave it to us, we will handle them. If both investigating officers turn up dead, that will overtake the message sent with Bell's death. The news will revolve around their murders and bring a different focus to the case. We don't want that."

"Can I just make them disappear?"

"Crux, knock it off. You are not to kill them, scatter their body parts, make them disappear or do anything else that will draw attention. That is not negotiable." The client sounds like a parent talking to a child. Julien bristles over the tone, but says nothing. He may be a killer with no compunction about ending lives, but even he knows not to cross the Covenant. They brook little interference with their plans and could make him disappear just as fast as the detectives.

"Tell me about the exchange spot," the client demands. "I know it a little but haven't been up there lately. What are the sight lines?"

"Open prairie, tall grasses, trees here and

there in groups. The picnic area is surrounded by field and has a couple of tennis courts. There's only one way in and out."

"No houses or buildings nearby?"

"Clear."

"Good. I want you to scout and make sure there are no patrols lurking in the area. I will try and secure reinforcements for you, but it will be tight. There may not be enough time to react. If I do get some, I will let you know."

"Okay, but I don't need them. I can handle this." Julien resents the idea that his client thinks he requires help. It's just two local detectives, one with a foot out the retirement door and the other in over his head on his first case.

"Understood. Now you understand something: We plan for contingencies, we backup the backups and we leave nothing to chance. That is how we will succeed."

When Julien doesn't respond, the client repeats himself. "Confirm you understand."

"Yes, yes. I understand."

"Good. Take this meet and act accordingly. We will overcome."

Julien clicks shut his phone and looks over at Griff. "I have to be honest, Detective Toms. I don't like how this is playing out. They won't let me just kill everyone. That's sloppy."

"I can completely feel your anguish. What are they thinking?"

"Well," Julien says with a smile. "At least we will always have this time, won't we?"

THIRTY SEVEN

Gwen stares out the windshield, watching cars pass the other way but not seeing anything other than her mental turmoil. The detective's voice drifts in and out of her mind, a distant sound that sends promise of a coming storm.

Dweldon held up his end of the bargain. After he, Jimmy and Deandre took turns with her, he drove them all to Deandre's place.

Once there, he departed quickly and Deandre disappeared to the back of the house, saying he needed to make some phone calls. Jimmy remained, eyes fixed on her like a hawk's. His pale skin and tattoos were the marks of recognition for her. She noticed that he had braided his dirty blond hair into cornrows since the last time she'd seen him.

He sparked up a bowl and offered it with a smile. But it was not the smile of a friend. There was little conversation between them, no words necessary or sufficient. They both knew what would happen to her. His eyes glittered with excitement, her eyes dulled to a disinterested gaze.

When he stood up and walked over to her, Gwen realized there was something more to this bowl than usual. He'd spiked it. Ketamine maybe. Her world spun in circles, narrowing down to a far distant point, the Special K working its magic.

As her mind detached, Jimmy dropped his pants and pushed roughly into her mouth, gagging her. His guttural laugh promised more of what she'd already endured at the *Hangout*. She complied, allowing him to thrust with abandon, trying to keep from choking. Her grip on reality disconnected, taking her away until the detective's entrance brought her back.

***

She slides a glance towards the detective. He's speaking into his cell phone with determined tones. His nose is strong and straight, his skin dark mocha. He seems young but talks like a man much older. Somewhere he picked up a burden that aged him, and she wonders what it could be.

Gwen feels nerves rattle in her spine. He's going to want her to identify the man who killed Noah Bell and she won't be able to do it. If that killer is lined up against a wall with several others, she will not be able to pick him out, especially if the others resemble him in height, coloring or build. Maybe they could stand him up with a bunch of blacks or Mexicans to help her out.

The wind blowing through her open window tugs the detective's jacket off her shoulders once again. She looks down at her exposed breasts and stomach, with a sense of detachment. They could be the body parts of someone else. She's known so much disconnection with other people, it extends to her own body.

Somewhere along the way she just stopped caring.

Bruises trace up her hips to her rib cage. Gwen thinks they are the result of being hit by a car, but it could also be from the boys back at the house. A few of them were pretty rough. They liked to debase her, make her gag, call her dirty whore, choke her. It gave them a power trip. She endures scenes like that because they get her high beforehand and she doesn't have to pay for it. She pays in other ways.

The truth was, they didn't need to get her high. Gwen would do it anyway. It's the only time she can feel connected to another human. If it has to be a group of boys having their way with her, it's still better than being alone all the time. The pain of their abuse is the price of her affliction.

"The beginning," the detective says and snaps his phone shut.

He stays silent for a bit, steering the stolen police car through the grid of streets. They take a number of turns, heading in a general northwest direction.

"Gwen," he says eventually and reaches over to tug the jacket back up. It's the second time he's had to do that. Both times she thought he was going to feel her up, take her someplace quiet and have his way with her. It's what she expects and she's willing to let him do what he wants if it keeps her safe. She doesn't move as he covers her. Maybe he doesn't want her.

"Gwen," he repeats. She turns her eyes to him. "I have to bring this thing to closure. It's more than the death of Noah Bell. Can you understand that?"

His eyes are brown, intense, piercing her.

She takes them in, knowing the next time they cross gazes, his eyes will look different to her. Now they are direct and forceful. Next time, who knows?

"No," she responds. "I don't understand. I've already told you I can't help. I won't recognize the man."

"I don't need you to. The sequence of events will be important to know, but I may not need you to pick out the guy for me. It may not come down to that. I just need him to think you can."

"You said he has your partner."

The cop nods, frowning deeply. "He does. He'll kill him."

"Like he killed Dweldon?" At the name of her dealer, Gwen feels a slight twinge. She had no friends, but if she were to count the people who knew her, Dweldon would have been in that friend category. She wonders who will be her source now.

"Not if I can help it. But I need you for this."

She turns and looks at him again, searching the eyes of a stranger for some kind of reassurance. "I get it. What are you going to do with me?" Her voice tremors and she doesn't try to hide it. She is scared.

"There's no one in my precinct who can -

or will - help. They have their orders. So that leaves me down to very few options, but I think I know someone who can." He pauses and returns her stare. "This is my promise, Gwen. I will not let anyone hurt you, I'll die before that happens."

She nods numbly. These are words she's heard many times, in different forms, different sentences, from different people, but the sentiment is always the same.

And it's always a lie.

The detective pulls out a business card from his pocket and starts dialing a number in his phone. "I have to make a couple calls and then I need to talk about your grandmother."

THIRTY EIGHT

I pull the cruiser over to the curb on Harrison Street, several miles north of Cicero, in a small area called Forest Park. The Eisenhower Expressway sits a couple blocks away, heard but not seen through the trees standing tall.

There's a Park District complex on the north side of Harrison: gated entrance, baseball diamonds, fenced soccer field, basketball courts, even an ice rink for hockey when the weather turns cold. In contrast to the park by Middle Plains, this place is a country club.

The south side of Harrison is lined with houses, two-flats, small commercial buildings with upper floor rentals. Everything is neat and tidy, the curbs bright yellow, the street signs unmolested. It's a nice area.

My attention is on the apartment building one block west of our spot. It's small, only ten units, but well kept.

"Where are we?" Gwen asks, looking around.

"We need to hide out and get you cleaned up, plus I need some time yet to get things squared away. I've got a plan, now I just have to make sure we are clear on the details."

"We? You and me?"

"No, someone else."

Gwen drops it. She'd heard my phone calls, heard me talking and planning. She shifts topics. "Are you taking me to your place?"

"No, this isn't mine. We can't go to my place. It's too easy to find me there."

She lets out a sigh, as if she knows what's coming but is resigned to it anyway. In that sigh is the surrender of will. I don't have any more words to reassure her.

There's no sign of police surveillance, not that I expected any. There are no links from me to the apartment. The parking lot is half full, most tenants out at work. I pull the squad into the lot and park it under a tree in the far corner. It's not visible from the street, blocked by other cars. The tree's foliage will prevent air patrols from spotting it. Thankfully Chicago PD doesn't use tracking technology like the Lo-

Jack on the BMW.

The radio chatter has dropped back to normal levels. I'm not fooled. They know I have access to a radio in the car and switched to another channel. I could probably figure out which one, but don't have the time. Plus I don't know how much that would truly help me. In thirty minutes I'll be out of this area and beyond their cordon.

"Come on," I say and exit. We cross the lot towards the back entrance, a tall black guy in a dress shirt and tie, and a tiny waif of a white girl, wearing his jacket and nothing else. We make for an easy memory should anyone see us, but there's little I can do about it.

We take the back stairs to the second floor. This side of the building overlooks Janura Park to the south. It's little more than an open acre with tended lawn and a couple of benches along a walking path. Chicago is really into parks. The cluster of tall oak trees around the park perimeter provide some measure of cover from cars rolling along the cross streets.

I punch in the code to enter the building and lead Gwen down the hallway. Sheila keeps a spare key on top of a light fixture over her door, not the most original location. She needs to drag over the Ficus plant sitting in the corner so she can stand on the rim and fetch the key. On my toes, I can just catch it with my fingertips.

The inside of the one bedroom apartment is quiet. Except for an under-cabinet radio tuned to a local AM news station. Sheila always has to have some kind of noise playing, whether music, TV or radio. The place is sparse of decoration, she's never been the type to hang pictures, flip through home decor magazines or worry about the furniture matching. Everything is in its place though. That is one thing she's adamant about. Right down to the different size forks. If I ever put salad forks in the same tray with regular ones, she'll rearrange them.

I glance at my watch. Just under an hour before the meet with Julien.

"Alright Gwen, we have some time."

She gives another sigh, avoiding my eyes, and walks closer. The coat slips off her shoulders as she gets down on her knees, head tilted back, mouth open.

I take a step back. "What the hell are you doing?"

"Isn't this what you brought me her for?" There's a look of confusion on her face. "I thought that's what you wanted."

"What? Why? Why would I bring you here for that?" I'm off balance and step back to create space between us. Her nakedness is alarming, but more so, her submissive nature and body language tell a tale. That tale is: Take me however you want, it's what I'm used to.

"No one does something for nothing. Everything has a price." She shrugs one shoulder.

I can see the bruises on her pale skin, stippling her thighs, dotting the ribs that stick out. Gwen's body reveals a callous story of those around her and it occurs to me that the scene in Deandre's house wasn't the first time. Her attractiveness, her petite frame, those are her chips for barter, the coins with which she purchases the necessities required to get her through the day.

"Well, I'm not like that," I shoot back, angry at a world that demands such a toll. "Go back to the bedroom and get some clothes. Clean yourself up."

I turn my back to her so she won't see how hard my jaw is clenched.

My phone vibrates against my belt and I welcome the distraction. As Gwen gets to her feet and heads into the hallway, I flip it open and answer.

"Arch! Talk to me! What the fuck is going on?" Sheila gets vulgar when she's frightened. It sounds like she is outside somewhere, maybe driving with the window open. "The scanners lit up with your name an hour ago, now they're silent. Talk to me."

"Sheila, it's not what it looks like..."

"Well, it looks like you shot your partner and no one can find him. There's a manhunt for you!"

"I know. Listen, things went sideways on the Bell case." I turn on her TV and flip to NBC. Sure enough, the news alert banner scrolls across the bottom of the screen. To one side a vertical panel squishes aside a daytime soap opera show. A male news anchor with a serious expression is reporting the latest. My official police photo fills the lower half of the panel. I don't bother turning up the sound.

Before Sheila can pepper me with a thousand questions, I forge ahead. "This isn't a case of gang members mugging Noah. Everything has been staged, a scene created to make the general public think one thing. I'm not sure I can describe much because I don't fully understand it myself. But the guy that staged everything has Griff and wants to trade him for our witness."

A sharp intake of breath. "You have the girl?"

I can practically hear the wheels clicking in her head. If she scores the first interview, it will shoot up her career. It's calculating and cold, especially at a time like this, but I know where her drive comes from. It's all to secure a better future for Anna, and for that I accept her rationale.

"I do. In fact, we're at your place now."

"Mine? Why?"

"She's going to borrow some of your clothes. Long story."

"And then what, Arch? What are you going to do?" Now her voice changes, shifting from aggressive possibility to potential fear. "You're not seriously considering this, are you?"

"I have an idea how to close this up. It's probably the only chance we have."

The TV screen switches out my picture for a live shot of the Kedvale house, shot from a helicopter hovering overhead. A dozen squad cars block the intersection, lights whirling, surrounding the BMW. I can see Rollins standing in a group of cops, including Hecker. It looks like he's describing my attack on him.

Sheila's tone softens, still scared but tacking at a different angle. "Honey, this is crazy. Don't risk everything we've worked for. Turn yourself in. If there's truth to your story, it will come out. The department has professionals to deal with this kind of thing..."

I interrupt her. "*If*? You don't believe me?"

"I want to, I really do, but think about it. What you're describing is way out there. It's like a movie plot, an unbelievable one at that. How am I supposed to react? There's more to this than your obsession with making things right. What will happen if it doesn't work out? Think about Anna."

"I am. I always do. If this guy doesn't get what he wants, it's all over. I'm screwed then. This is my only way back to the truth. I need Griff to corroborate me."

"You're going to get fired. That's your best case. Worst case, you disappear. Do you really think someone willing to take hostage a cop is just going to let you walk?"

"I don't. But that's what I'm planning around. You have to trust me, Sheila. Please. There's only one way out."

She's crying openly now, stifled sobs. I can picture her, biting the index finger of her left hand to keep the emotion contained. Sometimes she wins, sometimes not. Right now is the latter.

"You can't go it alone, honey. What do you need from me? What can I do to help?" She's resigned herself to my determination.

"I won't be alone, but we need to think past this, past the resolution of Bell's death to the end game. Start researching a white supremacist group called the Covenant Church of the New Millennium. There's a story about them in all this and you will want your name on the byline."

There's silence and I can imagine the pieces clicking into place in her head. She's too smart not to grasp the picture I've just sketched. "The one from up north a couple of months ago? That Covenant?"

"Yes. That one."

She releases a loud sob. "My god, Arch. What have you gotten yourself into?"

THIRTY NINE

I turn to find Gwen standing in the hallway, draped in a pair of Sheila's jeans and sweatshirt. The logo proclaims 'Duke University' but it's faded so much that the words are barely legible. The sleeves hang down over her hands, hiding them. Sheila is taller by several inches but baggy clothes are better than no clothes.

She's staring at the TV with a perplexed look on her face that I'm coming to realize is her natural expression.

My image is back in place on the side panel, the live shot from Kedvale now gone. Gwen looks from that picture to me, and back, as if trying to reconcile the two. I wonder if I look the same to her.

"That was your girlfriend," she says. If there's any embarrassment from her submission to me, it doesn't show. Maybe she's so used to it that there's no longer any emotion attached. "She has a lot of fancy clothes. Is she a snooty bitch?"

I nearly laugh. "Um, no. She's not. She's actually nice."

Gwen sniffs. "Good. There aren't enough nice people in the world. Why don't you live here?"

I hesitate. I've only known this girl for less than an hour. "It's complicated."

"You don't know complicated," she mutters and moves into the kitchen. "I'm starving."

I glance at my watch, calculating. "You have ten minutes. Help yourself."

Myself, I have all the world's butterflies roiling in my stomach. The call with Sheila served to make me just that much more nervous. I've had to block out the consequences of my actions, the almost certain loss of my job, the chance that all this backfires on me. But I'm committed now, there's no turning back. I meant it when I said my only path free runs through Griff, and with Griff comes Julien, so he's in my path as well. On the other side of him lies my redemption.

I turn to Gwen as she pours milk into a bowl of cereal. "Walk me through what happened at Middle Plains." For the next ten minutes I listen to her version of events and everything clicks into place. It doesn't help calm my nerves, though. If anything, it makes them worse.

This guy Julien is one lethal dude.

***

We step outside Sheila's apartment to the sounds of police sirens approaching. It takes me a second too long to realize the truth: Sheila called me in. Despite all my reassurances, she let fear of the future overtake her. I know she's trying to protect me from myself, protect the life we're just starting for Anna, so I don't feel betrayed. The fact that I'm just hearing the sirens means she thought long and hard before placing the call. Otherwise, we'd have been trapped in the apartment. It can't have been an easy decision for her.

Gwen twists her head around, trying to identify the direction. "Are those for us?"

"It's a good bet they are. Come on. We need to move fast."

We're driving away from the parking lot when the first squad rounds the corner several blocks behind us. I hit the first right, then a left.

Hopefully he didn't pay attention and was focused on finding the right apartment building. The radio is silent, keeping secret the coordinated activity of my fellow officers. I'm working blind, so far out on a branch I may never get back to ground.

For her part, Gwen remains silent, staring with a blank gaze out the front windshield. She hangs onto the grab handle, swaying as I take corners at high speed.

I don't understand her, her mentality of living each moment as a distinct session with no connection to the past or future. She may not recognize faces, but she acts as if she can't recognize events either, or the impact they have on her. Her manner of interacting with men - it's obvious she's accustomed to being used by them - stuns me.

How can anyone go through life like that? What about tomorrow and all the yesterdays that made you who you are? If we are all a representation of our past experiences, a collected bundle of memory, event and experience, what does that make Gwendolyn Manner?

The whoop of sirens swells for a moment as another squad running on a parallel road crosses his intersection at the same time we cross ours. I glance down the block. He's going in the opposite direction. I can't tell if saw us or not, but to be safe, I swing onto an adjacent road.

We make our way west in a circuitous route, sticking to small neighborhood streets with heavy tree cover. Somewhere I can hear the thump of helicopter rotor blades but the mix of housing and nature scrambles my sense of tracking. It could be anywhere.

If we can get to I-94, traffic will help us disappear. At that point we will simply be another police vehicle navigating the stretch of interstate connecting Indiana to Wisconsin.

Out of the blue, Gwen says, "Have you ever been to Rollins Savanna? It's pretty."

I find it an odd question, considering the moment, but everything about this girl is a little off.

"No, I'm new to Chicago. Haven't had a lot of time to explore."

She gives a self-satisfied nod. "That explains your accent. You talk like someone from the south."

"You've been there, to the savanna?" Maybe she can help navigate. I've only got a cross section of roads and a general description of an area to go by. The description I provided to Julien was provided to me and I repeated it word for word.

"Yeah, once. I don't remember much. A guy brought me up there when I was stoned, last year I think. When I woke up the next morning he was gone, but I hung around for a while, just walking and enjoying the sun."

"Wait. You were brought up there and left? Who the hell was this guy to you?"

Gwen shrugs. "Beats me. I don't know how I met him. Maybe he brought me there to avoid getting caught by his girl. Guys will go way out of their way to get their knock on."

"And you just went with him? Gwen, that's not a good way to live. What if something happened?"

She looks over to me. "Like what? Rape? You saw me in Deandre's house. You think that's the first time? Or last? One guy is easy to handle." She gives a scornful laugh. "But he was a special kind of asshole. It took me forever to get back home. I didn't have any money and had to give blow jobs for bus fare."

Another laugh, this one less edgy. "At least I didn't go hungry."

I'm stunned into silence. There are no words in me to respond. At this moment, I'm smacked in the face with the gulf between her world and mine. I'm only nine years older, yet it feels like generations, like I'm some crotchety old guy who can't understand today's youth.

I look over at this girl, a ghost from the fringes of society, existing just outside our periphery, wandering through her own travails with no one to lean on. There is no one she can trust, especially now that Olivia is gone, and it's evident she doesn't rely on anyone. Even when I told her about her grandmother, she shed the tears of someone weeping over death, not the tears of someone who lost a loved one. Her inability to connect with others has made Gwen this creature that feels little, senses little, cares little.

She's not callous. She's numb.

That, above all else, is the impact of her face blindness.

***

We make the interstate with no further drama. Traffic is light but steady at this noon hour, so there's enough to provide cover without slowing us down. I nestle into a grouping of semis, tucking between two of them in the right lane. Together we march northward out of the Chicago suburbs. Our destination isn't North Haven, although given what I know so far about the Covenant angle, it would be fitting.

I have a map on the seat next to me. I glance at it every time we pass another exit. A deep vibration comes from the passenger side tires as I drift off the lane onto the rumble strips.

"Let me do that. You focus on the road." Gwen takes the map and studies it. "Go another ten, twelve miles. Then look for Belvidere road and take that left."

"You mean west?"

"Whatever direction that way is," she motions towards the west side of the interstate.

I find the exit and turn onto a four lane road. The pavement is smooth and free of potholes. Far too soon for my liking, the sign for Rollins Nature Preserve looms up before us. I pull over at the entrance, just outside a set of stone pillars with iron gates mounted to them. The gates are swung wide open, inviting us in.

Looking over at Gwen, I ask, "You ready?"

She shakes her head. "No, but what else am I going to do?"

PART FOUR

FORTY

"No, but what else am I going to do?" Gwen says, and means it.

The detective stares out the windshield and she can tell he's thinking. He gnaws at his bottom lip then turns to her. "You don't have to do this, Gwen. I'll understand if you want to run."

She can see the leap of faith he's taking. This cop isn't like most of the others. He's young and from what she's been able to glean from his numerous phone calls, he went through a lot to get this job. It means everything to him.

He didn't give in when she offered him a blow job, which is unusual. More importantly, he seemed actually shocked. Maybe it's because he's new to Chicago and the way things work. Maybe that's just his nature. Either way, in that moment she understood. He was treating her on level ground and not as someone vulnerable who he could use at his leisure. He stepped back from her offer because he didn't want to use her. Yet, in a way, he does.

He wants her to risk her life for him.

Oddly enough, in Gwen's mind that's preferable. He's not just taking without giving back, he's asking that she stand beside him as they both risk much to close this thing out.

"Do you think it will work?" She asks, knowing her voice sounds small.

He sighs. "It has to. I'm backed into a corner."

"Sometimes I think I live in a corner." Gwen chews on a fingernail, spitting out the bits. "Let's go. The sooner we do this, the sooner we can go back to our lives."

The detective puts the car in gear and they roll through the open gates of the forest preserve entrance. Gwen remembers this area from her last visit. It's a park pavilion setting for families to come with their kids. Playground equipment, picnic tables and small lake in the background. She'd sat at one of those picnic tables after waking up, watching the sun rise over the trees. And even though it was cold and she shivered constantly, Gwen still thinks back to it as one of the most beautiful things she's experienced. There seemed to be this sense of happiness, of life fulfillment, soaked into the wood of the table.

She'd studied all the carved initials in the table, tracing them with her fingernail. Many were simply initials, some were sayings that looked more like runic characters. But each one - to her - represented a moment when someone sat with someone they cared for and spent effort to memorialize their existence at this place and time.

Gwen knows she is not likely to ever have anything like that. She can't look to the future, she knows it will be filled with blurred faces and strangers. There is only the existing moment, a short space in her life when she has come to know who is standing next to her and doesn't have to strain to place their features.

They drive through the pavilion and enter the preserve grounds, driving for another twenty minutes until a small park setting finally appears to one side of the road. The cop pulls into the empty lot and parks off to one side.

There is no sign of anyone else. They are

deep in the heart of the forest preserve, surrounded by a thousand acres of nature.

Despite the bright and beautiful cast to this scene, Gwen feels her nerves tremble again. If anything, the beauty of natural growth hides danger behind every copse of trees, the tall waving grasses, under the surface of the small lake. She's not sure there's been a better metaphor describing her life: This is a place where predators lurk in the weeds for prey like her.

And she came willingly.

Near the road are two tennis courts surrounded by chain link fencing with a green mesh laced through the links. She can see through the mesh. Beyond them is a basketball court, a tether ball pit and a small jungle gym for kids.

"What now?" Gwen wraps her arms tight around her waist, as if squeezing hard enough will keep her fear from spilling out. "There's no one here."

He gets out of the car. "Let's walk."

A gravel path leads off the back of the clearing and deeper into the grasses. Large trees line the path, held back by a border of wild weeds. This was part of what Gwen originally loved about the preserve but the glow of those memories is far away. They are heading into close quarters with a man she saw kill multiple people without flinching. She has no doubt he could smile into her eyes and pull the trigger.

After a few minutes the path opens into another clearing, nested up against the shore of the lake. The cop pulls her into this little oasis. It is oval shaped, with the path at one end, and an opening to the lake at the opposite end. She can see all the way across the water to thick stands of trees on the other shore. A single wooden bench has been placed near the water's edge.

Her grandmother's love of gardening pays dividends as she recognizes the many different types of growth. It pains her to think those days of sitting together, paging through wildlife books, are now gone forever. She feels a swelling wave of emotion at the thought of Olivia and forces her attention elsewhere. There's no time right now for weakness. She may be prey, but that doesn't mean she has to be *easy* prey.

Cat tails ring the edge of the lake, giving way to Bluestem, Indian grass and Switch grass. The clearing is choked tight by these grasses that grow straight up. The wild Bluestem soars even above the tall detective's head. Soft summer winds move the tips back and forth in a slow dance under the hot sun. Any other time, she could spend all day soaking in this beauty.

"It feels like we're the only people alive here," she says. "There's no sign of anyone else."

"That's on purpose," the detective responds and starts loosening his tie.

"What are you doing?"

"Stripping down, to show I have no weapons, no wires. This guy is smart, Gwen. It's not his first time. Just do as we discussed, keep your head down and let me handle it."

Gwen nods and looks around, as if trying to discover the danger lurking in the grasses. She thinks of those shows with lions padding softly through the African plains, tracking a wary gazelle or zebra. The behavior of prey is what always sticks in her mind. They know every moment holds a threat to their existence, but they cannot see it. All they can do is move with care and be prepared to run when the attack comes.

In the world of Man, in Cicero, the predators were just as well hidden, using circumstance and need as cover instead of trees or bushes. The predators were Dweldon and his sexual trades for pot, or Deandre and his fixation on running trains. It was the guy who heard about her through those two and took her somewhere to have his way, usually in exchange for something she needed.

She realizes those guys were not true predators but scavengers.

The man from the factory, he's an apex predator. He may not be as big or physically threatening, but he stands tall above the rest. Sharks are not the largest creatures, but they are feared above all others. Like those sharks, this guy trawls waters of a different type, adapted in much the same way.

None of this is making her feel better. She turns her thoughts onto something else and turns back to the detective.

He's standing naked, folding his clothes and setting his shoes atop them. She takes in his lean form, the corded sinew and tendon in his arms, the ridges of his rib cage. Her eyes drift lower.

"What are you looking at?"

She nods in approval. For a brief moment her fear fades as she considers other things. It's suddenly easier to keep her mind from the consequences of their situation.

He shakes his head and hands her the stack of clothes. "Go put these on the bench and stand by it. Don't be frightened."

She takes one last glance at his nakedness

and walks towards the bench by the water. The momentary distraction flees her mind, disappearing like a puff of smoke. Her limbs grow numb with dread and she can feel the burn coming to her eyes.

It all comes down to this.

FORTY ONE

I watch Gwen walk down to the bench. She sets my clothes on the seat and I can tell by the rigid nature of her spine that she's afraid. I am too. Julien has to be somewhere close by, monitoring our actions, but as I swivel my eyes around, I don't see him or Griff anywhere.

He could have already killed Griff and even now is training his weapon on my forehead. I'm not fool enough to believe his claim that he couldn't kill cops. The guy has already displayed an ability to kill in whatever manner he needs. His work at the basketball court showed close quarters combat with multiple targets. He created a peaceful scene with Olivia that, if it were taken out of the context in which we found her, would not raise an eyebrow. Then, his clinical dissection of

Dweldon demonstrated the monster that hides deep inside of him.

Against that knowledge, the idea that he could be lurking through the weeds is enough to make me want to wet my pants, if I was wearing any.

Standing completely naked, out in the open like this, I feel vulnerable. Smart Julien, increasing his mental advantage over me by stripping me down. It worked. I have to forget that I'm naked.

At least it's not cold.

I step back to one side of the clearing, within a couple feet of the tall prairie grasses. I've never seen any grow this tall, but it's fortunate for me that they do. In order for my plan to work correctly, Julien cannot be weaving his way through those grasses. I need him out in the open.

"Okay," I call out, voice echoing. "We're here. I'm standing on the east side of the clearing. Show yourself."

Everything feels surreal, like a bad movie. Here I am, waiting on a killer and my wounded partner, conducting an exchange of hostages with a secret plan in my back pocket. Unfortunately my pocket is twenty yards away and my star witness doesn't know who she's looking for. This is worse than a bad movie.

I just hope it works out.

Movement at the entrance to the clearing catches my eye and I snap my head around. Griff edges around the thick grass stalks, limping greatly. His skin is waxen and pale, slicked with sweat and I can see raw agony on his face with every step. A strip of cloth has been tied around his thigh, binding both wounds. It's soaked with blood.

Behind him comes Julien, up tight to my partner's back, presenting a smaller target. Griff's bulk easily hides the killer, all I can see is the top of his head and one eye peeking around the shoulder. They stop.

"All alone?" He calls. "No tricks?"

I keep my hands hanging away from my body, showing I'm no threat. I need to keep his attention on me. "None. I'm following the script. Griff? You okay, buddy?"

"Just perfect," he replies in a sarcastic tone. "I've got another name for my Christmas mailing list."

Julien laughs. "He's lying. I know for a fact he never sends cards." Even as he talks, his head swivels back and forth, assessing the scene. It's like the scene from the first *Terminator* movie, where Arnold is driving a car and scanning his surroundings with infrared vision. Julien moves his head in the same controlled manner, like a killer robot.

None of this is making me feel better.

They make their way deeper into the clearing, coming even with me across thirty feet of open space. It's a long distance, one I know I can't cover quickly enough to survive. Crux pulls Griff close to him and steps back towards the wall of grass at his back. I can see the muzzle of his weapon, buried in the flesh of my partner's neck. If this really was a bad movie, Griff could just spin and disarm him, ending the threat.

In reality, my partner can hardly move, much less with enough speed to overcome Julien. I doubt he could do it on his best day. There's going to be no help from that quarter.

"Send her over here," he says, eyes boring a hole in me.

"No, you send Griff down there. I want her to make sure he's okay." To Gwen I call out: "Stay where you are."

Julien flicks his eyes from me, to her, to the surrounding area. He knows something is up, there's no way he can't know. Everything about this guy tells me he doesn't leave much to chance, that he didn't get to where he is now by being careless and sloppy. His every move is premeditated, calculated. I can't give him time or space to adjust his plans. He needs to be forced off his game and the only way to do that is by looping the noose around my neck.

I take a step forward. "This is the only way it goes down, Julien. You'll never get out of the city. We'll lock this place down until even the cockroaches will need IDs to move between spots."

That produces a smirk. "Wow, can you overestimate your abilities any further? If you think my actions are dictated by a fear of the law, think again. I work to a different directive." He shoves Griff in Gwen's direction, immediately re-focusing his weapon on me with a two-handed grip. He takes another step back, settling his balance on flexed legs. The adjustment is reflexive and smooth, showing his ease with a weapon. Behind him, the grass is like a solid backdrop, stalks of green and tan soaring high, waving in the breeze. The wind makes a continuous sigh, rippling over the tips.

My partner makes his slow way down to the water's edge. He leans heavily against the back of the bench and I can see him whispering to Gwen. If I know him like I think I do, he's probably reassuring her that things will be alright, no matter how it may look. The fear in her eyes is visible to me from my distance so there's no way he doesn't see it. She nods and responds back.

Now comes the moment of truth.

I start moving forward. This is the part that chills me to my core. I've seen what this guy is capable of. There's something keeping him from simply putting a bullet in all our heads. I don't know what that thing is, but I'm counting on it. It is literally the largest gamble I've ever made, with my life as the chip.

"You know I can't just hand her over," I say. Another step. "Put the gun down and let's decide what needs to happen."

"I can hold it for you," Griff offers.

Julien takes an equal step back. His hands hold the weapon rock steady, trained on a spot between my eyebrows. He's right up against the grass wall. One step and he'll disappear behind the stalks. I have to keep him in position.

"Don't," he says. "Just don't. You think there's some heroic move you can make, some plot twist that will change everything. There isn't, detective. This ends only one way. The only people who can help you are already all here. You have no support system. I'd hate to have to kill you."

"Because you know it's wrong."

A puzzled expression comes across his face, like the concept of moral imperative is completely foreign. "No, because it would be an unpaid kill and my client forbid it. But I can certainly maim you."

He aims the gun downward, mouth tugging up into a smile. "This might hurt a little."

I take off running, sprinting away from Griff and Gwen, making for the entrance of the clearing. It looks like I'm running away from the situation, abandoning the other two and leaving them at his mercy. At least, that's what I hope it looks like, to Julien in particular. I can't have him thinking otherwise.

Immediately the assassin swivels his hips and crouches deeper into a firing stance. That's all I need from him.

"KILLING! NOW!"

FORTY TWO

Julien swivels, training his sights on the running detective. He's got to place the shot just right, wounding him enough to take him down, while not killing him. It's against his nature to purposely avoid the kill shot, but orders are orders.

"KILLING!" The detective yells. "NOW!"

A rustle, from behind him. A split second to place the sound. Then realization.

Julien spins, weapon tracking ahead of him, but he's too late. Far too late.

Rick Killing launches out of the tall grasses like a great white ape. His arms are spread wide and he's coming fast, a look of sheer determination fixed on his face. Julien is a fraction of a second behind. He fails to get his weapon in play before the large football player impacts him. Breath explodes from Julien's lungs when they land, absorbing the full weight of the other man. He struggles to maintain a grip on his weapon, but it flies out of his hand, to be snatched out of the air by Killing.

Julien feels a sense of frustration. *Seriously, this guy? Again?*

Suddenly other hands are grabbing him, pinning down his arms, and he realizes Arch has joined the fray. He yells for his partner to bring cuffs. Julien gets a glimpse of the old cop hobbling towards them, propped up by the girl.

She should be his, her life suborned to his own. This girl saw him; she's the one who can tie him to the Bell murder. He cannot allow her to sully his record of witness-free kills. Anger surges through him, at the injustice of getting caught by these yokels, at the thought of failure, at the idea that he could be made to stand trial. This is not what Julien Crux wants.

He expects more.

Killing and White haul him up to his feet. Both tower over him.

"I can't believe that actually worked," Killing says. "I've seen more realistic endings in soap operas."

White coughs a laugh into his hand. "Yeah, innovation is not my strong suit. I was desperate and had nowhere else to turn. This all could have turned out much worse. You didn't need to answer my call, so I can't thank you enough." The relief in his voice is almost a tangible thing. He thinks it's over and he's safe.

He's wrong.

"For starters, put some clothes on. It's starting to get weird. And you're welcome. I learned the hard way. When it comes to anything Covenant, there is no option to ignore the call. If you don't cut off one of the heads early, more will spring up to join it. This," he motions to Julien. "This right here feels like a win, but don't think you've won much. There are going to be other gears turning, other games being played behind the curtain. This guy is a pawn, whether he realizes it or not. He's just one piece of a large puzzle that no one else can see."

"Well, at least I wrapped up my case. That's all I can control for now."

Griffin and the girl limp up to them. The old detective's eyes are wide as he looks up at Killing. "That was incredible. I think you broke the little puke in half, man."

She hands White his bundle of clothes and Julien notices she glances at his body. Then she turns her gaze to him. There are tears in her eyes, like she'd been struggling to hold them back. The stare is glazed and distant, as if she's looking just past his eyes to the inner part of what made him human.

In a flash, Julien realizes she doesn't recognize him. Whether from shock or the dark of night from their encounter, she's trying to square his features with that of the man who came after her.

The cosmos has played a sick joke on him.

Julien relaxes his posture and lets out a low laugh. "She was never a threat to me, was she?"

White shakes his head. "Probably not. But that doesn't change things." To his partner he says, "Want the honors?"

"Damn right." He limps up to Julien and pulls out a set of cuffs. "You have the right to remain silent..."

Killing maintains his grip but White lets go and starts to get dressed, pulling on his boxers. To everyone here, this episode is over. They've caught the bad guy, put the world back into some semblance of order and now it's only a matter of process and procedure.

Julien has been here before, in this situation. Different place, different time, different officers, but same predicament. He expects the same results. It's all within his capability, he's not worried.

Relaxing his body another degree, he feels Killing's vise grip loosen in answer. He purposely keeps his expression loose, moving his eyes back and forth.

As Toms finishes his Miranda recitation and reaches back for his cuffs in their belt case, Julien goes.

He drops low and spins, sweeping out the legs of White. Toms and the girl are not the threat. White and Killing are. The detective is already somewhat off balance, pulling on his pants, so he goes down in a heap with a shout.

Julien shoots up from his crouch, aiming for a stiffened palm strike to the chin. Done right, it snaps back the victim's head so violently that blood flow to the brain is cut short and unconsciousness is immediate. He's made it happen more than once. This is where his smaller size benefits him.

Killing jerks his head back, taking part of blow on his chin. The move is just enough to avoid the intended effect. His eyes ignite in fury and he surges forward before Julien can center his stance enough for another strike. The man has incredible reflexes. Julien suddenly knows his error.

He feels his body ridden down once again, taking the full weight of Killing. This is the worst outcome. All his training, all his striking skill, those are nullified by the size and weight of Killing. He throws a few strikes to the ribs, but doesn't think they are even felt.

A forearm blow smashes his forehead. By itself it wouldn't hurt that much, but his head is pinned to the ground, preventing any movement, so the strike is fully felt. The second blow catches his mouth and he feels a tooth crack off.

He thinks he absorbs another five or six elbows and forearms but things get a little hazy.

Then he feels himself being lifted back to his feet. The world spins and swirls, and there's something in his right eye. He suspects blood.

"What is it with you kung fu guys?" Killing states. "Physics, man. Large smashes small."

Julien lists to one side. He's absorbed significant damage but this is not over. Free flowing blood looks worse than it feels. His head rings, his nose aches and he can feel tooth fragments inside his mouth. This is far from the worst beating he's endured. As long as he can keep the others off-balance, he can control the situation. They are on alert now, realizing he won't go down as easy as they thought. He needs to appear as if he's given up. Running his tongue over broken teeth, he forces a smile. "I was a liberal arts major."

He faces the lake, using that movement to scan the area again. Toms and Gwen are on the right, next to Killing who is gripping his arm much more tightly now. White stands to his left. The wind has stilled and the water is smooth as glass. It's a perfect scene, one worthy of painting. He can clearly see to the other side, to the thick stands of trees, even through his blood-soaked vision. The canopy of leaves darkens the ground below, the trunks cluster together like bystanders trying to crowd an accident scene. Instinctively he realizes the frame that has been created. His experience and history is founded upon scenarios set up in a similar manner. It's been his stock in trade. That someone has finally subjected him to the same should come as a shock, but deep down, he always knew it would one day come to this.

When he sees a flash of light from across the lake, sparking within the darkness of the trees, there is no surprise.

FORTY THREE

I'm pulling on my slacks when a thick meaty grunt emerges from Julien. It's followed immediately by a crack from across the lake. I've never heard the sound of a high-velocity bullet impacting flesh up close like this.

I hope I never hear it again.

I fall back and time stutters to a stop. Everything is frozen in my vision, letting me know I will never forget this moment.

Killing pulls away from Julien, arms thrown up to shield Griff and Gwen. His face has a look of anger, like he should have known to expect this. Griff looks shocked. Gwen is still staring at Julien's face, trying to reconcile his features with the man she saw kill Noah Bell. I see her eyes slide to me even as Killing drags them down into a heap covered by his bulk.

My pants are only halfway pulled up. I trip backward, sprawling to an ignoble position on the ground.

The world resumes normal speed.

Julien stares down at the hole in his chest. It pierced him on the right side, near the top of his lung. Already I see a blood bubble poke out and pop. The look on his face is bemused confusion, like he doesn't fully understand what just happened but is willing to accept it if only someone told him why. Even through the blood caking his features I can see his thoughts.

He was set up.

I start to scramble back up, feet snagging in my trousers, when Julien looks over at me. He opens his mouth to speak but it's lost under the clap of another gunshot.

The next round takes him clean through the forehead. The back of his skull explodes and red droplets splatter all over Killing's shirt. It came from across the lake. I dart a glance that way. The far shore is cloaked in trees, making for a perfect vantage point.

Whoever Julien was working with knew he'd be here, knew he'd be in the presence of police, and moved quickly to close the security breach he represented. They did it all within

426

the sixty minutes, from our call arranging this meet to the time we arrived. There's a lot to be inferred from that realization, but I'm more worried about getting out of here alive.

As Julien's body drops back into a lifeless crumble, I scramble over to the other three. It had to have been a large caliber round, maybe even .338 Magnums. And whoever pulled the trigger is no novice, not from that range and the target size. Head shots are no easy task.

Killing swears and dives towards the wooden park bench, yanking it over onto its back to provide us cover. "When you woke up this morning, were snipers on today's agenda?"

The bench shudders from the impact of another round. The crack of the rifle rolls across the flat water.

My eyes are fixed on the remains of Julien's face. "Someone followed us and killed him to eliminate a potential leak. If we arrested him, we could have gotten to the truth behind Bell's murder."

"How many times do I have to tell you?" Killing asks. "The Covenant does not play around. They tried to assassinate Dee in the same manner. It's probably the same damn shooter and rifle, too. Asshole."

There's silence in Rollins Savanna. Either the gunman is done, is repositioning, or is coming for us. I don't want to find out which.

Gwen is pressed up tight to my side, head down, balled fists pressed to her eyes. "Are you okay?" I ask her.

"No. No! Who could be right now? You're supposed to make things safe for me."

"I will, Gwen. We're all getting out of here."

Griff shifts his injured leg with a grunt and looks me in the eye. "Got to move, partner. Like now. You got a radio on you to call in backup?"

I look down at myself, in my white undershirt and dress slacks snagged around my knees.

"I'll take that as a 'no' then."

"There's a squad parked near the entrance, about two hundred yards away." I nod my head in the general direction. The car is hidden by a curve in the tall grasses and the slope of land.

Killing glances over at Griff's leg. "I don't think Santa Claus here is sprinting anywhere. We'll have to improvise."

Before I can respond, he directs a pointed look at me. "Help him up and follow my lead."

Killing heaves the wooden bench up and

holds it vertical. The thing must weigh over a hundred pounds, but he doesn't show any strain. "Get in front of me everyone, single file like school. Cookies and milk if we survive."

How can he be making jokes at a time like this?

I help Griff get to his feet, blocking out his grunts of pain. Gwen stands in front of him, helping with a steadying hand.

"Move into the weeds and make for the car," Killing barks. The bench shudders again as another round drives into the wood. Killing swears in response, drowned out by the gunshot echo. It came from a different angle so whoever is manning the rifle is moving.

That spurs us on.

We plunge into the grass. Killing keeps the bench at our backs, providing some measure of protection even though we are no longer visible to the sniper. That doesn't give me much confidence though. The ripples in the top of the stalks reveal our movement, at least in a general direction.

Griff is panting, sweat drips down his face, off the end of his nose. His eyes are bloodshot. "Hang in there, partner," I say through gritted teeth. His weight drags me down and I stumble more than once. He stays silent, focusing his eyes straight ahead as if he can see the car. Gwen's hands are no longer helping me, but clench tight to my arm and her head jerks wildly around, watching for someone else.

Two more shots ring out in the quiet savanna but neither finds a home in the bench. The sniper is firing blind now.

It feels like hours, but in reality only minutes before we reach the edge of the grass. The car is twenty yards ahead, alone in the parking lot. I don't know where Killing stashed his vehicle. When we planned this out, he said only that he'd hide it and work his way through the woods to us. He obviously knows this place well since it was all his idea.

"I'll get the car and back it over here. We pile in, tear out of here and call it on the move," I say, lowering Griff to the ground. "We can circle the savanna and stay close until all units arrive. If we get help here quick enough, we can set a cordon and maybe trap this guy in."

No one looks ready to talk me out of this stupid plan.

"It would be nice to see who's shooting at us," Killing remarks. He sets the table down on its edge, propping it up as a shield, and gestures to the car. "Your honors."

The small asphalt area is completely exposed. I know the lake isn't in view from here, but if the sniper moved far enough, he could have a good angle. I fish the keys out my pocket. "Get ready to move."

My shoulders are hunched so tight it seems like they will cramp as I sprint to the cruiser. The dread of a high caliber round piercing my spine chases me across the hot blacktop. I have socks on but no shoes. The plus side to that is my feet don't burn and I can run faster. I expect to hear the metallic ping of a bullet piercing the vehicle's skin, but there is only the sound of my lungs heaving.

I round the backside of the car, and slam up against the door with my body, keeping it between me and the shooter's general direction. Sliding into the seat, I fire the throttle and throw it into reverse, head low, driver's door open so I can lean out and steer my way back.

"Go, go, go!" I yell. As the three move forward, I see the size of the hole left in the table by one of the bullets. It's definitely high caliber. If the shooter takes aim on the car, it will punch through one side and out the other.

Killing shoves Griff into the back seat, along with Gwen. Then he darts around the front and tumbles into the passenger seat next to me. "No way I'm fitting back there."

"And how do you know this?"

"You'd be surprised. Now go. Get us out of here."

I gun the accelerator and send the cruiser rocketing forward. We bounce out of the lot onto the road in a squeal of tire smoke, heading in the opposite direction of the attack, engine roar following along. The lack of impact sounds against the Crown Vic tells me no other shots were fired at us. So where did the shooter go? Did he abandon the effort? Or is he repositioning himself to cut off our escape?

So many questions, no answers.

I pass the radio through the opening in the cage separating front seat from back. "Griff, call it in. And call Gonzales. We need to clear this up." I know it sounds selfish that I'm more worried about my job at a moment like this, but again: justification for the greater good. This is Anna's future we're talking about, not just my tin.

Killing points down a side road. "My car is a half mile back, under some trees. You can drop me off."

There's a sense of relief inside me. We tracked down the man responsible for Noah Bell's homicide. We have a witness to the crime. We should be able to tie Julien's DNA to the factory, the basketball court, and Olivia's house, resolving multiple cases in one fell swoop. My hands are shaking, but in a good way. Everything has been neatly wrapped.

Killing's voice doesn't reflect the same emotion. It's conflicted. He's had more experience with the Covenant, he knows the sniper signifies something else.

To me, that's another case. One for a task force with specialty in this area. I'm not passing the buck, but I know when I'm out of my league. He, apparently, does not.

As Griff grunts into the radio, calling for response units, my phone rings. At some point it came unclipped from my belt as I scrambled into the car, falling down into the foot well. I slide my left foot around, feeling for it.

Out of the blue, Killing looks over at me. "Did you hear what the guy said just before his head exploded? It looked like he was talking to you."

I shake my head. "No, I couldn't understand it." *Ah, there it is.* I kick the phone closer and reach down to grab it. "Did you?"

Killing shrugs as I look down at the screen and see Sheila's number. I flip it open to answer. "It sounded like he said a girl's name. Anna, maybe?"

Sheila's scream is all that comes through the speaker.

FORTY FOUR

Gwen feels confused. They escaped the park. The detective got them out safely. Next to her, Detective Toms speaks urgently into a radio. It sounds like he's talking with his boss, explaining what's happened to him. The tale sounds complicated.

She notes a heavier flow of blood from his injured thigh. The movement through the grass, the rush to climb into the car, those things opened his wound up. It runs down the pant leg, pooling on the vinyl seat. She doesn't know what to do to help him so she presses her palm against his wounds. That elicits a shout from him and he swats her hand away even as he continues to talk into the radio.

The black detective is frantic, driving like a maniac. She'd heard the scream that rang through his phone, but doesn't know what it means. The name Anna came from him several times. He yells at the muscular man in the passenger seat, that man yells back. There's so much noise and commotion she feels overwhelmed. Nothing makes sense, she can't comprehend what's going on.

The car swerves and careens along the savanna roads, tires squealing in the turns. The detective is driving out of control, yelling at everyone and no one. She doesn't grasp any of his words.

Then they are skidding to halt on the side of the road, tucked under a grouping of trees. She sees a sports car, a Mustang she thinks, parked near the largest trunk.

Both men vault out of the front seat. Her door is yanked open by the detective and his face is mere inches away from hers, shouting at his partner. The partner shouts back. They are both yelling over each other, words mashing together. She gets the sense the other two men are leaving, chasing something else.

The Mustang roars to life with a loud crack, echoing off the overhead branches. Gwen jumps from the sudden sound, startled.

The detective turns to rush away but spins back. He grabs her arm in a fierce grip.

"Stop being a victim, Gwen," is all he says.

And then he's gone, carried away on a wave of thunderous exhaust. The Mustang disappears around the bend.

She leans back in the seat, mind jumbled, thoughts in disarray. She doesn't know what just happened, or why she's left with Detective Toms. Is this it? Is she free to go back to her life? Gwen has no idea what to do next.

Suddenly she realizes there is only silence. Detective Toms is no longer speaking into his radio. He's tilted over against the opposite door, eyes closed. The radio lies on the floor, squawking with unintelligible sounds.

Blood soaks his side of the back seat. Gwen sees this and the fear comes rushing back. Did he die?

She leans over to him, calling out his name, pushing on his shoulder. It doesn't look like he died, she can see his chest rise and fall. In desperation, she presses again on his wound, hoping the pain will wake him. But he remains silent and still, and she understands what's just happened. He's fainted from blood loss.

She's on her own. Again.

Gwen steps out of the car and looks back at Toms. She can't leave him here like this. What if he dies before help shows up? Even though he's a cop, she doesn't want anything to happen to him.

But she doesn't know how to drive. She can't bring him to someplace close for help, because there is no place close. Yet she's afraid to sit and wait, in case it's too late. She doesn't even know if he told anyone where they were. All the yelling in the car kept her from keeping track of who said what.

Indecision freezes Gwen.

Then she shakes her head, physically shaking away all the fears and hesitation.

Don't be a victim.

She knows what the detective meant. It was more than a reaction to how she let guys use her body. She thinks it's about taking control of her life, of no longer running from the affliction that has shaped her every interaction. She's always known this, but until the detective said it, she never boiled it down to one simple statement.

Gwen reaches back into the car, grabbing the radio off the floor.

"Hello? Anyone? We need help. I'm with Detective Toms." The radio chatter continues and she doesn't know if they heard her. She twists the knobs next to the antenna and repeats her plea, but this time there's no response. Gwen realizes she switched away from the channel and doesn't know how to get it back.

Panic threatens to overtake her, but she fights it off. His breathing appears regular, like he's napping. The blood continues to seep out of his leg though. It comes out in slow pulses, which isn't a good sign.

Gwen looks around. There is nothing but trees, prairie grass and open meadow surrounding her. There are houses and neighborhoods bordering the savanna, but she's not exactly sure where. If she can get to one of them, she can get someone to help, call for an ambulance, direct the police here.

Gwen runs out to the road and looks both ways on it. There's no sign of life nearby, so she'll have to pick a direction and start moving. She tries to estimate direction. Detective White said they needed to head west when they drove to the forest preserve, so if she returns east, there were houses along the way.

Staring up, she can't tell which way is east. The sun sits high overhead, not appearing to lean one way or the other. In desperation, she lets loose several shouts, hollering for anyone in earshot. Maybe there are people out of sight, someone taking a walk along the path, or having a picnic in one of the other park areas.

But a thousand acres is a lot of space. It's easy to get lost in that kind of acreage. If the sound of gunshots didn't bring people running to investigate, it's not likely her yells are going to be heard. She needs to hoof it until she finds someone. And the sooner the better.

With rushed steps, Gwen starts running along the road, eyes peeled for any kind of help.

She's barely six blocks away when that help appears. The road bends around an outcropping of tall pines. Two boys emerge from the trees just as she nears. She doesn't recognize them of course, but they look to be around her age.

"Help, I need your help!" She shouts at them, pointing back the way she came. "Someone's hurt. Do you have a cell phone?"

The boys stop their motion. Both have light hair. One has both hands behind his back, as if he were out on an afternoon stroll with an old friend.

She slows her frantic steps. Something's not right.

They look at each other. "Yeah, we have a cell. Why?"

Gwen stops completely, staring closer, trying to pierce the veil of their features. "There's a guy, a cop, back there. He's been shot." Out of instinct, she takes one step back even as she speaks. It's a reflexive move from someone who lives as prey.

She notices a strap over the shoulder of one boy. It's wide, like a camera strap, or something else. The sense of foreboding crystallizes in her core.

"Too bad. Cops suck," he says and shrugs. The motion brings around front a rifle hanging off the shoulder strap. Her blood goes cold.

"Thanks for making this so easy, Gwen," he says. "Now let's go get your friends."

FORTY FIVE

I pound the dashboard of Killing's Mustang in frustration. "Come on, man. Move it!"

"Hey, easy there pal. This is my only car."

Sheila's call was incomprehensible, full of crying and gasps and bewilderment. She was at Anna's group home but could not describe the scene through her horror. My heart sank, from fear for my daughter, from the uncertainty of what I would find.

Once again Julien was a step ahead. He knew about Anna, he knew all about me. He took insurance against getting caught, long before we were even sniffing his trail.

I held her off from calling 911 right away, giving me time to get there first. She didn't want to, voice shuddering in panic, but I didn't relent. I'm breaking every law enforcement protocol, violating the moral compass points we are supposed to steer by, but this kind of day was never covered in academy training.

I'm working blind here, reacting as best as I can to keep it all together.

"Wait," I say. "This is your only car? I thought you were some hotshot pro athlete. Shouldn't you have a fleet of these things?" It's the most inconsequential of thoughts, given our situation, but it's out of my mouth before I can censor it.

He jams the shifter into fifth and glances over at me with his icy gaze. I can't help but think when someone wants to draw up the ideal Aryan man, they'd use this guy. He and I are exact opposites, in nearly every way.

"That's rich. Stereotype much? That would be like me looking at you and thinking: Young black detective. Now way he's qualified enough. Must have sued someone to get that position."

Touche.

"Just hurry up."

He lifts his hand off the top of the steering wheel, glancing at the speedometer. "I'm at 90 already. You going to keep me out of jail if we get pulled over? I don't even know where I'm going."

"Don't worry. Drive."

***

We skid to a halt in front of the church and I'm out of the door before the engine shuts off. I sprint back to Anna's convalescence home. Sheila's car is out front and she gets out of it as I approach. Her makeup is smeared, her eyes puffy and swollen from crying, her hands shaking.

She collapses in my arms and I hold her tight, looking over her head at the front door. Nothing seems amiss from my visit yesterday. I peel her away and look down into her eyes. "Sheila." I try to keep my voice gentle, but she doesn't respond. "Sheila! What happened?"

"Anna. Inside. Michelle is...there's blood, and Anna is...Arch, what the hell is going on?" Her words aren't much clearer since the phone call. She's an experienced field reporter, she's been on site of some awful accident scenes. She's stood just outside the tape of some nasty homicides. I've never seen her quite this rattled. That's not a good sign.

Sheila's eyes drift past me as I turn her towards the house. "Who are you?"

"His long lost twin," Killing says back. I want to punch him for the flippant comment at a time like this.

She pulls back. "I'm not going back in there."

I nod. "Okay, stay here. Killing, can you watch her?"

"I don't babysit," he snaps back and vaults up the front steps in one leap. There's a haunted look in his eyes and I suspect he's reliving some nightmare of his own that the Covenant brought. I clamp down on my angered reaction and steer Sheila over to the side.

Then I follow Killing into the house.

At first glance it seems the same. The kitchen is empty, dishes washed and in the drying rack, table set for the next meal. But where there is normally a quiet borne of care and giving, today's silence carries a different tone. Something ominous underpins the lack of noise. There's no squeaking of floorboards from upstairs as someone walks along the hallway. The sound of soft beeping monitors is absent. I can only hear Killing at the back end of the house, walking through each room with swift steps.

Dread stalks me as I move down the hallway to Anna's room. I have to see it, but an inner voice screams at me to run, to leave this place and stay oblivious and unanswered.

Michelle is first. She's lying prone just

inside the doorway. Her eyes are open and staring along the floor. A third eye has been opened in her forehead, courtesy of a close range bullet wound. The edges of the hole are darkened with what I suspect is powder burn, meaning someone held the muzzle to her forehead and pulled the trigger. Blood trickles down her skull to the floor joining the partially dried pool under her head. Only the center of the pool is still wet. That says something about the time line and it makes my blood turn to ice. The dread becomes a tangible creature, heavy in my stomach, pinching the back of my neck.

The rest of the room is empty.

There's no Anna. No sign that she ever existed here. No bed, no equipment. Even the picture of Sheila, her, and me that we'd framed and hung on the wall is gone.

They took her, bed and all. While my gut twists into knot, my head sorts through the logistics. The Stryker bed carries a backup battery supply for the life-giving equipment plugged into her, good for 24, maybe 30 hours. It's been just over one day since I last saw her.

But all that is secondary. She's completely helpless in the hands of her captors. They don't know what kind of needs she has, nor do they care. If they rolled the bed somewhere and simply left it, that's as much a death sentence as if they'd unplugged all power supplies. My eyes burn, with anger, fear and a host of other emotions. I want to curl up and sink down to my knees, paralyzed by every worse-case scenario flooding my mind, but if ever I needed to keep my head, now is the time. I take a deep breath, squeeze eyes shut for a moment, and push the emotion back down. I stuff it into a compartment deep inside my guts and lock the lid. Later, when I have a chance, I'll unpack everything.

I reopen my eyes, clear and focused.

In the place of her bed is the rest of Dweldon. His head sits on the floor. Both arms and legs are arranged as if he were lying down, except his torso is still back in Olivia Manner's basement. The stench of death is thick in the air, smelling of bile.

Killing's feet track down the hallway towards me. "You have to call this in, pronto. There's another dead lady upstairs. All the kids are still in their rooms but who knows how long they've been without care. The only other one killed was a small Asian girl. The bastards left all the white kids alive." Somehow I hadn't even noticed he bypassed me and went through the rest of the house.

His voice cracks as he talks. I have to remind myself that he's already been up close and personal with this kind of carnage from the Covenant. It doesn't get easier no matter how many times you see it.

There's a piece of paper clutched in Dweldon's hand. I'm numb as I step over and look closer at it. There is only one word visible, written in pencil: *White*. Many meanings can be attached to that single word.

Without another thought, I pull it out. All the procedures for preserving crime scene evidence flies out the window before my personal stake. Killing has contaminated the house with his movement, I'm tampering by moving the paper, but none of that matters any longer. I've broken so many rules today, what's one more?

I unfold the paper. It's from a hotel, from the notepad they provide on the nightstand by the telephone. The Holiday Inn logo is stamped in the top corner.

More letters in pencil. Sloppy, slanted to the right and masculine in nature. One more word: *Call*, followed by a number with a Chicago area code.

Killing glances at it. "Those assholes like to leave messages."

I don't know what he means, nor do I care. There's no need for further discussion. I turn and stalk back towards the front of the house, exiting onto the porch.

Sheila has her phone in both hands, clutching it tight to her stomach. In the distance I hear sirens. She meets my eyes and I see the agony in them. Twice now she's called me into my own department. "I'm sorry, Arch. This is too much. I don't know what you've gotten yourself mixed up in, but I can't not do anything. Michelle's dead. There are body parts in there. Our daughter is gone." Her voice chokes off.

I nod and look off into the distance, as if I can see the racing squad cars. They've been racing around all day, chasing me, chasing my story. There's no question that my chase will continue. I give no thought to waiting around for responding officers, to explain and try to get help for Anna. Everything I've accomplished over the last year is being undone. The Covenant has cut my knees out from under me, isolating me against my fellow officers and any support I might be able to muster. The realization that someone can create such an intricate plan on the fly should frighten the hell out of me, and maybe someday it will. But for now there is room for only one thought.

"I have to get Anna," I say, as Killing emerges from the house.

Sheila twists the phone in her hand as a door two houses up slams open to disgorge a lady. She's in sweats and t-shirt, looking around to see what's worth seeing. When her eyes land on us, she takes on step back, hand still on the doorknob.

"Arch," Sheila says, but I cut her off.

"You were right to make the call. Stay here. Give the police everything you know. Don't hold back. I don't know what's going to happen, but after today our lives will no longer be the same."

Her mouth opens to speak, but words fail to come out. She doesn't know what to say. There is nothing to say.

I look at Killing. He has no stake in this, other than social obligation to walk a moral path. His past experience with the Covenant is critical but I'm not sure I have the right to ask him. We barely know each other, yet we've been pressed together by circumstance, forced into a vise by events beyond either of our control. In an odd way, we might know each other better than anyone else.

He speaks first. "You need a ride to wherever you're going. If you think I'm giving you my keys, think again. Like I said, it's my only car. Let's go."

Without waiting, he heads down the steps

and up the block towards his Mustang.

I take a step to follow but Sheila grabs my elbow, pulling me back. "Arch, do what you need to do. I'll back you no matter what. You have a strong core, I trust you to win." She pulls my head down and kisses me fiercely, almost violently. When she steps back, her eyes search mine, conveying many messages.

The look demands a response. "When I come back, there will be an 'us' again, Sheila. It's time."

Then I'm running after Killing, chasing my future.

FORTY SIX

I take a deep breath, hold for two long seconds, then blow it out. Killing looks over at me as he rows the gearshift. "If you don't make that call, we're just going to drive around in circles. I'm billing you for gas in that case."

Is everything a joke to this guy?

I look down at the piece of paper. Maybe I'm projecting, but the letters scream a message of hate, of callous disregard for human life and decency. The author of this note holds the life of my daughter in his hands and there's a very real part of me that's scared to make the call. I'm scared of what I will hear.

Or what I won't.

As the sound of police sirens falls back into the distance, buried under the sound of

Mustang exhaust, I take out my phone and flip it open. The call is answered on the first ring.

"About goddamn time, nigger White. I was getting impatient." The voice is smooth and young, slicked with malice. The racial slur doesn't impact on my brain as I try to process. Have I heard this voice before?

"What do you want? Your assassin is dead and the truth about Bell is going to come out. Too many people know now. You don't need my daughter for anything."

"That's where you're wrong, rookie. I need her to get you here. And bring that asshole Killing with you. We all owe him one."

"Why? Why do you need us?"

"You monkey-fucked your way into the middle of this case and managed to screw it up, but we can still bend things to our favor. Words are a tool like any other. Your version, the girl's version, these are all opinions of what happened. The evidence left at the scene will only serve to muddy up the waters further, since it will be inconclusive on several fronts. We can shape the story that comes out but we need to close any potential gaps."

"Fine, I'll do what you want. Just let my daughter go. You don't understand, she needs constant care."

"Or what? She'll become more of a retard

than she already is? Oh no. How will we cope with one more mulatto drain on society? Trust me, boy, I'm doing her a favor." He drawls out the word 'boy' and I hear some natural Southern in it.

Red murder roils in the corner of my vision. I'm going to pull the trigger on this guy until the chamber is empty. And even then I'll only pause long enough to slap in another clip. I crumple the paper up and throw it in the backseat, earning a look from Killing.

"Tell me what you need," I say through teeth gritted so tight they hurt.

He rattles off an address in Burbank, about ten miles south of our present location. "You can't miss it. Look for an abandoned church. Back door is open." The connection clicks dead.

"So?" Killing says. "Who wants to kill us now?"

I squeeze my phone so tight I feel it crack as I stare out the window. "We didn't exchange names." Outside the passing houses blur from the stinging in my eyes.

Anna just turned six. Yesterday.

"Doesn't matter," he says back. "They'll disappear after this. Poof. Tell me where we're going."

I give him the address and he wheels the

Mustang southward along Harlem Avenue. "What do they want?" He asks. For the first time I notice how white his knuckles are on the shift knob. Killing plays the joker, but he's nervous too.

"They're trying to salvage the Bell homicide, to spin it so the narrative fits their agenda."

He nods, staring out the windshield with fixed eyes. "And that narrative would be that Bell was killed by black thugs?"

"Yes."

"It's similar to the narrative they wanted to paint with my friend Dee. Black leader rises up, gathers together the public in an attempt to bring us all closer, then is assassinated. In this case, they didn't need to prop up Bell, didn't need to create an activist, he was already doing that on his own."

"But why? How does that incite minorities to rise up against whites? If they want to provoke blacks to start targeting whites so they can step in and create a race war, you'd think they would pin Bell's murder on someone else."

"Like I said, it's part of a larger end game. I'm guessing they don't need blacks and whites squaring off against each other yet, for whatever reason."

456

I shake my head. "I can't keep up with the conspiracy stuff. It's too out there. Who thinks of all this?"

"Smart guys who drive Jaguars and act like CEOs, that's who." Killing looks over at me again. "You know they will try to kill us, right?"

I meet his gaze before turning my attention back out front. "I don't care. All that matters is my daughter."

"Keep that focused in the front of your mind then, White. You'll need it."

***

We pull up on a side street, across the intersection from the old Nazarene Church of Christ. The sign out front has been stripped of lettering, but the name is still visible from the sun-fading on the wood. Cardboard covers all the windows from the inside. Red brick clads the outside walls, offset by white trim and steeple. The parking lot is faded and gray, yellow parking lines long gone, weeds growing up in spots.

A *For Sale* sign is staked in the yard, listing to one side. It's been here for a long time, judging by the condition.

We're dead center in a residential neighborhood. The houses are spaced farther apart than what I'm used to seeing, but the style remains post-war three box structures. Tall green trees line the street, bushes and flower beds delineate boundaries.

I look around. "Is this right? We're in a bunch of houses."

"I think they have a thing for residences. I almost died in the three car garage of a million dollar Victorian. Stupid neighborhood watch program was on break." Killing opens the door and gets out.

I do likewise. "I can't tell if you're being serious." My head swivels back and forth, scanning the street.

"It's for sale now, just for your information."

We cross the street. The lot loops around back and I see the tail end of a black Tahoe sticking out from the corner of the building. The license tag matches the surveillance photo Towney provided. I direct my feet that way, Killing follows.

Sure enough, the back window features a star-shaped crack pattern. Dead center I can see the impact point. "You must have really whipped that rock." I poke my finger through the hole in the glass.

He grunts in reply, looking around.

Beyond the back of the parking lot is open

yard, a couple of acres maybe, butting up against privacy fences for the houses on the next street over. Somewhere I can hear kids yelling and laughing, deep in their summer break, enjoying days without structure. It's surreal to think there are stone-cold killers waiting for us with this as our setting.

I don't have my gun. It's lying back in Rollins Savanna, atop the rest of my clothes. I don't know what the punishment is for abandoning your weapon, but compared to everything else I've done today, I'm not stressing over policy violation.

I am stressed about not having a weapon, though. We're walking into this setup without any kind of protection. Killing doesn't have a weapon either, except his sharp tongue. That's as likely to harm us as anyone else.

"Do you have any plan?" I ask as we stop at the corner and peek around. There's a van backed up against the rear door, also black in color. On the side the words *Covenant Church of the New Millennium* are branded in white letters. The symbolism in color choice is obvious to me. Above the name is a logo design that resembles one of those old Viking runic characters. It's the perfect camouflage. Bystanders would assume another religion is checking the place out, perhaps moving in.

Killing looks at me. "Why would I have a plan? This is your gig, I'm just your driver."

"You have more experience with the Covenant. I just thought..."

"You thought what? That I know them so well I can tell you their modus operandi? Sorry, pal. This group doesn't work that way. Everything they do is compartmentalized from other cells of the church. They killed Bell, but don't think for a second that this is all about Bell's death. They are setting up something else and he was a piece they needed. I'd guess the guys we're dealing with don't even know why Bell died, just that he did."

"So, what? We just waltz in there and figure it out on the fly? I'm not willing to wager Anna's life that way."

He stops and stares across the yard for a brief moment. Then turns back to me. "Here's the one thing I do know, and you won't like it: Everything you have, everyone you care about, is already in the wager. Didn't you wonder how they knew about your daughter? Where to find her? That isn't some random coincidence."

My first reaction is that Griff told Julien about Anna, but the more I think about it, the less sense it makes. The timing doesn't work. Michelle has been dead for hours. Julien must have struck last night. I open my mouth but no response forms.

"While you're at it, ask yourself why Bell took up your cause. Did he ever tell you why he decided to help you sue your way into a job? That's not the type of work he normally did. He served underprivileged youth, the at-risk kids from minority origins. He made his mark as someone who thought on a global scale, like incarceration rates for blacks, or migrant labor stemming from illegal immigration. A guy like you, bucking the system to get a promotion, you don't quite fit those kinds of societal needs."

That freezes me. I never thought about why he contacted me, why he offered to champion my suit. In my desperation to get Anna to Chicago, I didn't care why, only that he did. I remember the sense of relief and gratitude that someone understood my case, someone who could actually do something about it.

"What are you saying then?"

"I'm saying not to underestimate these guys. If there are people who can manipulate one of Chicago's most prominent activists to their own ends, it should make you question everything that's happened to you. Bell was a pawn. It's entirely possible you both were.

461

Are."

The enormity of that angle is huge. Bell was a smart man, very smart, nobody's fool. If someone had talked him into my case, for whatever reason, that implied a vast amount of influence. Who had that kind of sway?

But I already know the answer.

William Travian.

Travian has the smoke of the Covenant all around him, and where there's smoke, there's fire. It doesn't matter that Griff found only circumstantial links. You are defined by the company you keep. Too many connections exist. Travian and Moller and the Covenant. The degrees of separation are minimal.

"Okay, waltz in it is," I say, edging around the corner and heading for the back door. "Keep my daughter safe. That's our only goal."

"Beating up some white supremacists would be fun too," Killing adds as he falls in behind me.

We enter into the darkened building.

FORTY SEVEN

It's silent and shadowed inside. The back door opens into a large vestibule. It's empty of any furnishings, only a forgotten coat rack stands off to the left. A glass wall separates the vestibule from the narthex. I can see across the vestibule to the front door entrance. The floor slopes upward as we enter.

On the other side of the glass wall the ceiling soars high up, a hundred feet at the peak. Light streams in through multiple skylights, making it look like sun rays poking through heavy cloud cover. I wonder if it was an intentional effect by the architects. At one time this had to be a thriving congregation if it needed so much space. There are at least fifty rows of pews in the nave, leading down the sloped floor towards the front. Three steps lead up from the nave to the chancel.

Killing sees it at the same time I do. We both stop.

Anna's bed sits dead center on the altar, symbolic in its placement. The core instruments are mounted at the head of the bed and I can see lights still blinking. At this moment, the batteries are enough to keep her breathing. How much more power do they have?

At the feet of the bed sit Gwen and Griff, on the floor.

My partner lists heavily to one side, eyes closed, nearly falling over. Only Gwen's grip on his arm keeps him upright. A bruise spreads across her left cheekbone. His body is so limp I'd think he was dead if it weren't for her grip.

"Out of the frying pan..." Killing mutters. "Maybe we shouldn't have left them on their own."

I don't answer. He's right. In my haste to get to Anna, I assumed they would be fine, that the local cops would arrive quickly enough to keep the sniper from being a further threat.

My assumption was wrong.

It also means these guys came across them quickly and rushed them down here. This plan was made on the fly, without much time to consider all aspects. Such haste might play into our favor. They have to be off-balance as much as we are.

Behind the bed stand three kids, one of them a girl. They are young, barely out of their teens. A fourth stands off to the left, behind the pulpit lectern, rifle trained on us through the glass.

"Son of a bitch," Killing breathes.

"What?"

"I know two of these punks."

Without further explanation, he pushes through the glass doors into the nave and stops behind the last row of pews. I follow quickly on his heels, off guard. It should be me taking charge, it's my daughter in the noose up there, yet Killing's move took that momentum from me.

"Casey Barton, Todd Layton. Long time no arrest."

"What are you doing?" I hiss to him. "How do you know them?"

"They shoplifted from me a few months ago."

The girl, Casey, says nothing but there's a look of anger on her face. Her hair is short and curly, dirty blond in color. Her expression hints of conflict somewhere between them.

The one with the gun - Todd - shrugs and snugs the rifle up to his shoulder, sighting through the scope. This is the guy that shot at us in the park? It doesn't fit. He barely looks old enough to drink. His dark hair is cut short, nearly at military length, and he's whip-lean like me. There's something in his eyes, a desperation, a willingness to take that first step over the edge of the cliff.

"Not so smug now Killing. It's different when someone has the barrel pointed at you, isn't it? Where'd all your smart ass comments go?"

"They went 'otway'," Killing replies, then glances over his shoulder at me. "Inside joke. It's the name of his hometown in Ohio."

This kid isn't who I talked to on the phone. The voice is different. Despite his solid grip on the weapon, his words tremor ever so slightly. I'm doubting whether he was the shooter. Maybe that's not even the same gun, it looks more like a standard hunting rifle. If it's a .30-.30 or .358 caliber, there's no way Todd was the sniper. The distance across the lake was too far for a deer rifle.

I have to take back control before this gets even worse. We're already behind the eight ball. Whoever pulled the trigger up in the forest preserve has ice water in his veins, I can't take the chance it's this young kid standing before me.

"We're here," I say, stepping in front of Killing to assert myself. "Just as you said. I'm going to walk up there and check on my daughter."

Without waiting for a response, I start down the center aisle, steeling myself for the flash of gunfire. Both boys standing behind Casey unholster handguns and train them on me.

Todd shrugs, casual and dismissive of the life being sustained by fading batteries. "Don't worry about your little retard kid. She's alive. Everything is still beeping and blinking like it did before."

At that, Casey looks over to Todd, an expression of concern on her face. In a flash it comes to me: She's the one who ensured Anna stayed okay. It's one thing to join a group with a mission to change the world, no matter how twisted. It's another to watch a helpless child die right in front of you. Maybe she's not fully vested in the Covenant program, maybe she had some motherly instincts kick in. It doesn't matter. All that matters is my daughter.

"Casey," I direct my words to her. "Is she okay?"

"Don't talk to her," Todd states. "You deal with me."

I ignore him. "Casey?"

She glances over at Todd then back and gives a quick nod. "I think so."

I see Anna's head turn, a fraction towards the sound of my voice, and it hardens my resolve. These guys made a huge tactical error. They assumed my daughter would introduce an angle to weaken me, but they're wrong. I'm focused on only one goal to the exclusion of all others. None of these young shits understand this father's drive to protect his child.

"From stealing digital cameras to rifles," Killing says. "Looks like you graduated up the ladder. Must be because your leaders are either dead or breathing through straws. How's that make you feel, Todd?"

Why is he instigating someone holding a weapon?

"Shut up and stop moving." Todd nods to the two other boys. They round Anna's bed and come to the edge of the chancel, training their weapons on us. Behind them Gwen looks around, at Griff, at Todd, at us. I can't tell what she's thinking but our stares cross.

"Gwen, Griff? How you guys doing? Sorry about leaving you alone."

She shakes her head. "I don't think he's doing good. There's a lot of blood and his skin feels kind of cold."

Griff cracks open his eyes. "Arch, what the hell, man. Leaving me with a young attractive girl? You know how they can't control themselves." His voice is weak, a poor imitation of the sarcastic tones that were his default. He makes no effort to hold himself up, letting Gwen be his support. That worries me, but I can't let it show.

This is about as bad a situation as you can be in.

Todd swivels his rifle to point at me. "Enough chattering. Hands up."

I place my hands on top of my head. "Fine. I'm stopped. I've done everything you asked. Now what?"

"He probably wants to shoot us but he's too chicken to do it," Killing taunts.

"For Christ's sake," I hiss over my shoulder at him. "Would you shut up?"

One of the boys smirks. The gun is rock steady in his grip, not a good sign for us.

Todd lowers the rifle and reaches into the lectern. He pulls out a cell phone. It's already flipped open. He holds it up to his ear and speaks. I can't make out his words, they're soft, but it's clear to me what's going on. He's on a leash from someone else, somewhere else. Behind the virtual curtain there's a puppet master pulling his strings.

That's the guy I spoke with, he's the danger. I know it. Could it be William Travian?

Would someone with his power be involved at this level? To the point of giving instructions to a lackey holding hostage a disabled child?

Travian can't be that stupid. There has to be layers between him and the person pulling the trigger. Fine. I'll start with whoever is on the other end of the call and track back until I land on Travian's doorstep with a warrant and over-stuffed binder of evidence.

We stand there, an uncomfortable silence arising. Both boys with guns stare at us. Killing stares back. At one point he blows a kiss to them. Gwen struggles to hold up Griff while Anna's instruments beep softly behind her.

Todd continues speaking into the phone, casting frequent glances over to me. I can tell by his body language he disagrees with the speaker on the other end. There has to be a way I can leverage that.

"Is it me, or is this getting awkward?" Killing suddenly blurts out. "It's worse than a blind date with someone who doesn't speak your language. Don't ask me how I know."

"Shut up," the boy on the right says and waggles his weapon.

"Or what? You're going to shoot me?" Now a nasty edge tinges Killing's voice and I get a glimpse of the mean streak hidden below his joker image. He may annoy people with his relentless nature and off-hand remarks, but there's a guy underneath the clown mask who takes things very seriously. This is the Rick Killing to be reckoned with. This is the man I need to match by raising my own game.

I take a step forward. "Let's get this over with. Whatever you think you're going to do, it won't work. Backup is on the way. All four of you are going to end up deep in a cell, but things haven't gone too far yet. Tell me who held the rifle up in Rollins and there might be a way out from all this."

Todd laughs as he snaps the phone closed. "That line probably works with the weak-minded niggers and spics that infest this area, but I'm not stupid. We set up at a distance up in Rollins in case you tried to sidestep Crux and bring backup. But if you didn't do it then, I'm pretty confident you didn't do it now either."

He descends from the pulpit, placing himself at the end of Anna's bed. The rifle is left leaning up against the lectern. Casey is behind him and her eyes dart between him and us. She's really nervous, which means she's not aware or okay with what's to come, which means I'm not either.

A pistol appears in Todd's hand and I notice he's wearing a latex glove. He lifts the weapon up. "You guys have been looking for this? It's an important piece to your case."

"On behalf of the Chicago PD, thanks for bringing it to us," Killing spouts. "I don't have any of my own gloves, can I borrow yours to carry it?"

Todd cocks his head to one side, looking at us like he's bemused at our inability to take this situation seriously. I don't know what Killing is thinking, but I'm quaking and sweat trickles down my back. My eyes keep darting between Todd, the boys on guard, and Anna's monitors.

"Jesus, you just don't stop, do you?" He says. "Maybe this will shut you up."

He swings the pistol around, pointing towards Anna, and fires.

FORTY EIGHT

The monitor mounted to the head of Anna's bed explodes, shards of crystal glass flying through the air. Casey screams and ducks, hands over her ears. Both guard boys flinch but keep their eyes trained on us.

In an instant, the readouts for blood pressure, pulse/ox, tidal volume and respiratory rate wink to black.

I roar and charge forward. Red floods my vision and vengeance propels my motion. Killing is a half-step ahead of me, teeth gritted, muscles straining in his thick neck. This guy doesn't know me from Adam, he has no personal stake in this, but he's reacting like any decent human being would, if they had the physical capability.

Instead of firing at us, both of Todd's guard dogs take a step back and train their muzzles at my daughter. Todd swings his weapon to us. Now there's one pointing forward, two pointing back at Anna.

This freezes me. Killing also stops, glancing back over his shoulder at me.

"Swear to God," I pant through a dry mouth. "If she's hurt in any way..."

"Shut up, Oreo. The retard is alive. I can hear the pump still going."

Casey stands up, slowly, looking at the shattered monitor. An expression of dismay flushes across her features. "Todd, what the fuck did you do?"

He doesn't take his eyes or his aim off us. "What are you talking about?"

"She's just a kid, a helpless kid."

"No, she's a niglet, a mulatto niglet. The world is better off without these kind of parasites."

Casey stares at Anna's face, conflicting emotions writ large.

"You better not tell me you're getting weak," he continues. "We both have the brand of the Covenant on our neck. It's an oath, a promise to our kind that we will pave the way for a better America. That means something to me and I'm not turning it over for anyone, even a little cripple girl. It better mean something to you too, all of you."

Casey says nothing in reply, continuing to stare at Anna. The two guard dogs cross glances, with each other, with Todd, and re-grip their weapons. My daughter squirms her head, reacting to the noise.

Hang in there, baby. Daddy's here.

He needs us for something. There's a reason Todd hasn't simply shot us. I need to find out what that is.

"You obviously have your orders," I say, arms hanging loose at my side, forcing me into a relaxed posture. No matter how much my insides are howling, I will not give him the pleasure of playing the victim. Next to me, Killing crosses his arms, letting me talk. "Otherwise you would have just shot us. Tell me what you need. My only concern is getting my daughter out of here safe, so whatever it takes, I will do it."

On the floor next to Todd's feet, Gwen looks back and forth from him to me, eyes wide with fright, hand locked on my partner's arm. Griff gives a soft grunt and moves his head slightly. His eyes stay closed.

"Good guess. Between you, Killing the idiot clown and Crux's weird stubbornness, everything has bent sideways. The scene we wanted to stage is gone, but there's a still a way to salvage it all." He wags Julien's gun. "And this will be key."

I shake my head. "No, it won't. Others in the department know the truth behind the murder. The evidence won't match up to whatever scenario you cook up. The idea that Noah Bell died from an attack of black gang kids won't sell anymore. All the public relations in the world can no longer whitewash that fact. You're going against data and your racist agenda won't hold up."

"Not only that," Killing interjects. "You aren't smart enough to do the simplest things, like spell 'idiot'. It's T-O-D-D."

At that, one of the guard boys barks a laugh. Todd shoots him a hard look and he shuts up.

"Go ahead, keep cracking, asshole." Todd taps the gun against one of the metal rails of Anna's bed, producing a loud clink that rings harsh in the vast sanctuary. "Ballistics will match this weapon to the basketball court. It will also match slugs found in your partner's head, when his body finally shows up. When they find your prints on it, that's when things start to get fun. So many questions needing an answer: What happened this afternoon? Why would a young black detective shoot his partner and the witness to a crime he was investigating? If he was so close to Noah Bell, then where is he? Why did he disappear and leave behind a trail of bodies?"

He smiles and looks me direct in the eye, watching my reaction as his intent becomes clear. I feel the blood drain from my face, but maintain my composure. It takes a Herculean effort. He doesn't know Griff already called in to explain, but that may not make sense in the face of the evidence.

"Sounds stupid. Like Sesame Street stupid, but the intelligence level is a match," Killing replies. His voice sounds steady, but I can hear the cracks in it.

"Yeah?" Todd spouts back. "What about when wanted detective Aramis White is spotted near the scene of a famous white athlete's murder in a few weeks? Like maybe some local guy that just got drafted after being a failure most of his life? What about when his prints turn up in connection with that case? Neither of you understands. It's all about sowing confusion and uncertainty. Crime scene evidence can provide some facts, but no one will really know what happened without a witness. And unfortunately, those are scarce nowadays. In that void of knowledge, the media will create their own, mold stories and speculation, spawning scenarios that sell to the sheep. The niggers will get uppity at the perception that it's a racial thing. They'll cry persecution and demand all sorts of shit from white people in positions of power. Out of social guilt, those white people will give in and make stupid public statements, but everyone knows deep down they mean nothing. This all feeds into the war. We're going to turn this kettle up so that when it blows, it blows big. Armies will erupt overnight. Blacks attacking whites, attacking other blacks, acting like the animals they are. But the Covenant will be ready. We all will. When white is ready to take back this country, we'll be there to lead the way. So, Sesame Street that, Killing."

"It's still spelled T-O-D-D."

Leave it to Killing to drag someone down to his level and beat them with experience. "The Mollers sounded the same way and look where that got them. Tell Lance 'Hi' when you guys bunk together in prison."

"Yeah, whatever." Todd points at him. "Fuck you..." Then he points to me. "...and fuck you." His voice echoes back against the rows of pews behind us, amplifying the hate. I have no doubt he could pull the trigger now. The nervousness that caused his hands to tremble earlier has been wiped away by anger at

Killing's mouth. We should have had a better plan.

He looks down at Gwen, sitting on the floor at his feet, silent and small. "Sorry you had to get stuck in the middle of this. Wrong time and place for you. Too bad. You have a nice body and you're white. We could have had fun."

Todd ratchets a shell into the chamber of Julien's gun and points it at Griff's head. He looks over to me and smiles. The two guard boys step towards the head of the bed, getting out of the way.

I feel everything tangled up inside me, knots keeping me from movement, paralyzed by fear and desperation. *Anna.*

Casey makes a strangled sound.

Killing inhales deeply, nostrils flaring, filling his body with oxygen to ignite his own explosion.

Todd turns an annoyed look to Casey. "What now?"

"The pump," she points to a spot under Anna's bed where the mechanism is mounted. "It stopped."

I shout.

Killing leaps.

Gwen screams.

FORTY NINE

The sound of Todd - she heard someone say his name - chambering a shell into his gun startles Gwen. She jumps and releases her grip on Detective Toms. He slumps over to his left side with a soft moan. Even through the haze he's still feeling pain. She shouldn't have let these kids press on his bullet wounds until he awoke. Toms screamed so loud in the back of the SUV, she thought he might rupture a vocal cord.

Todd is aiming his gun at old detective, standing over her like she doesn't even exist. His words rang in her head. *You have a nice body and you're white.* That's all he saw in her, a sex toy, a thing to play with and discard when done. This jerk has never met her before and he's already treating her like everyone else does.

We could have had fun.

Anger burbles up inside her, at circumstance, at the injustice of it all, washing away the fear that always grips her. She just wanted to be alone, to slink away from civilization and strange faces and stranger encounters. Gwen, her chalks, and her drawing. Is that so much to ask?

Instead she saw something she wasn't meant to. Chased by a killer. All the kids on the basketball court who were shot simply because she ran to them. Dweldon died for her, even though he also used her. Her grandmother. The little crippled girl in the bed behind her.

Now, sitting in this empty church, full of echoes, she feels the weight of it all descending upon her shoulders. Everything has been her fault. They are all here because of one thing she did. Or didn't do.

She didn't run to the police. Instead she tried to hide on her own.

She didn't recognize the two boys with guns back at Rollins, allowing her and Toms to fall back into their hands. These same two boys stood next to her, guns gripped tight in their hands. The idiocy of her actions fuels her anger further.

Stop being a victim, Gwen.

Detective White said that, just before he ran off and left her alone with Toms. One simple statement. It struck something deep inside of her, a something that took root back at the savanna and continued to grow on the way here. One sentence, heavy with other meanings that carried little weight to anyone else in this church.

She's her own victim, hiding behind weakness and excuse, letting others have their way because that's how you trade for what you want in this world. Her face blindness keeps her isolated from society, but it doesn't have to be that way. She'll never be good with faces, but she can be good with other things.

So why did it take a detective - a complete stranger risking his life and his daughter's life for her - why did it take someone like that to say the one sentence that changed her?

Tears start to flow, like they always do, but now the source reason is different. The fear is still there, it will always be there, but these tears come from another place, one of anger and frustration so deep she's never looked that far down. Things could have been different all this time.

Gwen squeezes her eyes shut, squeezing the tears out and clenching the anger in. It's such a different feeling than the uncaring haze of her highs, she's not quite sure what to do with it.

Griff shifts in her grasp and lifts his head, looking over at her with unfocused eyes. He's in a bad way.

Todd stands over her, ignoring her presence like she's inconsequential to anything in his life, except the potential for "fun." He looks over at Detective White and smiles, an evil expression pulled straight from a source of hate. He's going to shoot Toms and watch the reaction.

On the other side of the table, the girl gasps and says, "The pump. It stopped."

Everything explodes. Detective White roars with anger and desperation so complete it fills the sanctuary. The large man with him lunges forward, blinding fast for someone his size, aiming for the two boys near the head of the bed.

Gwen responds in kind. This, this moment; this is where her emotion and tears can be aimed.

As Todd points his weapon at Toms and squeezes the trigger, she lets out a primal scream and shoots straight up from her sitting position.

The gun fires.

She punches Todd's arm upward, loosening the weapon in his grip.

Then the detective is on him. They collide in a heap of sound and striking limbs. The gun clatters to the floor of the chancel and bounces down three steps. It slides under the first pew.

Motion, sound and violence surround Gwen. The anger and dark emotion flees her tiny body, dropping her back down in a crouch with hands over her ears. Feet scuffle the floor just inches away and she scurries towards Detective Toms, half to protect him, half to hide near his bulk.

His breathing is shallow and rapid. She can barely hear it against the loud shouts and gunfire rolling overhead. Sweat greases the hair flat on his scalp. It sticks to her cheek as she presses against him.

"Hey," she whispers forcefully. "Hey! Get up!"

He doesn't respond, other than to expel foul-smelling breath from cracked lips. It's a rattling sound that dies off at the end. His limbs go slack, becoming dead weight but he twitches, once, twice. That has to be a good sign, right? Gwen shifts her body to support him, feeling the leg of someone smack up against her backside, and cradles his head in her arms. She continues to slap at his face and yell his name, at a loss for what else to do. She is oblivious to the action gyrating around her, the present danger of two men against three, trying to keep everyone alive.

There is only the helpless detective in her arms and the need to end her run as a victim by protecting someone else. Blood slicks her arms, significant in meaning.

FIFTY

Killing is a full step ahead of me, vaulting forward with an explosive leap that catches both of Todd's buddies off guard. The speed with which he moves is incredible for someone his size. It shocks them and they are late bringing their weapons to bear.

Everything in my vision goes white and narrows down to a tunnel focused only on Todd's face. I see Gwen jump up and hit his arm at the same moment he fires. The look of released anger colors her face, turns her ugly and raw in that moment. She doesn't need to know his face to recognize what he is, and it's clear she hates him.

Her blow catches him as he's still looking back at Casey with a look of annoyance. The gun loosens in his grip and his expression flicks to dismay.

And then I'm on him.

An upward chop finishes the job of disarming him. The gun clatters away somewhere, leaving us equal. We're nearly equal in height and weight too, but I've got the distinct advantage over him: I'm a father protecting my daughter.

I don't hold back. All the rage, the pent-up anger at Todd's social poison, the need to lash out in the name of a great man who can no longer defend himself because a hate group decided to make him a pawn in their twisted game; it all boils to the surface in an explosion of strikes.

Counting on Killing to handle the other two, I ignore any threat from that quarter and smother Todd with hammer fists and kicks and screams full of rage. My world coalesces to a point, fixed on Todd, and there is nothing else. A gunshot goes off somewhere, sounding like a shot from across a vast canyon. Shouts are everywhere, floating across the background of my awareness, but I pay them no heed. There is only this young racist punk and the threats he made to my daughter.

Stand up for yourself, stand up for someone else.

Todd ducks and tries to escape my assault, but there's no way I'm letting up. It's an awkward fight, clumsy and sliding, lacking any of the grace that marks Hollywood scenes. I attack him with everything I have, swinging for the fences. I've never had any formal combat training other than what was taught at the academy, but this isn't about that.

It's about bone on bone, crushing what the other represents, and surviving.

He reacts like many people do, curling his body away from me to create space so he maneuver to a different angle. I don't give him that space. I press forward, landing blows on his upraised arms, kicking at his gut and legs. He yells and tries to level a few blows at me, but fails to inflict much damage.

The pump. It stopped.

I'm driven by a need that he will never be able to match. No matter how much despite he carries for others not like him, it's less than the love I have for my daughter. It always will be and that gives me strength far exceeding his.

He shoves off in order to swing back, or scramble for his weapon. I don't know and don't care. His calf smacks up against Gwen's back as she huddles over Griff, tripping him, sending him in a tumble off the chancel to the nave floor below. He goes down in a heap, arms flailing, and lands heavily on his back. The pistol is somewhere under the first pew, too close for comfort.

We both realize it and make our moves simultaneously.

He scrabbles over, reaching for the weapon. If he gets it, I'm a sitting duck, standing in clear range above him. There's no time to process thought or consider consequence. There's only reflex birthed of emotion and desperation.

I launch myself off the chancel, leaping high in the air, bent at the knees. This is not going to end well for one of us.

He's just rolling to his back, swinging the gun around to fire, when my right kneecap impacts his chin. My full weight drives his skull back down against the concrete floor. Thin industrial carpet covers the surface, but it's for show, to provide a layer of warmth over cold. It's not there to give any cushion.

I feel something crack, followed by a strangled scream from Todd. It's mercifully short, an indictment on the severity of my strike. The hand holding the weapon drops like dead weight back to the floor and the rest of his body goes limp. I snatch the gun from his now-slack grip. He doesn't move. He may never move again.

But I'm already spinning away.

I jump back up to the chancel, coming to Killing's aid. He's a huge guy and in shape, but it's still two to one, and both of those two have guns. Nine millimeters can bring down two hundred plus pounds pretty quickly.

He's on top of one kid, hammering at him with elbows and forearms. The other kid is staggering back to his feet, blood running down his forehead, drawing his weapon down on Killing. I don't waste time shouting a warning or anything else required by my badge. Protocol and policy have no place here.

I fire three shots into his back. He cries out and drops to his knees, then tilts off the chancel. I follow him to clear the weapon, but he's not a threat. He lets go of the gun to grasp at his back. The cries that come from him are piteous and loud. They are the cries of someone who got a lot more than he bargained for when Todd came knocking.

Throwing the gun to the far end of the sanctuary where no one can get it easily, I jump back up to Anna's bed. My peripheral vision registers Killing getting to his feet, the kid limp on the floor. Gwen is still cradling Griff's head, staring down at him. Her face is hidden by her hair so I get no hint of her emotional state. Griff's face is slack and relaxed, eyes closed.

All that passes through the background of my mind, unchecked, pushed aside by exigency and mortal fear for my daughter. It's only been a minute since the pump stopped, but it could be a lifetime. My daughter's lifetime. There is only her and her frail form in my vision.

Casey is standing on the other side of the bed, eyes locked on Anna, tears streaming down her face. Whether from fright at her circumstances or other emotion, I can't tell. I draw a bead on her forehead. She gives a startled cry at my action and raises her hands, backing away. She wants no part of me or what I'm bringing. There might even be a part of her that's wrapped up in the plight of my daughter, a sliver of decency hidden under the hate symbol branded into her neck. If so, there may be hope for her yet.

Hang on baby, daddy's here.

Anna's face is still and drawn. The ventilator tube jutting out of her mouth looks obscene, a useless instrument now that the pump no longer works. I don't know if the batteries ran down or the damage to the monitoring equipment sent a shutdown signal.

None of it matters. My daughter needs help breathing, whether from machine or man.

I yank out the ventilator tube and start blowing into her mouth. From me to her flows the oxygen her lungs can't pump on their own. There's nothing else in my sight other than her face, the face that just turned six years old. Somewhere I hear someone calling my name, hear shouts from Killing, but the sound doesn't penetrate the noise of my own distress. I'm calling my daughter's name over and over, tears and stars blurring my vision, maintaining a constant rhythm of life on her behalf. That's what a dad does: He lives in order for his children to live. If they can't breathe, he breathes for them. If they can't stand up for themselves, he stands up for them. I gave life to my daughter in one moment of passion, I sustain her life now in a moment of extreme passion, propelled by emotions that had no role in her conception. I brought this life into the world and I'll die before I release it.

That's what a dad does.

My eyes grow dark, the world swirls around me, constricting. My throat goes raw from the effort to choke back my own screams of despair. There's a tightening of the noose around my neck as I work to save Anna. Breathe in, breathe out.

That's what he does...

EPILOGUE

Clouds roll in slow tumbles far above our heads, darkening the earth and the moods of everyone present. Not that anyone needed prompting to remain somber. Funerals are like that on their own. I keep my head down, hands clasped tightly into fists before me, as we listen to the Catholic Rites of Committal. A casket is suspended over the freshly-dug grave, draped in flowers and ribbons, ready to be lowered by the winches holding it aloft.

I can't take my eyes off it.

Sheila is next to me, heartbreaking and beautiful in black, silent except for an occasional sniffle. Hundreds of people are staged around us, also silent and respectful for the ceremony and what it represents.

The priest's words bounce off my ears, acknowledged but unheard, as he closes out the interment service with the Lord's prayer. My lips move in numb reflex, reciting words I've known since childhood, but have dreaded saying in these circumstances.

"Our Father, who art in heaven, hallowed be thy name…"

The cemetery echoes back the prayer, ringing out with meaning and loss, and there are very few dry eyes. Me, I'm dried out, hollowed by the emotion and events of the last week. There's nothing left to give, my mind has been carved up into a new shape that will be my template in the days going forward. On the other side of the casket, Rick Killing is visible towards the back of the crowd, taller than everyone else. Detective George Warren is next to him. They both meet my eyes and Killing nods. He was there when it all happened; this guy, who I have nothing in common with, stood next to me at a time when literal life and death hung in the balance. Without pause, he put his head in the crosshairs and dared the Covenant to pull the trigger.

"…your will be done…"

So, they did. The hate group tried to stake their claim, but in the end we were equal to the task, by luck, by skill, by sheer desperation. Todd survived, barely. His fractured skull required many hours of surgery, I heard. Good. He deserved it.

"And lead us not into temptation..."

The other boy I shot in the back also survived, although he'll require months, maybe years, of rehabilitation to walk properly again.

Killing pummeled his kid to the point of reconstructive surgery to his facial structure. Casey stood down, crying at the extremity of their actions that day in the church. She never thought they'd go so far and when it all came down the final chips, she didn't have the stomach to kill an innocent child. There's still a cell in her future, and it will be filled with minorities who will see the brand burned into her neck. If she's lucky, they won't recognize what it means.

"...but deliver us from evil. Amen."

The priest gives the final sign of the cross and steps back. Motion ripples through the crowd as everyone begins to shift and move, dispersing in slow degrees, speaking to others at this time of shared loss. The voices are low, the words subdued, as appropriate for a cemetery setting.

I look down at Sheila. She squeezes my

forearms and smiles up at me, but it's a haunted expression. She processes her emotions on the surface and the last week has taken as much of a toll, if not more, than it did to me. We're in this together now, my trial is her trial, our lives coming into a shared direction.

"How are you doing?" She asks, for the thousandth time today it seems. The golden fire in her eyes burns with a different glow, with compassion and understanding. I return a nod in response, revealing an answer only she can interpret.

Then I tug her through the crowd to Griff's widow.

Elizabeth Toms stands with Gwen; the woman who spent her life with Griffin Toms and the one who spent the last few minutes of life with Griffin Toms. Gwen's action to prevent Todd from shooting my partner was noble and right, but a heartbeat too late. The slug took Griff behind his right ear.

Gwen looks at me as I stop before her. That vacant gaze is still in place, but I can see there's something more underneath it. A self-promise to change. She's told me things will be different with her, that she will stop being the victim. I didn't realize my parting words to her that day up in Rollins would have such impact, but I'm honored to know they did.

I've given my respects many times to Mrs. Toms, and I will give it many more times, because it's all I can give. He was my partner, my friend, my shield against the interoffice politics. For that and that alone, I'll always carry a part of him with me.

We speak for a few minutes, hushed words of sympathy and grieving. She accepts them with red, swollen eyes, keeping her gaze fixed on the casket of her husband.

There's a slow dispersing of the crowd, people moving in bits and fits towards their vehicles. Hundreds of police cruisers line the roads coming into the cemetery, lights whirling in recognition of a fallen brother. Uniformed cops stand at alert beside each patrol car, paying their respects with presence and solidarity. They know someday this could be their scene.

Warren and Killing approach as we disengage from Elizabeth and Gwen. Warren met me once, we spoke for a total of thirty minutes. But he knew Griff for many years. There's an awkwardness built into those degrees of relationship. He doesn't really know what to say to me, nor I to him. We occupied different phases of Griffin Toms' life.

Killing looks down at the handcuffs

linking my wrists together. "They couldn't cut you loose even for this? What a bunch of dicks."

I nod with my head over to the edge of the nearest road. David Hecker stands in front of an unmarked cruiser, several of his police captains with him, staring at me, waiting with barely restrained emotion until he can escort me back to the station. "It's mostly that guy. He's giddy with the thought I might get bounced from the squad, all because of what happened."

Warren shakes his head. "Guy was always a jack, even when we were cubs coming out of the academy together. Don't sweat it, White. It's all due process now and just takes time."

He's right, and I have to keep telling myself that. My prints were all over the gun, which matched ballistics to the rounds that killed many people over a three day period, including a well-liked and respected police detective just months from retirement. This isn't Hollywood where the final scene wraps up everything in a neat bow designed to make the audience feel good. Griff's statements to Gonzales over the radio, along with corroborating evidence and statements from others, will help clear up the reality of my case. But there's a holy mess of evidence that will take time to process and the case itself is complicated to reassemble. Until then, I remain in custody. Hecker will make sure I do.

"Thanks for coming down," I say. "I've said it before and I'll say it again, Rick: I don't have the words to thank you. Nothing I can say or do will erase the debt I owe."

He shrugs. "No biggie. Slow day on TV anyway, what else did I have to do?" He's got his wiseass character back in place, but we've each seen the other's core, when the trappings of life have been stripped away to expose who we really are and what really matters. "Your kid doing okay? Doctors still giving her thumbs up?"

Sheila fields the question. "Yes, thank you. She's in another home for now until they reopen hers. They said there wasn't any measurable damage done from oxygen deprivation. You and Arch did a fantastic job with her until the ambulance arrived."

As Warren excuses himself to talk to another cop, Killing nods. "Good to hear. Kid's a fighter. As for you," he looks at me. "I told you the Covenant played for keeps. Todd and his merry band of pranksters weren't the key play. You know that, right? Todd was just a minor cog."

"Yeah, I get it. There was someone on the

other end of that call, directing those kids. We tried to process the cell phone, but it didn't turn up anything, just pointed to a number that's never been assigned, according to the cell company."

"Figures. Those assholes probably own the cell company for all we know. Never underestimate their reach and influence."

It's not the first time he's said something like this. Frankly, I'm getting tired of it. Two weeks ago I'd never heard of them, now they're central casting in my life story, the looming antagonist shadowing my present and future. Whenever I think of them - of Todd and Julien Crux and the thick file folder of Grand Haven or Middle Plains - I sense the threat. It lurks just out of sight, a creature stalking in the distance. Perhaps it stalks me with intent, perhaps it only poses a threat if I make myself known again. I don't know.

We fall silent for a moment, all of us, working towards an ending. Even Sheila says nothing, staring off into the middle distance, patient, not understanding of the bond formed between Killing and me.

Finally, he breaks it. "So, what's next for you? Besides getting the cuffs off for good? Any plans?"

I meet his eyes. The ground slopes away

from me, just enough to put us at equal height. We both know the true question being asked. For this I do have the words.

"Plans? Yeah, I have them. They revolve around a man named William Travian."

Rick Killing holds my stare and there are many things unsaid in that minute. They don't need to be said.

In the distance, a police siren whoops, once, twice, clearing a path for the champions of law to move forward.

~end~